coded history

- My Life of New Beginnings

Barry Dwolatzky

Cover Design © 2022 Tessa Wagener

Typesetting © 2022 Paperhearts Publishing

Cover Photography © 2022 Edwin Wes

To my family, the bridge between the past and future

foreword

He wrote without fear about his impending death. He wrote about a weariness that few have experienced. The all-encompassing exhaustion one feels when every cell in your body craves oxygen. All but the most vital systems in your body start shutting down. His body slept for eighteen then twenty then twenty-three hours a day. His brain kept working as it bubbled up a long lifetime of memories into his subconscious in the form of vivid dreams that filled his hours of sleep. He used his last remaining hour or two a day of wakefulness to share some of his memories with his life partner who sat at his side watching him fade away. With his last tiny package of energy, he shared his experience of dying with friends and others on Facebook in a final post as his life slipped away. And then he died. It was late 2018.

I read this final post. I hadn't met him, but I knew who he was. A fellow academic. A powerful force in his field who had influenced those he taught and those who read what he wrote. He was about my age and we had moved in similar circles. He had died of leukaemia. I knew exactly what he meant when he wrote about 'all-encompassing exhaustion'. As I read his Facebook post, I also felt that deep weariness. I too was dealing with the effects of leukaemia. In my case, however, modern medicine was winning the battle. I felt stronger and less weary every day. The Cladribine that was being injected into my body every day was working its magic. My red-cell count was going up. The supply of oxygen to my cells was increasing.

Reading his account had a profound effect on me. It gave me a preview of what my own death might feel like if the Cladribine and other treatments stopped working for me. I thought a great deal about his memories. How he described them bubbling away. Once we are gone, so are those memories. Some might say, 'who cares?' But I care about my memories. I care about them because they represent a thread – a very tiny thread, but a valuable thread in the history of our world. And history is important because it is the foundation for future knowledge and future actions. Without history, there can be no innovation, no progress.

So what do I do with the added lease on life that Cladribine has given me? One important item on my to-do list is to capture some of those memories. Put them in safe places where they won't be lost when my life ends, however that may be. With that note-to-self safely tucked away, I recovered from my treatment and went back to life as normal, chasing deadlines and filling my days with other people's priorities.

And then in November 2019, something changed. A young man, Tiyani Nghonyama, who had been inspired by some of the things I have done, was named South Africa's IT Personality of the Year. In his acceptance speech, he said that he wanted to 'be like Prof Barry'. He spoke about what I had done to inspire him, but I realised that he knew so little about me. I had so much more to share with him and others in his generation who would, hopefully, carry on the work I have initiated. I remembered that item in my mental to-do list, still waiting to be ticked off: 'Put my memories in a safe place.' I set to work on producing podcasts capturing some of these memories.

And then in March 2020, the world as we knew it changed. The COVID-19 pandemic swept the globe. Like everyone else, I'm taking time to process the short-, medium-, and long-term consequences of this tiny coronavirus. But, in my case, another factor has come into play. In 1987, when I was first diagnosed with hairy-cell leukaemia, my spleen was removed. Although, as I write these words, the consequences of being spleen-less and contracting COVID-19 remain uncertain, my doctors advised me that I'm in the high-risk category. To put it bluntly, the virus will probably kill me, if I let it get to me. As a respiratory illness, COVID-19 seems (from the little I've been able to bear to read) to lead to the kind of death I read about on Facebook. Cells starved of oxygen, weariness, memories bubbling away. This could be me, and this time there is, so far, no treatment with the magical qualities of Cladribine waiting to pull me back.

It is with these thoughts, and this sense of urgency, that I feel driven to write this book. What I thought of as a long and thoughtful project, filled with research and reflection, has now become a rush. I hope it isn't a race between me getting it finished and the coronavirus finishing me ... but I have no way of knowing.

Locked down at home, Johannesburg 12th May 2020.

note to readers

This memoir is written with the intention of sharing the whole story of my life. It straddles all aspects of my life, both personal and professional. These aspects are intertwined in a way unique to my own story. My political beliefs and activities are just as important to me in telling my story as the work that I did in software engineering. My family and the communities I've lived in are as important as the academic environments in which I've worked.

I've made a conscious effort in writing this memoir to not indulge in the obscure disciplinary jargon for which my profession, software engineering, is notorious. There might, however, be sections of this narrative that the "non-technical" reader might choose to skip over. Please feel free to do so.

I should also note that as an academic I've been trained in a style of writing that places great emphasis on cross-referencing and fact-checking. In this memoir, I have taken on a very different style. While everything I write is an accurate and true account of what lies in my own memory, and while I have checked each fact and piece of information as best I can, there might still be errors. In the interest of transferring the memories in my brain onto these pages, I decided to forego the rigours of academic writing. Please forgive me if you spot any errors. An incorrect date or name here and there should not detract from the story I share.

Barry Dwolatzky, October 2022.

acknowledgments

I wish to acknowledge several people who helped me in transforming a set of Word files into the complete book you now hold in your hands. Jane Rosenthal gave me many valuable suggestions and encouraged me to share what I had written with a wider audience. My daughter Jodie was my first reader and shared many thoughtful insights into how what I had written could be improved. My wife Rina and son Leslie added their own valuable comments and guidance. A huge thanks also to Melanie Pleaner for reading an early draft and sharing her advice, enthusiastic encouragement and support. Moira Niehaus shared a treasure trove of long forgotten letters that filled gaps in my memory. I owe a particularly huge debt of gratitude to Helen Lunn who edited what I had written and helped me see my words through the eyes of a reader. Megan Moll was my meticulous line editor, who became the first fan of my book. Finally thank you to Samantha Hogg-Brandjes and her team of experts who took on the multitude of steps required to create this book and get it out into the world.

Some of the photos included in the book were taken by

one of my oldest and dearest friends Edwin Wes.
Thank you.

part one

chapter
one

KNOCKING ON HEAVEN'S DOOR

1987

I don't recollect his name, which is strange as what he told me transformed my life. He was about five years younger than me and wore a starched white coat and a very uncomfortable expression on his face. He introduced himself and then perched uncomfortably on the chair next to me, determined not to make eye-contact while he fiddled with a small pile of papers in a beige folder. At last, he looked at me and, in a shaky voice, told me that I was about to die.

'Five to six months,' he said.

My first reaction was to comfort him. I felt sorry that he had to be the one to bring such terrible news. But then the gravity of what was happening to me began to sink in and shock set in. His voice grew bolder but seemed to come from a long way off. I don't think I spoke. I struggled to listen to the words coming out of his mouth.

It was Wednesday 23rd December 1987. I was thirty-five years old, alone, and would soon be dead.

Two days earlier, on Monday 21st December, my alarm clock had woken me as usual at 5:45am. I lay under my warm duvet for a few extra minutes thinking about the week that was about to start. The research lab where I worked would be closing at noon on Thursday 24th, Christmas Eve, and would stay closed until 2nd January. Eight days off would be a welcome break.

'Four more early morning commutes until Christmas', I thought as I dragged myself out of bed and prepared for another long day.

I felt desperately tired, run-down, unfit, overweight, and stressed. The past year had been tough. A few days earlier someone had asked me whether I had any plans for the Christmas break. I replied, half seriously, that all I wanted to do was to spend the week in my pyjamas sleeping, eating and reading. Two days later, my wish came horribly true.

I pulled on my big puffy green duvet jacket, grabbed my briefcase, and stepped out into the dark cold early morning London drizzle. With my head down and my glasses misting over, I walked from my house in Lavers Road to the bus stop in Stoke Newington High Street where I joined the stoic queue of familiar strangers. It was only a five-minute walk, but I was breathless when I arrived at the bus stop.

'God, I'm unfit!' I thought.

Thirty minutes later, I was climbing off the number 149

bus at Liverpool Street Station from where I boarded a train to Chelmsford and another bus to Great Baddow. Door-to-door, my daily commute took ninety minutes each way. No wonder I was perpetually tired.

I arrived at work, as always, at 8:15am. I was already sitting at my desk, working on my year-end report, when my colleagues began to arrive. The mood in the lab that morning was light-hearted and festive. Someone had strung up Christmas decorations. The wonderful Tetrabot, an innovative and unique industrial robot designed and built in our lab, was standing in the corner looking like a huge Christmas tree with streamers and baubles attached to its two metre-high frame.

I really enjoyed my job. I worked as a postdoctoral research associate at the GEC-Marconi Research Centre on the outskirts of Chelmsford in Essex. The team I worked with was part of the Industrial Automation Division. Our major project brought together an international consortium of companies and universities and was funded by the European Union as part of the ESPRIT Programme. We were developing new technologies that used artificially intelligent (AI) robots to assemble manufactured products. In retrospect, we were pioneers of the Fourth Industrial Revolution – thirty years before the term was coined by Klaus Schwab, founder and executive chairman of the World Economic Forum.

At about 10am, Ian Powell, our team leader, came into the lab to remind us that the NHS Blood Bank had set up a blood donors' station in the staff canteen area. As a registered donor, I decided to head over and donate a pint of blood. Steve Sanoff, a fellow researcher and a good friend, joined me.

In a corner of the canteen, a few hospital beds had been set up. On each of the beds, a donor lay connected via a thin plastic tube linking a needle in their arm to a transparent bag. Next to the cluster of beds, a small group of people sat and enjoyed tea and biscuits, their reward for parting with a pint of blood.

When it was my turn to lie on one of the beds, the nurse jabbed my finger with a sharp needle. She squeezed a drop of blood onto a paper test-strip and waited for it to change colour. She looked at the strip and then walked over to consult with one of her colleagues. She came back to my bed.

'You're a bit anaemic,' she said. 'We won't take blood today, but I'll take a sample to send to the pathology lab. I don't think there's anything to worry about, but if the tests do show up anything of concern, someone will call you. Please make sure that we have your correct telephone number.'

And then with a conspiratorial smile, she added, 'If you still want some tea and biscuits, I won't tell.'

On the way back to the lab, Steve asked why they hadn't taken my blood. I told him, and when I saw a look of concern cross his face, I assured him that I wasn't worried. Finding out that I was 'a bit anaemic' didn't surprise me. I'd been feeling run down and exhausted for weeks. We went back to the lab where I continued working on my report.

The following day, after lunch, I was putting the finishing touches to my annual report. The phone in the corner of the lab rang and Steve picked it up.

'Barry, it's for you,' he said.

I walked over and answered, 'Barry speaking.'

'Dr Dwolatzky,' said a voice at the other end, 'I'm calling from the pathology lab at Broomfield Hospital. We've tested your blood sample and we will need you to come in as soon as possible for a few more tests.'

I thought about the very important task I had to do that evening, and the report I needed to finish, and said, 'I won't be able to come today, but I'll be there first thing tomorrow morning.'

'Okay,' she said and put down the phone.

Only then did I think of several questions I should have asked.

After work, I commuted back to central London and went to a popular pub in Islington. It wasn't very crowded when I entered. I ordered a half-pint of bitter at the bar and went to sit alone at a corner table with my back to the wall and a clear line of sight to the door. I watched people coming in and going out as I sat reading The Guardian.

At exactly 6:30pm, Riaz, the man I was waiting for, came in and headed towards the bar. Our agreed all clear signal was for me to carefully fold the newspaper and put it on the table next to my beer. Riaz glanced my way and then ordered an orange juice which he carried over to my table. We sat together talking softly. I continued to watch the door as we spoke. Riaz told me that he and his partner Muff

Andersson were leaving London early the next morning. They would be away for several weeks. He took a large brown envelope from his coat pocket and quickly slid it under my newspaper. He whispered instructions. I listened very carefully. He finished his orange juice, stood up and left. I carried on sipping my beer while watching the door. I needed to make sure that no-one followed him out of the pub.

Fifteen minutes later, I slipped the newspaper and the hidden envelope from the table into my briefcase. I stood up, put on my coat, took my briefcase and left the pub. As I had been trained to do, I didn't immediately walk toward the bus stop, but stood on the corner smoking a cigarette while I kept an eye on the pub door to make sure nobody followed me out.

Before I caught the number 73 bus home to Stoke Newington, I bought two large heads of lettuce. When I got home, I sat in my bedroom with the door closed. I took the brown envelope out of my briefcase and tipped the contents onto my bed. There was a huge pile of fifty Pound notes. I counted them. Twelve thousand Pounds which was more than half of what I earned in a year. I stuffed the cash back into the envelope, sealed it and put it back into my briefcase.

I then went and sat in the kitchen, where I turned my attention to the lettuces. I munched my way, leaf by leaf, through both. This was my way of cramming for the blood tests that awaited me the following morning. Surely all that lettuce would deal with my anaemia?

My long commute early on Wednesday morning took me to the Broomfield General Hospital in Chelmsford. I had told my colleagues that I would be a little late for work that morning but didn't say why. I walked up to the hospital at about 8am and paused outside the entrance for a cigarette. I was feeling nervous for two reasons: the uncertainty about the blood tests and why I needed them, and the brown envelope bulging with cash that I was carrying in my brief-case. I had to be at a secret rendezvous at exactly 7:30pm that evening in Central London to hand over the envelope to someone I had never met. If he or she didn't receive the money in that envelope, carefully laid plans would fall apart, the consequences of which would probably be very serious.

I felt impatient. I didn't want this check-up at the hospital to take up too much time. I had so much to do that day.

I stood at the hospital's reception desk waiting to be noticed. Eventually a clerk came over and asked for my name. He ran his eyes down a handwritten list of names on the page in front of him. He suddenly stopped and stared at me in horror. This was the first indication I had that my life was about to take an unexpected and dramatic turn.

'How did you get here?' he asked.

'Train and bus from London,' I replied.

'But you shouldn't be walking!' he said. 'Sit on that bench and I'll bring a wheelchair.'

I stared at him, convinced that he had mistaken me for someone else. Before I could ask him to check his list again, he rushed off in a panic in search of a wheelchair. From that moment, I found myself being processed as a passive participant in a rapidly unfolding sequence of events. I was wheeled into a curtained cubical. Someone appeared and extracted several test tubes of blood from my arm. Someone else gave me a folded green gown that tied at the back and told me to change into it. People in white coats drifted in and out, poking and prodding me, not saying anything. For long stretches of time, I lay on the examination table alone in the cubical, thinking, 'What's going on? When will someone fill me in on what they're looking for and what they've found?'

I tried to ask questions, but nobody had the time or authority to answer. I kept checking my watch, becoming increasingly worried about arriving late at work.

At last, a doctor who seemed to be in charge came and introduced himself. He sat on the chair next to me and said, 'We're not happy with your bloods. Your counts are so low that by any standard you should be unable to walk, let alone catch trains and buses. We're not sure what the cause of your anaemia is, but we've decided to refer you to Barts in London. They have a very good department there.'

I wasn't really taking it all in.

I said, 'I know why I'm anaemic. I'm sure it has a lot to do with what I've been eating and how hard I've been working. I would prefer to go to work now. I'll get some rest over Christmas. I'll see how I'm feeling after the break.'

He shook his head. 'I don't think you've understood what I said. You're very ill. I've arranged for an ambulance to take you to St Bartholomew's Hospital in London. The nurse will come in soon to arrange some paperwork and then we're going to give you some blood.'

That was it. Britain's famous National Health Service had taken charge of my life.

I travelled back to London lying on a stretcher in the back of an ambulance. I watched two bags of blood drain into my arm. A uniformed paramedic sat next to me taking care of the blood transfusion with a disinterested look on his face.

'This all started when I volunteered to donate some blood, and now I'm making a withdrawal from the Blood Bank,' I thought as the ambulance crawled along, sounding its siren from time to time as we inched through the London traffic.

We stopped, the back doors opened, and two hospital porters wheeled me out of the ambulance, through a pair of swinging doors, and then along brightly lit corridors. They left me in a passageway and disappeared. I read a sign above the door: Saint Bartholomew's Hospital: Haematology Oncology Unit. I wasn't sure what oncology meant.

A nurse appeared and pushed my trolley into a long narrow ward. There were about twenty beds, most of them occupied. We stopped at an empty bed. In a rack under the trolley was a bag filled with my clothes. In a separate wire bin, I saw my shoes, green duvet jacket and briefcase. 'Thank goodness the briefcase is still there!' I thought. She helped me arrange my possessions in the small cupboard next to the bed. I waited for her to leave and then I quickly

11

pulled my briefcase onto the bed, opened it, and looked inside. I breathed a sigh of relief. The fat brown envelope was still there. I locked the case and propped it up next to the bed.

This was the first time since my early childhood that I had been in hospital. I had no idea what to expect, but all around me the staff in the ward confidently went about their tasks. Everything seemed to run like an efficient machine. I felt that I was in good hands. From time-to-time, strangers appeared at my bedside. They took blood samples, monitored the drip that was connected to my arm, recorded my temperature, checked my blood pressure, tapped my chest and stomach. I still had no idea about what was happening and why they all looked so worried.

I lay there for several hours in a sort of numb state, trying to process everything that had happened that day. It was then that I met the young man with the white coat whose name I cannot recall. I do remember that he told me he was a registrar, which is hospital-speak for a trainee specialist. He pulled at the heavy green curtains to create a private space around my bed and sat on the chair next to me and told me that I had something called hairy cell leukaemia.

'It's a very rare condition,' he said. 'If we look at statistical probabilities,' he said, showing me some bell curves he had photocopied from a recent journal, 'without treatment, it is definitely fatal. Even with treatment, it's very serious. There are a few treatment options available to us and we will need to decide on what action to take, but you need to understand that, statistically speaking, you have a life expectancy of five to six months, even with treatment. I'm sure you will understand (I see that you have a PhD in Electrical Engineering) that we are speaking about probabilities and averages. You, as an individual, might be anywhere on this distribution curve. The good news, if there is any good news,' he said with half a smile, 'is that you are in a unit headed by Professor Andrew Lister, arguably one of the top authorities in the world in this field of medicine. Professor Lister will see you later this evening. He will discuss treatment options and answer any questions.'

The young registrar was more relaxed now that he had finished the speech he had been sent to deliver at my bedside. He asked if there was anyone I would like him to call. I thought about the two huge problems I had to deal with and weighed up who I most needed next to my bed at that moment. Was it a good friend to hold my hand and comfort me as I came to terms with the fact that I had something called hairy cell leukaemia that might lead to my death within the next few months? Or was it someone I could rely on to take the cash-stuffed envelope to the secret rendezvous point in Central London at 7:30pm that evening?

I asked him to phone Francis McDonagh, my housemate for the past five years. Francis was both a good friend and someone I could rely on to undertake my secret mission. As I flipped through my address book looking for his phone number, I noticed that my hands were shaking. I was in shock! The doctor wrote down the number I gave him and disappeared through the curtains, leaving me alone and shivering. A nurse appeared a few seconds later with some tablets and a glass of water.

'Take these, luv,' she said in a familiar Manchester accent.

I swallowed them and shut my eyes.

I must have fallen asleep because when I opened my eyes Francis was sitting in the chair next to me. Words poured from my mouth. So much information to share, all of which was shocking to him. I told him what little information I had gleaned from the nervous registrar and then informed him about the envelope in my briefcase and my secret life that neither he nor any of my other closest friends knew anything about. He absorbed this torrent of information with a somewhat flabbergasted look on his face and tears in his eyes, but then rapidly pulled himself together to focus on the task at hand. He listened carefully to my instructions – including secret passwords and other precautionary measures – about where to go and what to do with the brown envelope. Having absorbed the shock of my revelations, he suddenly seemed to be quite excited to find himself participating in this cloak and dagger mission. I reached for my briefcase and gave him the brown envelope which he carefully pushed into his coat pocket before setting off into the cold London night.

'Oh shit,' I thought, 'I can't die now. I'm only thirty-five and there's still so much I need to do!'

I lay back on my bed and allowed myself to sob big wet tears for the first time in many years.

———

IT WAS THURSDAY MORNING, CHRISTMAS EVE, AND MR LISTER stood at my bedside. I was intrigued that in the UK medical system specialists are given the title "Mr" rather than "Dr" to denote their higher status. He was a youngish man, about ten years older than me. He was completing his ward rounds and stopped at my bed. He was accompanied by a retinue consisting of three or four registrars, including the young man who had sat at my bedside the previous day, and the matron in charge of the ward. He sat on a chair and flipped through my file.

It was obvious that he and his team had already had a long discussion about my case. He looked at me as he spoke, but he was also sharing his comments and observations with his entire retinue. He repeated some of the information the registrar had already given me. He used some medical jargon that I didn't understand. One of the words he used was splenomegaly. I looked it up weeks later and found that it means an enlarged spleen. He explained that my spleen, which should be the size of my fist, had expanded to such an extent that it was now the size of a rugby ball and filled most of my abdomen.

'Didn't you notice anything strange?' he asked.

'I thought I was putting on weight,' I said.

He explained that there was a very serious risk that my very large spleen would rupture, in other words, burst.

'If this happens,' he said, 'you could bleed to death. You're really lucky. You've been walking around with this bloated spleen for months. It could have ruptured at any moment. The first step we will take is to do a splenectomy, in other words, remove your spleen. You're booked into theatre this afternoon. I hope they haven't let you eat anything this morning!' he said, looking at the matron. 'After the spleen is removed, we will consider various treatment options.'

The retinue moved on. A nurse appeared and adjusted the drip attached to my arm.

'Your brother, Hilton, phoned about an hour ago,' she said. 'He has spoken to Mr Lister.'

I was relieved. Making contact with my family had been one of the other major worries filling my head. I had been anxious about when and how I would share news about my predicament with my family, none of whom lived in the UK. Hilton, my younger brother, is a medical doctor living in Israel. My parents lived with him and his family. I wondered how Hilton had found out about what was happening to me and that I was in St Bartholomew's Hospital. Then I realised that Francis must have called him.

'Thank you, Francis!' I thought.

Late that afternoon, I was gently manoeuvred onto a trolley and wheeled out of the ward. I spent Christmas Eve 1987 in an operating theatre having my giant bloated spleen removed. I had no idea what a spleen was and why we needed one.

I have a very hazy memory of Christmas Day 1987. I was heavily sedated and in a lot of pain. I slept a lot and was woken from time-to-time by doctors and nurses poking and prodding me and asking me questions. I remember having vivid dreams, or was I hallucinating? I was vaguely aware of friends and work colleagues sitting next to my bed either in tears or with encouraging smiles on their faces. Were they there or did I only imagine them to be there?

My clearest memory of that Christmas Day is of a group of angels (or people dressed as angels) coming into the ward and singing Christmas Carols. Mr Lister and the matron were pushing a trolley around the ward, offering patients whiskey and vodka. He stopped at my bed and poured whiskey into a glass.

'Have some of this,' he said.

'Do you think that's wise?' asked the matron.

'Let him enjoy something today,' said Mr Lister. 'Who knows how long he's got!'

I drank the whiskey which burnt my tongue and throat. To this day, I have no idea whether this is an actual memory or one of the many drug induced visions I had that day.

chapter
two

1960s to 1972

I t was about 6am. I sat alone on a patch of grass, a cup of instant coffee in one hand, a cigarette in the other. In front of me stretched an amazing display of rugged mountain peaks poking out above a sea of grey mist. Behind me squatted a small stone building flying a Red Cross flag on a pole. The Kena Clinic was the size of a small Johannesburg suburban house and sat neatly in the middle of a square of carefully mowed lawn edged by rose bushes. The sounds of goats and clucking chickens came from the direction of the cluster of round stone huts to the left of the clinic. A rooster crowed and I pulled the blanket I had draped over my shoulders a bit tighter. Winters in the Lesotho mountains were very cold – particularly just before dawn.

The sky in the east changed to a reddish pink. I felt I had never been in a more beautiful place in my life until I focused on Kena village as people started to emerge from their homes to face another day of endless struggle. Two young girls, followed by a skinny dog, were setting off with buckets to fetch water from the stream several hundred metres down the hill. Their day began with the ritual lugging of heavy buckets of water back up the hill. The first bright yellow edge of the sun appeared on the horizon and again the sky changed colour. I sipped my coffee and puffed my cigarette deep in thought.

———

IF SOMEONE WERE TO ASK ME WHEN I BECAME POLITICALLY AND socially conscious (in those days, we used the word consci-entisation), I would choose that early morning moment in the Lesotho mountains as one of the key turning points. The stark contrast between the natural beauty of that remote village and its grinding, hopeless poverty deeply disturbed me. It was June 1972. I was a second-year electrical engi-neering student at Wits University. I had neither the language nor the theoretical understanding to adequately describe the socio-economic reality I was encountering for the first time in my life, but it felt really wrong!

The first twenty years of my life had been spent enclosed in the bubble that was white South Africa. My parents were the children of Lithuanian Jews who had arrived in South Africa in the early 1900s to escape the rising tide of anti-Jewish persecution that would ultimately lead to the Holocaust. My father, Jock, was born in Roodepoort, west of Johannesburg, in 1918. His mother died in the Great Flu epidemic shortly after his birth. He and his four older brothers were raised single-handedly by his father who moved them to the small Orange Free State town of Senekal. My mother, Masha, was born in Lithuania and was five years old when she arrived, with her mother and four older siblings, to join her father who worked as a tailor in Benoni, east of Johannesburg.

I grew up in Orange Grove and Highlands North, suburbs in the north of Johannesburg. I went to government schools and socialised with school friends and neighbours, many of whom came from a similar background to mine. I would never have thought of myself as privileged or well off. My parents owned and ran a small retail shop in Bramley, called H&R Drapers, which sold clothing and haberdashery. They worked incredibly hard, five and a half days a week throughout the year. The business did well enough to support our family of five, but money was always very tight. I often felt envious of my friends and my extended family, many of whom lived a far more affluent life than we did. They wore smarter clothes, had fancier houses, and went on exciting holidays every year. We had very few family holidays. My brothers and I either helped in the shop, or we were shipped off to our uncle Abe who had a farm near Messina on the Rhodesian (current day Zimbabwean) border.

Only those who grew up in Apartheid South Africa will understand how successful that system was in keeping people in racially separate universes. It was like living in two different countries. I lived in white South Africa. The only black people I encountered did menial jobs. Even though we weren't well off, we had a live-in maid and a part-time gardener. There were the garbage collectors who appeared twice a week hanging off the back of a smelly truck that was driven by a white man. There were cleaners in the shops, delivery men on bicycles and diggers of holes at the side of the road. I hardly ever spoke to a black person and when I did it was very difficult to communicate. They seldom spoke much English, coming mostly from rural areas where they had little or no education.

The same separation was true for black South Africans. In general. the only white people they ever encountered were in positions of authority. Policemen, government officials, doctors in hospitals and bosses in all shapes and sizes. A black South African boy, born in the same city and in the same year as me, certainly lived a very different life from mine.

And yet our separate worlds stood geographically side-by-side. Orange Grove, where I spent my early childhood, is about 8km from Alexandra, one of Johannesburg's oldest and most notorious black townships. One of my earliest childhood memories was seeing thousands of black people walking along Louis Botha Avenue, the main arterial road linking Alexandra to town, as we called the Johannesburg city centre. I remember hearing chanting and shouting and seeing sticks and flags and banners waving around. I remember feeling scared. What I was witnessing was the famous Alexandra Bus Boycott of 1957 during which

Alexandra residents walked a forty-kilometre round trip to get to work and home again. They did this rather than pay an increased bus fare. In my childhood, I lived through the Treason Trial, the Sharpeville Massacre and the Rivonia Trial, and yet none of these momentous events made even the slightest impact on me. My world consisted of school, teachers, friends, acne, girls, rugby, and cricket. Although I was an engaged and sensitive boy, although I read a great deal and followed the news, I knew more about Britain, Europe and the US than I knew about the world that the maid who worked in my home came from. That was the reality (and the success) of Apartheid.

Despite the success of the system, there were events that penetrated through the bubble of my ignorance, particularly in my late teens when I caught glimpses of life in the parallel universe. I remember the day Mr Odendaal, our Afrikaans teacher, came into class in tears and told us that the Prime Minister had been assassinated. I was in Form 2 (South African Grade 9). Dr Hendrik Verwoerd, known as the principal architect of Apartheid, had been stabbed to death in the Houses of Parliament by Dimitri Tsafendas, a parliamentary messenger. I remember one of my classmates cheering at the news, which enraged Mr Odendaal. I remember feeling puzzled and uncomfortable because I didn't understand why anyone would kill the Prime Minister, why Mr Odendaal should be so upset, and why my classmate was cheering.

Another early memory I have relates to the arrest of Bram Fischer in 1965. Bram Fischer was from a highly respected Afrikaner family and yet he had represented Nelson Mandela and others in the 1963-64 Rivonia Treason Trial. Soon after Mandela and some of his co-accused were convicted, Bram Fischer was arrested and charged under the Suppression of Communism Act. While he was out on bail, he disappeared and there was speculation that he had fled South Africa. In fact, he was living, in disguise, in Bramley, Johannesburg, as Mr Black and often came into my parents' shop, H&R Drapers. My mother became very friendly with him and was intrigued that he often came in with a young black child to buy clothes for her. My mom was deeply shocked when kind and friendly Mr Black was arrested in November 1965 and turned out to be the infamous "communist terrorist" Bram Fischer. This also left me puzzled and unsettled. Why would a successful and famous white Afrikaner advocate join the communists and land up in prison?

These and other pieces of evidence simply didn't make sense to me. It was like finding pieces in a jigsaw that came from another puzzle.

————

MY POLITICAL AWAKENING PROBABLY BEGAN TOWARDS THE END of my time at Highlands North High School and certainly during the nine months I spent as a conscript in the army in 1970, the year after I matriculated.

I don't have many fond memories of school. I had a stutter and was often mocked and teased. I was the perfect target for bullying – the fat boy with glasses who stuttered. In high school, most of the teachers either ignored me or joined in with the teasing and bullying.

I linked up with other boys (it was an all-boys school) who also didn't fit in all that well with the crowd.

Philip Bert had been my best friend since Grade 1 at Linksfield Primary. We were in the same class for all 12 grades at school. Phil had a sharp mind and loved to argue. He always took a contrary position. I might have said that the Springbok cricket team was better than the Australians, and he would immediately argue that they weren't (even if he really thought that they were). Phil also spoke very fast. His words ran into each other, sometimes making it difficult to catch what he was saying. At one stage we were both seeing different speech therapists. While he was working on speaking more slowly, I was working on speaking faster. Phil was an avid reader. He introduced me to books I would never have otherwise come across. He loved classics translated from other languages – Dostoevsky, Gunter Grass, Hemann Hesse, Franz Kafka, Jean-Paul Sartre. We both read a lot and argued about the underlying meaning in these books. On many Saturday nights in our last year or two in high school, we would take the bus from Highlands North to Hillbrow. There we would browse in Exclusive Books, check out the new international magazines at Estoril Books, have a milkshake or a Coke float at the Milky Way, and then take the bus home. Phil contributed hugely to my intellectual awakening.

Percy Miller became a close friend when I started high

school. We lived a block apart and spent a lot of time together outside of school. We walked together to and from school every day. Percy was what we would now call a nerd. Like Phil, he was an avid and voracious reader. One day I overheard my mother telling a friend, in hushed tones, that Percy's father was "listed". I had no idea what this meant, but a few days later I asked Percy about his father. He told me that he was a communist and that he was no longer permitted to work in a proper job. He didn't know or wouldn't say much more. Percy's dad was often at home when I visited. He would playfully ask us thought-provoking questions, but never spoke about politics and the situation in South Africa. It was only much later that I learnt what "listed" meant. When the South African Communist Party (SACP) was banned by the Apartheid government in 1950, all of its known members were placed on a list and were subjected to a range of restrictions and surveillance. Mr Miller was on this list.

Roy Katzenburg was quiet and reserved. He was very interested in music and art. It was from him that I learnt about the type of music that my classmates had never heard of: Bob Dylan, Frank Zappa and Janis Joplin. I had acquired a reel-to-reel tape recorder and Roy and I swopped illegally recorded albums. Roy also experimented with drugs (it was the 60s, after all) and was by far my coolest friend.

The other person who had been in the same class as Phil and I throughout school was Hilton Schlosberg. We were very close in primary school. I remember when we were in about Standard 4 (now Grade 6), Hilton's father died. It was the first time I experienced a friend's parent dying. I visited his house while he, his mother and brother were sitting shiva, which is the seven days of mourning following the death of a family member in Jewish custom. Hilton and I sat in the garden both crying our eyes out at the terrible loss we felt. Hilton, like my other friends, was also academic and bookish. He was always top of the class. He was constantly bullied because he was seen as a teacher's pet. The word in use then was "shloop", which unfortunately had a similarity to his surname. So, to the bullies, Hilton became Shloop-berg. I always tried to take his side, which wasn't much help to him since I was also a popular target for the bullies.

At that time, all able-bodied young white men were conscripted into the South African Defence Force (SADF) after finishing secondary school. My nine months in the army were probably the worst months in my life but they contributed significantly to my burgeoning understanding of the reality of South Africa, and my place in it.

———

THE DAY I HAD BEEN DREADING ARRIVED. IT WAS AN EARLY morning in January 1970. I stood alone in a crowd of thousands of other seventeen- and eighteen-year-old white South African boys on the parade ground at the Drill Hall in central Johannesburg. At the far end of the parade ground, dozens of Bedford trucks were parked in neat rows. At the Drill Hall end of the parade ground, clusters of fierce-looking men in uniform stood sipping from mugs of coffee and talking among themselves.

Not a single one of my school friends had received the same call-up instruction. Phil was assigned to the air-force academy, Roy to the signals corps. My assignment was to Number 1 Maintenance Unit at Lenz Military Base. In my one hand was my dad's old brown suitcase, packed with underwear, toiletries and a pile of books which I hoped to read but never did. In my other hand were my call-up papers instructing me to report to Die Drill Saal at 7am sharp on that day. The actual building stood locked and shuttered behind a forbidding fence. Everyone appeared to be as confused as me, standing in groups waiting for something to happen. It was already 7:30am and I hadn't yet reported. I just stood there, watching, listening, with a tight knot in my stomach. I realised that nobody was speaking English. It dawned on me that in this army, Afrikaans was the medium of communication. 'Oh shit!' I thought, 'I'm even more screwed.'

Suddenly, at around 7:45, one of the fierce men in uniform detached himself from the others. He marched thirty or forty paces towards the middle of the parade ground, stopped with a sharp stamp of his foot and stood smartly to attention. And then, with an unbelievably loud voice, he shouted something that sounded like 'Tree Aan! Tree Aan!'. He repeated it several times. I watched to see how others would respond. Some of them seemed to under-stand what to do. They rushed over to stand in front of the man with the voice, forming themselves into straight rows.

I followed. The other fierce men in uniform walked among our haphazard rows, snapping at us like sheepdogs. They pushed us into neat ranks snarling words in Afrikaans. Every second word was 'fok' or 'fokken'. As a polite Jewish boy from Highlands North, I had NEVER heard someone in authority use the word 'fuck'. Now I was about to hear it in every sentence shouted at me for the next nine months.

We were counted off into groups of forty and made to run over to the Bedford trucks where, as soon as we were inside, the flap on the back was raised and secured, an order shouted, and the driver set off into Johannesburg's early morning traffic. In my truck, we were mostly silent, although a few of my truck-mates dealt with their nervousness by making wise-cracks in Afrikaans. I couldn't understand much of what they said.

The Lenz military base is about forty kilometres southwest of central Johannesburg. It's on the outskirts of the then-Indian township of Lenasia. It seemed to take hours to get there. When we arrived, we were again herded by the snarling, nipping, cursing sheepdogs into ranks on a dusty parade ground. I tried to get myself into a position near the back where no one would see me. I still clutched my dad's brown case in one hand, and my call-up papers in the other.

Again, we were shouted at in expletive-filled Afrikaans and then counted off in groups to be fed into a production line awaiting us. We were taken into a large hall where we were given a huge duffle bag for our civvies. We were told to strip naked and line up. I waited my turn to be given a medical examination by a doctor who grabbed my balls with his gloved hand and shouted 'hoes' (cough) and then listened distractedly to my chest with a stethoscope. An assistant grabbed the call-up papers I still clutched in my hand and laboriously copied my name and army number into his register. When he saw my name, he stopped and said to the "doctor", 'Kyk na hierdie poes se naam!' ('Look at this cunt's name!'). 'Dwo.. wat se ding?' ('Dwo.. what's this thing?'). From then on, I was at known to those in authority as "Dwo-wat se ding?", which was soon changed to "D-d-d-d-d-dwo-wat se ding?" when they discovered that I stuttered. The "doctor" also looked at my circumcised penis and said in a loud voice, 'Nog 'n fokken Jood!' ('Another fucken Jew!'). This gave me my other commonly used name in the army, "Jood".

After being examined and declared medically fit, we filed, still naked, into the quartermaster's store where we were issued with our items of uniform, which – so the joke went – came in two sizes: too big or too small. My size was mostly too big. At last, we were allowed to put on underpants, shorts and a tee-shirt. I was so relieved to at last be able to cover my circumcised penis which had become a major item of interest and amusement to the uncircumcised Afrikaans boys.

Finally, our heads were shaved, which was the final humiliation, and then in groups of thirty we each awkwardly lugged a steel trunk or "trommel" packed with our new uniform, and a duffle bag, to our bungalow. Each bungalow was long and narrow with fifteen beds lined up on each side and an empty space running the length of the bungalow, forming a corridor between the beds. We were instructed to put our trommel at the foot of the bed and our duffel bag under the bed. The concrete floor was painted red and was as shiny as a mirror.

At Lenz, the bungalows each had a name. There was Alpha, Bravo, Charlie, Delta, Echo. It took me a few weeks to realise that this followed the NATO phonetic alphabet for radio communication. I was in Bravo bungalow, which was to be my "home" for most of the following nine months. From the first day, I counted off the remaining days, starting at two hundred and seventy-five days. You could have asked me at any time on any day and I would have been able to tell you how many days I still had to spend in that awful army.

My time in the army consisted of two parts. The first part was basic training, which lasted for six weeks. It was an absolute nightmare. In the second part, I was assigned a job and that period was much more bearable, but still punctuated with dreadful moments.

When I came out of the army at the end of September 1970, I swore to myself that I would never go back into the army.

My time in the army brought me into contact for the first time in my life with that other group of white South Africans, the Afrikaners. In the 1960s and 70s, when I was growing up, the social separation epitomised by Apartheid was only one of the forms of social division in South African society. There were many other important divisions based on culture, heritage and class. In the late 19th and early 20th centuries, the white Afrikaner community had suffered significant discrimination and humiliation at the hands of the Anglophone community. The defeat of the Boers by the British in the Anglo-Boer War (1899 to 1902) had left huge divisions in white South African society. Generally, English-speaking white South Africans were seen as being aligned with the British, while white Afrikaans speakers were aligned with the Boers. The Second World War sharpened this division. Many prominent Afrikaner nationalists had aligned themselves with Hitler and the Nazis against the British. In the whites-only general election in 1948, the Afrikaner Herenigde Nasionale Party (HNP) came to power with a five-seat majority and only 38% of the votes cast, defeating the long-time pro-British Afrikaner Prime Minister Jan Smuts. DF Malan, leader of the HNP, became Prime Minister and set about settling old scores.

He introduced Apartheid, which formalised and legitimised a system of racial discrimination that actually dated back to British colonial rule. He also embarked on uplifting and empowering the white Afrikaner community and wresting both political and economic control from the English-speakers. By 1970, when I was conscripted, this project was well underway. While economic power remained in Anglophone hands, political power was firmly entrenched with the Afrikaners. BJ Vorster was Prime Minister at the time and the state bureaucracy was mostly Afrikaner. Parastatals such as SA Railways, the SA Post Office and the SABC were all controlled and run by

Afrikaners, while law enforcement and the military were firmly in their hands.

Not only did Afrikaners control the SADF, but they also filled most of its ranks. Career soldiers formed the permanent force (PF). A key strategy for the Nationalist Government was to implement an affirmative action policy to create jobs for poor white Afrikaners. The PF was a popular employment destination for unskilled, poorly educated Afrikaners who lacked the prerequisite skills to enter the civil service.

A lifetime of anti-English (and anti-Jewish) propaganda coupled with a huge inferiority complex, and often a psychopathic personality, came together to create the Afrikaner PF instructors and officers who ran Lenz military base in 1970. I represented the perfect target. Overweight, wearing glasses, useless at macho physical stunts like scaling walls and leopard crawling under barbed wire, English-speaking, Jewish and – best of all – I stuttered. They had a field day, spurred on by the Afrikaner conscripts who took great pleasure in seeing others suffer. My six weeks of basic training were filled with humiliation and embarrassment, marching up and down in the blazing sun, being shouted at and sworn at endlessly in Afrikaans, impossible physical tasks, midnight inspections, coupled with terrible homesickness. However, I wasn't alone! There were others who were having a similar experience to me. We formed a close bond and supported each other as far as we could. It was this bond that helped us all through those endless weeks.

After basics, each of us was randomly assigned to a job. Lenz was the base of Number 1 Maintenance Unit, which is that part of the army responsible for logistics. It provided drivers, clerks, storemen and cooks. I was assigned to become a cook. After four weeks of training in Pretoria, I returned with a bunch of others to Lenz where we were now responsible for feeding the two thousand or so soldiers stationed there.

It wasn't a bad posting. The work was relatively easy, and I became very good friends with some of the other cooks. I became particularly good friends with Steve Segall, who we called "Gully". He and I usually worked in the kitchen together. Sometimes we worked the night shift alone, preparing breakfast for two thousand early risers. During the night, we also cooked ourselves delicious meals and listened to music on LM Radio. We shared a lot in common, including our disdain for the PF cooks who managed the kitchen and ran a business on the side stealing and selling the best produce that was supplied to our camp. We kept each other going and left the army with many funny stories to tell our children. On the flip side, I remained an easy target for the PF bullies who didn't miss an opportunity to remind me why I hated that place and the system it represented.

———

AFTER THE ARMY, I HAD FOUR MONTHS TO LICK MY EMOTIONAL wounds and recover. I was so happy to reconnect with my loving family and some of my old friends, although when I first came out, Phil and Roy were still in the army. Their call-ups had been for twelve months. In many ways, I came out of the army stronger and much clearer about my country and myself. In February 1971, I registered for a BSc(Eng) in Electrical Engineering at Wits University.

Me with mom, dad and older brother Leon on Durban Beach in 1955 [Photo: Family Album]

Me in about 1961 [Photo: Family Album]

chapter
three

THE WHITE LEFT

1971 to 1972

After leaving the army, I decided, much to my mother's horror, to become a hippie of sorts. I grew my hair and beard into a tangled bush, dressed in tie-dyed t-shirts and bell-bottom jeans, wore sandals, clogs or walked barefoot, and replaced my unfashionable, black-framed glasses with a "cooler" gold-framed pair. I smoked dagga, but only occasionally since I didn't enjoy the muddle-headed paranoid feeling it left me with after the initial high. It's always been important for me to feel in control and dagga worked against that. I never tried any of the heavier drugs, such as LSD, which some of my friends were using. My version of being a hippie was to immerse myself in the literature and music of the late 60s and early 70s. I listened carefully to Bob Dylan songs trying to understand his ambiguous lyrics. I identified strongly with the struggle against the war in Vietnam, the civil rights movement in the USA, the international peace movement, youth culture and activism against "the system".

At first, my rising level of consciousness was located outside of the South African context. Having strong views about distant America's role in even more distant Vietnam was far easier than dealing with the complexity and contradictions of being a white South African. Although I knew a little about the anti-colonial struggles being fought all over Africa, I had so little information and understanding about them, that I preferred not to think about things happening closer to home. I was much happier hanging a peace sign round my neck and reading the poems of Allen Ginsberg.

I had decided to study engineering at the University of the Witwatersrand (Wits), not because I had a great passion or interest in working as an engineer, but largely because I couldn't think of anything else to do. I knew that I needed to do something that would give me a professional qualification. I worried a lot about how I would support myself knowing that I needed to become independent of my parents who continued to struggle financially. The professions followed by my peers were mostly medicine, law or accounting. Although engineering was seen as a possible career option, hardly anyone from the community I came from considered it. I remember my Bobba (my maternal grandmother) saying to me when she heard what I planned to study, "But Barry, that's not a job for a nice Jewish boy like you! Rather become a doctor."

In 1971, Wits University had a liberal reputation and was recognised internationally, as it still is today, as one of South Africa's top universities. Up until 1959, Wits and the University of Cape Town (UCT) had admitted students of all races. However, while academic classes were racially integrated, there was strict segregation of social and sporting activities. The other three English-medium universities were Rhodes, which was all-white, Fort Hare, all-black, and the University of Natal which admitted people from all racial groups but kept its classes racially segregated. The Afrikaans-medium universities, Stellenbosch, Pretoria, Potchefstroom and Orange Free State, were strictly for whites only. In 1959, the Afrikaner National Party government passed the Extension of Universities Act, which closed Wits, UCT and Natal to black students.

Wits had responded to this attack on their freedom to admit students based only on merit by protesting as strongly as they could in parliament and in the streets of Johannesburg, but ultimately they failed and continued as a whites-only institution. Academic Freedom Day, with talks and protests, was observed annually at Wits to mark the day that the Extension of Universities Act came into force.

When I enrolled at Wits, it did have a tiny number of black students. Since engineering and other professional qualifications were not offered at exclusively black Apartheid-created tertiary institutions, some graduates of what became known as bush college could apply to the Minister of Education for special permission to register at Wits for these disciplines. The few students granted permission were subjected to strict conditions, including not engaging in politics. There was one black South African student in my engineering class at Wits and three or four South African Indians.

————

ON THE DAY I REGISTERED FOR ENGINEERING AT WITS, I WAS convinced I had made the wrong choice. As I stood in the registration queue dressed in my new hippie garb, I looked around and realised that I stood out like a sore thumb. Every other first year engineering student in that queue had short, neatly combed hair and wore the same type of clothes that my father wore, although some wore short pants and long socks, which I couldn't imagine my dad wearing.

When it was my turn to stand in front of the dour and conservative-looking Professor Volckman, the then Dean of Engineering, he looked shocked. He didn't comment on my appearance, but he pointedly cleared his throat while he watched me struggling to sign a form while the pen became entangled with the tassels on my wristband. I saw the faculty registrar, Elise Barnes, and her assistants whispering to each other and giggling as they watched me. I'm sure that they were also convinced that I had made the wrong choice.

————

A UNIVERSITY IS A VERY DIVERSE COMMUNITY. WHILE generalisations are seldom accurate, it's true to say that certain academic disciplines attract certain types of people. At Wits in the 1970s, the stereotype shared amongst my friends was that medical students were the swots and high achievers, commerce and law students were the smooth operators, and architects were the creative slightly eccentric artistic types. Those in what we would now call the humanities were a mixed bag ranging from those who were mostly interested in participating in campus life to the radicals. And then there were the engineers. This was an overwhelmingly male group of super-conservative students who could always be counted on to take a pro-establishment stance. They drank huge amounts of beer, were fanatical rugby supporters, and tended to be staunch and unthinking supporters of the government and its policies.

I was horribly out of place in an engineering class. I really should have been doing a BA. I discovered, however, that I had the skill of a chameleon. I toned down my dress code and avoided topics of conversation with my classmates that would have led to political arguments. I soon noticed that my classmates did likewise. I sometimes walked in on a conversation that stopped as soon as I entered the room. They were usually speaking about "communists", "hippies" and blacks, usually using the K-word, regurgitating propaganda being pumped out by the government and its supporters. Although most of these classmates were academically very bright (electrical engineering was acknowledged as being one of the most challenging degree choices at Wits), the majority had never read books and articles that dealt with topics outside of their engineering studies. I was shocked to discover that, apart from set-work books at school, most of them had never read a novel.

What kept me sane and helped me to continue to grow intellectually was finding like-minded people around me at Wits. There were some who were also studying engineering. I became particularly friendly with Jean Bodart, a fellow electrical engineering student, who had been at high school and in the army with me. His family were French and he had grown up in various places outside of South Africa, which had broadened his perspective. I met David Berchowitz, who was studying aeronautical engineering, and Howard "Toy" Stassen, who was in chemical engineering. Through them, I met several others studying in other faculties. I also connected into a wider circle of friends and acquaintances, who shared my world view and interests. I began hanging out on the Wits Library Lawns, close to the Student Union building with its canteen that served huge plates of hot chips which we drowned in tomato sauce. Although I was a very conscientious student, I sometimes got so engrossed in a discussion with some of my new friends, or in doing the cryptic crossword in the Rand Daily Mail, that I missed a lecture here and there.

The big question discussed within my circle of friends was about how to get involved. The problem we shared was that our presence at university was a contradiction. On the one hand, we were all inadvertently the products of white privilege and, as Wits students, we continued to benefit from this privilege. On the other hand, we understood the need to change this very system. While my own level of consciousness in my first year at university was still in an embryonic stage, there were others in the group who were already making their mark as radical student leaders.

In my first year at Wits, I spent my time observing and struggling to understand the politics of the day. The Student's Representative Council (SRC) under its president Taffy Adler was very active. It frequently called mass meetings, issued pamphlets and waged campaigns. There were pickets on Jan Smuts Avenue, across the road from Pop's Café and the headquarters of SA Breweries (SAB). Wits students stood on the university side of the busy road while uniformed police and RAU students stood on the opposite pavement in front of SAB[1]. In my view, both the police and the RAU students were cut from the same cloth as the bullies who had tormented me in the army, and I took an instant dislike to them. I occasionally half-heartedly joined the pickets, which usually descended into the trading of insults and throwing of rotten fruit, but mostly stood with a bunch of other Wits students watching the picket from the fringes. There was also often a counter-protest on the Wits side of the road staged by students who were opposed to the picket. Most of the students in this group were my fellow engineering students. They stood in a group also hurling verbal insults at the protesters.

Although I knew that the issues being discussed and the

campaigns being waged were extremely serious and important, I saw student politics at that time as something of a game. Taffy and his fellow SRC members addressed meetings and wrote pamphlets using jargon and rhetoric filled with political terminology that went right over my head. Even though I read a lot and followed current affairs, I didn't understand the difference between liberalism and radicalism. I hadn't read the works of Lukàcs and Gramsci. I had no clue who Fanon was and thought of Lenin and Trotsky as villains, not heroes. While the radicals on campus studied political theory and debated false consciousness and spoke about the dialectic, I struggled to keep up with my very demanding engineering curriculum.

I was, nevertheless, eager to engage. I attended mass meetings and incomprehensible seminars, usually sitting near the back. I sat on the Library Lawn with my radical friends and asked lots of questions about the issues being debated. Thinking back to that time in my life, I realise now that I failed to make a connection between the reality of my existence and the issues being earnestly analysed and discussed. How could I feel a connection sitting in meetings hearing about migrant labour, rural poverty, exploitation of workers, solitary confinement and life in the townships, while spending my days as a privileged white student on Wits campus and weekends and evenings being pampered by my Jewish mother in our family home in Highlands North?

ONE DAY IN MY SECOND YEAR AT WITS (1972), I HEARD ABOUT an organisation called South African Voluntary Service (SAVS). They were organising two-week long work camps in rural areas in South Africa, Lesotho and Swaziland during the June/July winter break. They were looking for volunteers. Some of my new circle of friends were planning to join, so I added my name. My decision to spend a couple of weeks on a SAVS camp had far more to do with me wanting to go away with some of my friends than seeing it as some form of activism.

SAVS was a student organisation that took on development projects in some of the poorest rural communities in Southern Africa. Most of the projects involved building classrooms or clinics. During the year they would be approached by rural communities requesting support. Small teams were sent to carry out feasibility studies and a few projects were chosen for support. SAVS then approached companies and private donors to fund or contribute in kind to the projects. A project often required three or four two-week camps to be completed.

My first SAVS camp was in Kena, which was about 100km from the capital of Lesotho, Maseru. SAVS owned a five-ton truck, named Bruce, and a Toyota bakkie, called China. Early one cold June morning, a group of about twenty bleary-eyed Wits students gathered near the Students Union building on campus to load building materials and food onto Bruce and China. We were each allowed a small bag of clothing. There was only space in the cabs of the trucks for the drivers, Tim Haynes and Stan Sher, and a few lucky passengers. The rest of us climbed onto the open backs of the trucks where we created "nests" of blankets and tarpaulins in between bags of cement, concrete lintels, window frames and asbestos roofing materials. We also shared the space on the truck with a vast number of donated boxes of Pronutro and Black Cat Peanut Butter. This would be the bulk of our food for the camp.

Amongst the twenty SAVS campers were a few friends and many new faces. Phil Bert, my oldest school friend, was there. Eddie Wes, who I had met while I was in first year, was there. Some of my Library Lawn friends, including Mel Pleaner, Moira de Groot, David Dison and Gil Brokensha, were also on the truck. I didn't know it then, but among the group who set off that morning on a freezing, bumpy, uncomfortable journey from Johannesburg to Kena and Hansi, which was the site of another camp in Lesotho, were people who became, and still remain, my closest and dearest friends.

Our project in Kena was to build a new clinic to extend the existing Red Cross building. The most abundant and traditional building material in that part of Lesotho was stone. When we arrived in Kena late that afternoon on the back of Bruce, we were greeted by the school choir and a huge pile of rocks which the villagers had spent weeks gathering. There were about twelve of us at the Kena camp and we were given use of two classrooms in the school, one as our dormitory and the other as a storage space and kitchen. We were also greeted by Abram, the local master stonemason, who would be helping us with the building, although actually we were there to help him.

Kena was the first time I had really ventured outside of my white South Africa bubble. The first thing that struck me was that there were very few men in the village. Apart from Abram and a few other middle-aged men who filled specific roles, such as the priest, the headmaster and store owner, the only men present were a few old and sickly individuals. Women and children did most of the work: collecting water, cooking food for their families, caring for infants and helping on the building site. Where are all the men? I asked someone. 'Working on the mines', I was told. At that time, most working-age men in Lesotho were recruited to work in South Africa's highly dangerous, labour-hungry gold mines in the Orange Free State and Witwatersrand. Some, but not all, of these men sent part of their meagre earnings back to villages like Kena. Every year they would come home for a few weeks, make babies and return to the mines. Some returned from the mines with terrible injuries or chronic illnesses, such as silicosis. When they were too old to work, they returned to Kena to live out the rest of their shortened lives as burdens on their impoverished families. Some of the young women also left the village to sell their labour as domestic workers, farm labourers or in other menial jobs, in South Africa's towns and cities.

There was no local economy. The little bit of agriculture,

carried out in the rocky shallow soil, was only subsistence farming. People grew a little sorghum and some vegetables, and might have kept one or two cows, goats and chickens. The road leading to the village was almost non-existent. People mostly used Basotho ponies for transport. There was no grid electricity. The store had a noisy generator that powered a fridge and some lights. People used candles and a few paraffin lamps for lighting and cooked and heated water on fires fuelled mostly with dried-out dung.

What struck me and stays vividly in my memory, even now, was the extreme level of poverty. People had so little. They wore flimsy and tattered clothing. Many had no shoes and walked barefoot even in the coldest weather. Inside their homes, which were mostly traditional stone-built single room huts, there was hardly any furniture, very little crockery and cutlery, maybe a single aluminium or cast-iron pot, and very, very little food. Families ate at best one small meal a day. Many children had the extended bellies and other tell-tale symptoms of kwashiorkor. We heard that many children died of diseases we white South Africans thought of as minor ailments, such as measles and gastroen-teritis. It was the middle of winter and almost everyone in the village seemed to be ill with coughs and snotty noses. This was poverty as I had never witnessed before.

The school was only a primary school, and not all chil-dren attended. Those few children who continued on to secondary school went away to distant boarding schools. Several grades sat together in a classroom or under a tree with a single teacher. Most of the learning was done by rote. Day-in and day-out we heard children chanting the times tables or repeating sentences spoken by the teacher. One of the school's proudest institutions was its choir. The culture of school choirs seemed to have permeated all of Lesotho and schools competed in local, regional and national choir competitions. Kena's choir was particularly successful. Every day we heard the choir practicing for hours on end. One song they sang particularly beautifully was a multi-part harmony version of 'The Teddy Bear's Picnic', which opens with the line 'If you go down to the woods today...' and ends with 'today's the day the teddy bears have their picnic.' After school, the children would come to the building site to watch us work, giggle at the silly white people doing hard physical labour with so little expertise, and – for the bolder kids – to practice their English or teach us Sesotho. One day, Moira asked some of the children, 'Do you know what a teddy bear is?' One of them answered confidently, 'It's a little someone who goes to the woods for a picnic.' Moira then asked, 'And what's a picnic?' They didn't have a clue. When she explained that it was taking your food into the veld and eating it there, they roared with laughter. 'Why would you want to eat your food in the veld?' they asked. 'Why don't you eat it at home?' Good point!

Although that first SAVS camp was one of the most memorable and enjoyable experiences of my life, it shocked me deeply to realise that this was how most people in

Southern Africa lived. I finally made the connection in a very deep and meaningful way between rural poverty and migrant labour and my affluent and comfortable life in Johannesburg. Someone from Lesotho had to sell their labour for a pittance so that South Africa's gold mines could make a big enough profit and pay enough tax for me to live my life as a white South African. This realisation gave meaning to the jargon-filled radical rhetoric I had been hearing from student leaders and my radical friends over the past year and a half. I also understood that the real enemy was not the Afrikaner bully-boys who had made my life miserable in the army, nor was it the racism encapsulated in Apartheid. It was the whole rotten system.

————

IT'S IMPOSSIBLE TO CAST MY MIND BACK AND REMEMBER exactly how I saw the world then. However, virtually everything I've done since, and most of the decisions I've made, grew out of the way I began to view my world in 1972.

My revelation in Lesotho had been a moment of understanding the concept of underdevelopment. The entire South African economy from agriculture and mining to construction and manufacturing had depended on the creation and maintenance of a supply of cheap labour, and much of the historical thrust of the preceding eighty years had been about disenfranchising the majority of the population through underdevelopment.

When I was at school, there were two things that had clouded my understanding of politics in South Africa. The first was the way I saw Afrikaners, and the second was liberalism.

In the early 1970s, the true might of the Apartheid state was reaching its peak. Afrikaner control of government and its institutions had grown more confident and more complete. Although English speakers, who in many cases were proxies for international – and mostly British – interests, still controlled the economy, Afrikaner capital was increasingly asserting itself. Government-controlled entities such as Sasol and Iscor were being used to empower Afrikaner business. Within the circles that I moved in, a great deal of attention was focused on this divide between Afrikaners and English speakers. The stereotype created was that we – the English speakers – occupied the moral high-ground. We were the good guys while Afrikaners were the bad guys who were messing up the country.

What I didn't really understand until 1972 was that Apartheid wasn't the invention of Afrikaner nationalists driven by narrow-mindedness and racism but was actually a continuation of an ongoing and proactive underdevelopment strategy created by, and for the benefit of, capital, irrespective of language and cultural prejudice. According to the theory I came to appreciate much later, the stereotypes about English speakers and Afrikaners were maintained and nurtured to conceal that uncomfortable truth.

Liberal politics conveniently concealed this fact and dominated my broader community within white South

African society. It defined our relationship with black South Africans who were seen as poor and underprivileged. We never really went deeply into the reason why black South Africans were in such a state. We certainly never understood that our affluence and privilege was only possible because others were poor and underprivileged. The liberal response was to apply band-aids to the gaping wounds in our society and to trust the system. There were numerous organisations and campaigns devoted to feeding poor black children, collecting clothes for the poor, buying Christmas gifts for homeless kids and raising bursaries to educate deserving black students. While growing up, I was a sensitive and caring child who never missed a chance to join in when charity was required. I often gave my pocket money to "the poor". Liberals were continuously writing letters to the press, signing petitions and, in some cases, going to the courts or appealing to international bodies to challenge the excesses of the Apartheid government.

Some of the very same liberals who campaigned against Apartheid ran the mining companies, banks, and manufacturers that depended for their profits and very existence on the fact that rural communities lived in poverty. What I began to understand in 1972 was that liberalism was a cloak behind which those with a guilty conscience could hide. I became aware of the contradictions at the heart of South African society and the uncomfortable truth of my own place within that society.

At Wits University in the 1970s, this analysis, and some

of its consequences, was being put forward by a passionate group of students and young academics, and due to the work I did with SAVS I related directly to the issues being debated. I was developing my own political line and analysis.

The white Left, however, was far from homogeneous and united. There were numerous factions and divisions. SAVS and the work we did was criticised by some who saw us as liberals papering over the cracks and having negligible impact. I, on the other hand, saw SAVS as a huge learning curve for myself and others. While I accept that the handful of projects we tackled did very little to even scratch the surface of the Apartheid edifice, other very significant consequences flowed from the fact that through SAVS hundreds of white South Africans were given an opportunity to understand some of the harshest realities of the South African system. From this group, many people went on to make significant contributions in the struggle against Apartheid and to the building of our new democracy after 1994.

———

Barry Dwolatzky

SAVS school building [Photo: Edwin Wes]

Me with Cindy Meltzer (Balkin) [Photo: Edwin Wes]

Protest outside Johannesburg Magistrate's Court in
1975. Janet Love with Chris Marchand and David
Dyzenhaus. [Photo: Edwin Wes]

---

1. RAU was the recently established Rand Afrikaans University that was
being set up for Johannesburg's white Afrikaans speakers. They operated from a temporary site near Wits in Braamfontein while their
permanent campus was being built in nearby Auckland Park.

chapter
four

COMING OF AGE

1973 to 1976

The morning was cold and dark. There had been more snow during the night and the path to the bus stop hadn't yet been shovelled. My hard-toed fur-lined worker's safety boots sunk into the fresh snow as I trudged from the hostel to catch the 6:30am bus. I was careful not to slip on the icy path as I shuffled along, cocooned in scarf, gloves, hat and coat with my glasses misting over from my breath. The outside floodlights illuminated the side of the building I had just left and then I saw it, crudely painted in still-wet paint on the clean white wall of my hostel. The South African flag, with its orange, white and blue stripes, splattered with red paint like blood. Painted underneath it in huge untidy blood-red letters were four words in Norwegian: 'Sør-afrikanske rasister ute'. I couldn't read Norwegian, but I guessed it translated to something like "South

African Racists Out". It hit me like a punch in the solar plexus. It was a protest against **me**. People didn't want **me** there. With my head spinning, I continued on the slippery path to work.

It was December 1973 and I was in Trondheim in Norway as an IAESTE (International Association for the Exchange of Students for Technical Experience) exchange student. A requirement for engineering students at Wits, and all over the world, was that we were to do six weeks of practical work at the end of our second and third years of study. IAESTE made arrangements for international work experience. I had applied and been given the opportunity to work for six weeks in Trondheim hosted by the IAESTE Chapter at the technical university in Trondheim (Tekniske Høgskole i Trondjem). I was joined by another white South African engineering student, Dave, from the University of Natal. I worked in a job-shadowing role with the local municipal electrical power utility. Both Dave and I were given accommodation in a hostel on the university campus.

It was the first time I had been out of Southern Africa and the first time I had ever travelled on an aircraft. It was also my first experience of real snow. As a kid, I had seen a light sprinkling of snow once or twice on those very rare occasions when it snowed in Johannesburg, but Trondheim had the real thing. Being in Norway in the middle of winter was an exciting and magical experience.

The IAESTE Chapter were great hosts. They assigned some of the students in the hostel to take care of Dave and me. Outside of work, our lives were filled with drinking, hanging out at the Roundhouse, which was the students' social centre at the university, sight-seeing and more drinking. Norwegian students loved to drink, and I rapidly discovered that, like engineering students around the world at that time, our hosts had no interest in politics. They were curious about South Africa, but only about the wildlife and the sunny beaches. I was constantly asked whether there were wild animals in the streets of Johannesburg and whether we had real buildings or only grass huts.

The anti-South African slogan daubed on the outside wall of our hostel took me completely by surprise. I hadn't thought that anyone apart from our hosts even knew that Dave and I were there. When I came back from work at the end of that day, the flag and the words in Norwegian were gone. They had either been scrubbed off or painted over by university maintenance. Dave wasn't particularly concerned about it and our student hosts laughed it off as the work of the "Maoists". I, however, was both horrified and excited: horrified that I was being lumped together with the white racist minority who ruled South Africa; excited that there were students at this engineering university in remote and distant Trondheim who knew, and cared, enough about South Africa to paint that message on the wall.

I wanted to meet the Maoists to find out more about them and try and set the record straight about my own political views. Finding them wasn't very difficult. They had an office at the Roundhouse along with tens of other student organisations and associations. A few days after the slogan-painting incident, I plucked up courage and walked into their office. A few people were sitting around talking in a very untidy space. They didn't seem at all surprised to see me come in, and they certainly knew who I was: one of the South African racists who was neither welcome at their university nor in their office.

Nils, a tall, thin stereotypical Norwegian with very long, straight fair hair and a wispy beard stood up to confront me while the others looked on. I sensed that they were all ready for a fight. I can't remember exactly what I said, but it was something about agreeing with the words that had been painted on my hostel wall. This took them by surprise. They began asking me questions and throwing accusations at me about the way I 'treated black South Africans and starved their children'. A long conversation ensued during which it became clear to me that while Nils and the others had considerable insight into the nuances of international politics, they were ill-informed and naïve on the subject of South Africa. At best, they had read an article or two in left-wing publications or seen an anti-Apartheid documentary. Despite their ignorance, they were indignant that IAESTE was uncritically hosting white South Africans at their university. This was something I hadn't even thought about when I applied to participate in the student exchange.

The conversation in the Maoist's office soon became friendly and energetic. Illicit alcohol (many students brewed their own spirits in their hostel rooms) was shared as Nils and his comrades pumped me for information. It was agreed that they would organise a student's meeting on

South Africa which I would address. Dave and I hadn't previously spoken to each other about our own political views, and when I told him about this planned meeting he was horrified. He was convinced that the South African authorities would hear about me mixing with communists and anti-South African groups and would arrest me when I returned home. He wanted nothing to do with my new friends.

The following week, I participated in a discussion with a motley group of about twenty Norwegian students, all of whom held left-wing political views of some description and all of whom were eager to hear my views on Apartheid and the situation in South Africa. This was my first experience of international solidarity, a concept that played an important role in my life in the future.

Nils and some of his comrades became good friends of mine while I was in Trondheim. They shared many insights with me and taught me much about the nuances of left-wing politics. I hope they also learnt a little from me.

———

I RETURNED TO SOUTH AFRICA FROM NORWAY VIA LONDON. I took a ferry from Bergen to Newcastle in January 1974 as Britain went into a three-day working week in response to electricity shortages. The coal miners' union was on strike and the British Government, under Conservative Prime Minister Ted Heath, imposed drastic measures to conserve coal. My ferry wasn't allowed to dock and we stayed bobbing about in the stormy North Sea for two days as food in the cafeteria ran out. This lack of food didn't trouble many of us since everyone was horrendously seasick. Even the crew of seasoned sailors had turned sickly green and, like the rest of us, threw up constantly into stinky buckets.

When I at last reached London, that mythical city of my childhood story books, it resembled a scene from a Dickens novel. The shops in Oxford Street were lit by gas lanterns and candles. I found it charming, but I was also fascinated to witness first-hand workers' power and trade unionism, especially as workers' power was just beginning to take root in South Africa.

———

IT WAS FEBRUARY 1974. AS THE AIRCRAFT APPROACHED Johannesburg, I looked out of the plane's window at the familiar skyline. I had been feeling homesick and was filled with excitement at the prospect of being home. I would be going into my third year of electrical engineering. Partly because of my involvement with SAVS and my growing interest in student politics, I hadn't been a diligent student in my second year of study. I had failed two of my ten subjects, which I repeated in 1973. This gave me abundant time to enjoy university life. My trip to Norway was the cherry on top of a fantastic year in which I turned twenty-one and grew and matured in many different ways. Thinking about the year ahead as my plane taxied to the terminal building, I felt, for the first time since I had started university, excited at the thought of becoming an engineer. It was the first time I had felt that emotion.

As I came through the arrivals gate at Jan Smuts Airport, I saw my sister-in-law, Denise, waiting to meet me. I immediately saw from her face that something terrible had happened.

I had been away for two months. In that time, the only contact I had had with my family and friends in South Africa had been an occasional letter. My family had written but hadn't said much, and no one called because international calls were horrendously expensive. It was only when I returned that I found out that a number of disasters had befallen my family. Driving back from the airport, Denise was in tears as she filled me in on all that had happened. I was in a state of suspended disbelief as I listened.

Firstly, my Bobba, of whom I was very fond, had died. She was the only grandparent I had known. It was the first time someone close to me had died and I hadn't been there to share my grief with my family or comfort my mother. I felt deeply sad about that.

Denise then told me a long and complicated story about my parents' business, the little haberdashery shop in Bramley. Although the business was profitable enough to support our family's modest lifestyle, cashflow was always tight. In spite of this my parents assisted M, the husband of my dad's cousin, and someone who had the reputation of being a very successful businessman, by signing post-dated cheques against which he could borrow money. While I was in Norway, one of M's business deals went bad resulting in my parent's bank liquidating H&R Drapers. My parents not only lost everything but were obliged to sell our home in Highlands North. In the face of these financial shocks, my father, Jock, who was always prone to chronic depression, had suffered a major breakdown. He was in hospital receiving shock therapy.

The bottom had completely fallen out of our world.

By the time Denise and I reached home, I had decided that I could not even think of going back to university. My younger brother, Hilton, was about to enter first year at Wits Medical School and if any money could be scraped together, I decided that his education should be the priority at that time. I would need to find a job and earn enough money to support myself. I had absolutely no idea as to how I would do this. I couldn't imagine what job I would be able to find but I would have to do it.

My mother, Masha, was waiting for us as Denise's car drove up. She was in floods of tears as she hugged me and repeated some of the things Denise had told me. Although she seemed so small and vulnerable, I immediately detected in her a fierce determination to get things back on track, and remarkably that is what she did.

Before I could say anything, she said that, whatever it took, I would stay on at university and Hilton would join me. Although it was one of the most difficult things she had ever done, she had already approached Jewish community welfare organisations for help. She had always found it difficult to accept any form of help from anyone, and to have to go cap-in-hand under these circumstances to ask for charity had been the most difficult of all.

As it turned out, I didn't need money from Jewish welfare. Hilton was granted a bursary and I managed to organise a loan from Wits University. In the previous year, while I had been on my self-enforced semi-gap year, I had worked as a private tutor, teaching maths and science to school kids and first-year university students. I continued to do this for the rest of my time at university and managed to cover all my living expenses from the money I earned. My father recovered after a fashion. He continued to have bouts of severe depression for the rest of his life and was never able to find employment again. My mother was our pillar of strength. She held it all together. She went to work as a shop assistant in a jewellery shop. She was always cheerful, always positive and always eager to bend over backwards to help others. The example she set inspires me to this day.

Cousin M showed no remorse for the damage he had done to our family. He continued to live a comfortable affluent lifestyle. I took away many life-changing lessons from this most traumatic family experience. For me, it was an example of how heartless the capitalist system could be. It seemed then, and still seems, so unfair that my parents, Jock and Masha, who worked tirelessly to give my brothers and me the best opportunities in life, should be screwed in the way they were, and that people like M suffered no consequences.

Barry Dwolatzky

—————

My trip abroad and the trauma I had faced on my return had a profound effect on me.

I was no longer half-hearted about my studies. I desperately needed to have a qualification that would guarantee me employment and some level of financial security. I felt really privileged to have an opportunity to study at a world-class university like Wits in a discipline I was starting to understand and enjoy. I had also fallen in love with computer programming while on my enforced gap year. I had spent hours in the Wits Computer Centre on the ground floor of the Northwest Engineering Building learning to program in Fortran. I became a familiar figure in "The Barn", the area in the Computer Centre where we transferred our program from paper coding sheets to punched cards. I stood at the window between "The Barn" and "The Machine Room", which housed the huge IBM mainframe computer, and watched the operators at work. I was sometimes allowed to go into the Machine Room to help load paper on the line printers and separate sheets of printout. I often helped students who were new to computing as they struggled to debug their programs. I began to think that computers would feature in my future career, although I had no idea what such a career might look like.

My new interest in my academic studies became more evident in my performance as a student. I achieved good marks and attracted the attention of some of my lecturers and classmates. I was no longer the hippie misfit trying to remain invisible at the back of the engineering classroom. I became a popular member of the class with a reputation of knowing this stuff.

My social and political activism also became an important part of my activities and self-definition. In 1973, when I had had more time on my hands, I had become more active in SAVS. I had participated in feasibility studies in which a small group of us visited sites of potential workcamps all over the country. I went on several camps and gained a deeper understanding of how rural communities lived in different parts of the country. I started to become very interested in what we called "appropriate" or "intermediate" technology, which were low technology solutions that could be used to solve some of the most pressing problems in underdeveloped areas.

In 1974, my new devotion to my engineering studies left me far less time for SAVS and other related activities. I remained close to my SAVS friends but only managed to go on one camp at a village called Pitseng in Lesotho.

The 1973/74 period was a turbulent and critical time in South African politics in which the Wits campus and Wits students were at the epicentre of some significant developments. In February 1973, eight white left student leaders who became known as the "NUSAS 8" were issued with banning orders. Banning orders were a mechanism that the government had created to prevent individuals from engaging in political and social activism. A banned person was not allowed to attend gatherings, receive visitors, enter certain places, publish anything or be quoted, or leave the area in which they lived. Effectively, banning was a way in which government silenced and harassed its opponents. At the same time, eight black student leaders active in the newly emerging Black Consciousness (BC) movement were also banned. One of these was Steve Biko, its founder. Wits students packed the university's Great Hall in protest and picketed along Jan Smuts Avenue. I enthusiastically joined in, filled with outrage at the government's attack on some of those who I respected as my leaders.

In 1974, there were elections to the all-white national parliament and the Wits SRC ran a campaign highlighting the real issues facing the white electorate. There was a series of mass meetings on campus at which politicians from all parties presented their manifestos. All of the Great Hall meetings were jam-packed and most turned into political theatre in which white politicians were heckled and torn to shreds by some of the most articulate and sharp-witted students at Wits.

In 1974, I also joined a literacy training project run at Wits by the Wages Commission instituted by NUSAS. I was trained as a tutor and assigned to work with black Wits staff members who were illiterate. My favourite pupil was Richard Shezi, who worked as a security guard. Richard was a little older than me. He grew up in rural Natal and had never had the opportunity to go to school. When we first met, he couldn't even write his name. He brought me a document Wits had asked him to sign which had something to do with his pension benefits. I explained its contents to him and he signed it with a cross. Throughout the year, we met twice a week during which time he proved to be one of the most dedicated and conscientious students I've ever taught. He worked so hard and learnt so quickly using the training methodology we used that he was able to read and write enough to pass his test for a learner's driving licence by the end of the year. His manager at Wits taught him to drive and he was promoted from the lowest paygrade as an unskilled security guard to the higher grade as a semi-skilled truck driver. I continued to meet Richard regularly until I left Wits in 1979. Apart from English, I also taught him arithmetic and history. When I returned to Wits in 1989 after spending ten years in the UK, he was one of the first people I bumped into. He told me that he had passed his matric exams and was now a manager in the Wits support services. Through Richard, I learnt in a most practical way how lives change through access to basic education.

———

WHEN I GRADUATED AS AN ELECTRICAL ENGINEER IN 1975, I received a prize for being "the most improved student". My final year average was over 75% and I would have received a cum laude had I not failed subjects in my second year. I've always considered my prize something of a loser's prize, but my mother was the proudest parent in the Great Hall.

I still lived at home with my parents and my younger brother, Hilton. Home at that stage was a rented flat in a building called Xanadu in Yeoville. My older brother, Leon, with his wife, Denise, and their two daughters, had left South Africa to live in Melbourne.

I decided to stay on at Wits to study for my master's degree, mainly to avoid being called up to do military camps in the South African Defence Force (SADF).

———————

By 1975, THE SADF, EQUIPPED AND SUPPORTED BY THE WEST, was waging a low-level anti-insurgency war in Rhodesia (now Zimbabwe) and on the northern border of Namibia, which was still referred to by South Africa and its western allies as "South West Africa". South Africa was illegally occupying Namibia in defiance of a United Nations resolution. In 1975, Portuguese colonialism ended when its right-wing government was swept from power, and its two Southern African colonies, Mozambique and Angola, became independent. The liberation movements in both of these countries came to power, Frelimo in Mozambique and the MPLA in Angola, but the departure of the Portuguese did not mean peace. Western-aligned forces, Renamo in Mozambique and UNITA in Angola, proceeded to wage vicious civil war against the new Soviet-aligned governments.

South Africa waded into these regional conflicts claiming that it was saving the world from communism. At that time, the SADF was the best equipped and trained army in the region and supported Renamo, UNITA and Rhodesia's white government.

A large number of soldiers in the SADF were white conscripts whose period in the military had been substantially extended. By the mid-1970s, every medically-fit white South African man was obliged to spend two years in the SADF after completing school. In addition, they had to attend a four-to-six-week military camp every year until the age of forty. There were only three ways to avoid this annual call-up: you had to refuse to go, leave the country, or provide proof that you were a full-time student. If you declared yourself a conscientious objector on either religious or moral grounds, you were sent to prison. Many of my male peers in the White Left faced this difficult decision. My choice was to hang on to my student status for as long as I could. This was why I registered for a master's in 1976. I was lucky enough to be awarded a substantial scholarship which, together with the income I earned giving extra tuition in Maths and Science, made me financially self-sufficient. The time had come for me to leave the family nest.

Most of my friends lived in communal houses. Johannesburg's Berea and Yeoville areas were popular places for these communes. I decided to move into a big communal house on the corner of Tudhope and Honey Streets in Berea where some of my best friends at that time had been living for some time. The group included Eddie Wes, Suzanna Cross, Melanie Pleaner, Mark Centner, Helene Zampetakis and Moira Miller. There were others who came and left in a continuous ebb and flow. I have many happy memories of life in that house. There were frequent communal meals, funny stories and serious philosophical discussions over cheap wine late at night. All of this happened against the backdrop of me working conscientiously on my master's research. I often sat in my room pouring over my books or computer printouts as Eddie's infectious laughter echoed through the house.

There were also some bad moments. One of these was a few weeks after the world-shaking events of June 1976. Soweto had erupted on 16th June when police opened fire on school children protesting against the introduction of Afrikaans as the language of instruction at their schools. Hundreds subsequently died and thousands were injured as protests spread throughout the country and the government declared a state of emergency. Was this "the revolution" my friends and I had been anticipating? We were simultaneously scared, devastated and thrilled as events unfolded. The police were hunting down "ring leaders" in Soweto and many student leaders had gone into hiding.

Our house, and other communes in Yeoville and Berea, became temporary hiding places for some of these leaders. Skinny young kids, smelling of smoke, would arrive at the house, smuggled in by our friends from other communes. These refugees from the burning townships never said much and we didn't ask. We gave them hot food, a mattress and a pile of blankets in our lounge. We listened out fearfully for sounds in the night that might be a prelude to the arrival of the police. Thankfully we were never raided. After a day or two hiding in our house, the young refugees would be smuggled to another safe house or driven by one of our friends to the Botswana border where they would disappear into exile and an uncertain future.

Thinking back to that time, I have a vivid and lasting memory about something all of those young men and women had in common. It was the look in their eyes. An empty dead look, like the eyes of a fish. It was the look of deep trauma. Those eyes had seen things I couldn't even imagine.

Another bad memory from my time in that Honey Street house happened just before Christmas. All of my house-mates were away on holiday and I was left behind to mind the house, feed the cats, water the plants and work on my research. The house was rented and had come with a number of squatters who lived in the servants' quarters under the main house. In the world of Apartheid, small numbers of black South Africans managed to defy the strict constraints of racial segregation by pretending to be domestic workers and finding property owners who would allow them to live in their servants' quarters (which most houses had). The people living underneath our rented house had lived there for years but didn't work for us. Some of them went off during the day to do casual work in the area as cleaners and gardeners. Others brewed and sold illicit alcohol to domestic workers in surrounding blocks of flats and houses.

The house was structured so that the part we lived in was quite separate from these other residents on the prop-erty. Sometimes this changed, like the night when we were all awakened by blood curdling screams. When we rushed out, we saw two naked women confronting a half-naked man in our back yard. There was loud swearing, some punches were thrown, and everyone was screaming. Eddie bravely went downstairs to try to calm things down. I never found out what it was all about.

I was alone in the empty and quiet main house a few days before Christmas 1976. The downstairs part of the house was anything but empty and quiet. A large number of children who, I guessed, usually lived in the rural areas had come to join parents or relatives for the Christmas holidays. At 2am, there was loud knocking on the front door of the house. Half asleep and half dressed, I opened the door to see five or six policemen holding torches.

'Pass raid', said the one in charge.

At that time, all black South Africans were obliged to carry a document colloquially known as a "dompas". It contained various stamps and signatures that gave its owner permission to be in a white area. Anyone caught without a valid pass was arrested, charged and jailed. As I stood at the front door with some of the police, I realised that a bunch of other police were downstairs hauling people out of the servants' quarters and lining them up. I was shocked to see that there were about twenty-five people in all.

None of them had a valid dompas. They were therefore all illegally staying on what appeared to be my property. The policeman in charge called me aside. He said that he wouldn't arrest any of them now, but that he would be back the next day.

'If any of these illegal bantus are on your property when we come back tomorrow, we will arrest them and fine you for each illegal bantu here. There are so many. It will be a very big fine', he said.

With that, he and his squad left to raid the house next door. I stood there facing my twenty-five fearful neighbours.

'Please will you all leave tomorrow morning', I said.

'Where must I go, baas?' asked one of the older men. 'This is my home. My children are here for Christmas.'

Everyone else looked at me with pleading eyes.

'Please baas! Don't throw us out!' they begged.

I was not their "baas", and I had a complete and total revulsion at the thought of me enforcing Apartheid's pass laws, but what could I do? I could have taken a principled stand, but I guess I took the coward's way out. I scraped together enough money to give people bus fare or train fare to get out of Berea for the Christmas period. When the police returned the next day, I was the only person on the property. The policeman in charge seemed disappointed. I realised then that what he was really after was a nice fat bribe to make his festive season more joyful.

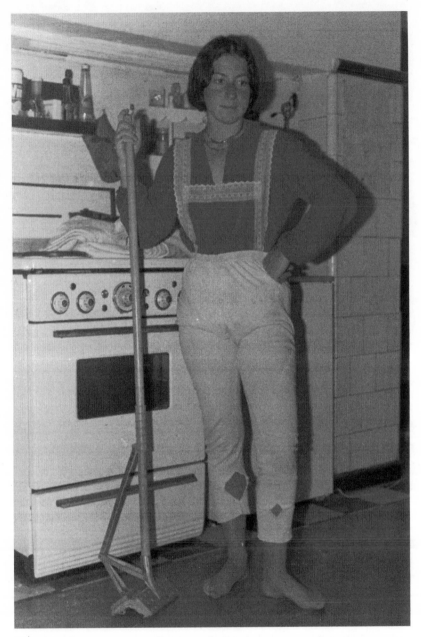

Melanie Pleaner in Honey Street communal house. [Photo: Edwin Wes]

Me with Moira Niehaus in Honey Street communal house. [Photo: Edwin Wes]

Me in Honey Street. [Photo: Edwin Wes]

chapter
five

CROWN MINES

1977 to 1979

S teve Barnet and I left at 4am in my old Renault R5. We
drove on the almost deserted roads to the Johannesburg Fresh Produce Market and were back in Crown Mines
by 7am, the car loaded with prime grade fruit and veg. An
hour later, we had divided our purchases into ten identical
piles, and I packed some of the bags back into my car so
that I could drop them off on my way to Wits.

By the time I returned home that evening, all hell had
broken loose. Steve and I had been summoned to the
Kremlin for an urgent confrontation.

Our crime was the purchase of prime grade produce.
Every week, a pair of members of the Crown Mines Veggie
Co-op were entrusted to buy supplies, and every week the
people sent to the market competed to show how much
they could buy for the fixed weekly budget. The trick was

to focus on quantity, rather than quality. A huge bag of Grade D sweet potatoes or a sack of tired withered cabbages were seen as a far better buy than a tray of juicy fat Grade A peaches. On the way to the market that morning, Steve and I had agreed that we were tired of eating lentil stew and mushy vegetable slop every evening. We needed something more exciting. What if we bought less, but bought quality? Surely everyone would be happy with that? We were wrong and had been summoned to explain our wayward bourgeois tendencies!

———

IN 1977, I HAD MOVED FROM MY FIRST COMMUNAL HOUSE IN Honey Street, Berea, to another house in the same street. Towards the end of that year, I moved again with some of my new housemates to a house at the end of a row of attached terrace houses in the bottom street of Langlaagte Deep in Crown Mines. The area was owned by Rand Mines Properties (RMP), who, following the end of the life of one of Johannesburg's first goldmines, were looking for ways to develop the real estate around it. RMP was willing to rent out houses at a ridiculously low rent while they decided what to do with these properties. After a while, Model Village and Royal Village were emptied and (very sadly!) demolished, but Langlaagte Deep remained. White lefties began to move from their communes in Berea, Yeoville and elsewhere to this village and some of the other remaining Crown Mines dwellings, like Peacock Cottage.

Our village had three roads. The middle road was tree-lined and had large double-storey houses on either side of the street which had been the homes of senior mine officials. There were about twelve houses in the middle road. At the one end of the road was a community centre, with a neat sign indicating that it had once been the scout hall. Adjoining it was a little playground for kids, complete with swings, slide and see-saw. The top and bottom roads as we called them each had two rows of small attached houses – about ten in each row. Each interior had a similar layout of three bedrooms, kitchen, lounge, toilet/bathroom and a verandah with mosquito netting in the front. There was a small patch of garden, with the classical South African servants' quarters, a tiny box of a room, at the back. Huge mine dumps of discarded mine rock crushed to a fine sand lay just beyond the houses in the bottom street. Although Langlaagte Deep village was less than 5km from Johannesburg's city centre, it had the feel of a small rural community. Neighbours popped in and out of one-another's homes, borrowing sugar and sharing gossip, which was not in short supply. Everyone knew about everyone else. Tongues wagged constantly as couples combined and separated. We all heard who was seen sneaking into and out of which house in the early hours of the morning. Added to this spice was political intrigue and another, more sinister and dangerous, form of gossip. Who were the security police agents in our midst? Who had been spotted meeting at a café in nearby Mayfair with a suspicious looking character who just might be their security branch handler?

Heather Bailey, a British woman who was slightly older than the rest of us, started writing a weekly newsletter which spread some of the hottest gossip, both personal and political. We all lived in fear of being mentioned in Heather's dispatches.

Our little village also imposed a strong code of political correctness. We were mostly young white radicals struggling to find our role in Apartheid South Africa. While we were all decidedly privileged, our backgrounds varied; some of us were self-supporting, some of us were relatively poor, and others had the backing of wealthy parents living in the suburbs. What we all shared was a conscious effort not to live out the white privilege Apartheid bestowed upon us. One of the worst labels that could be pinned on someone was to call them bourgeois. If you were seen wearing smart clothes, eating expensive food or drinking good wine, you earned this label.

A house whose residents became the self-appointed arbiters of political correctness was in the top street. Some of us referred to it as "The Kremlin" and it was to this house that Steve Barnet and I were summoned on the day we broke rank and bought bourgeois fruit and veg with the community's money. Fortunately, we weren't shot at dawn, but we did earn a severe ticking off and something of a reputation as deviants.

Crown Mines became a very important part of life in Johannesburg's white left and played a central role in many individual lives and relationships. I loved the community and living with my housemates, Gil and Sue Brokensha,

Eric Engelbrecht and Debbie Pilkington. While I was living in Crown Mines, my parents emigrated to Melbourne to join my brother and sister-in-law. While most of my friends and neighbours had a family home in the suburbs to which they could retreat when they needed some home comforts, my only home was Crown Mines. It provided a stable foundation for me as I worked hard on finishing my PhD and mapping out my future while focusing on my other all-consuming preoccupation: appropriate technology.

———

THROUGH MY WORK WITH SAVS, I HAD BEGUN TO concentrate on the role of technology in society. Working in rural villages in Lesotho and Natal, I was struck by the fact that life was so difficult for people, particularly women and children, who spent an inordinate proportion of their day acquiring the raw materials for their survival. It was a never-ending grind which all too often ended in defeat. Infant mortality was high, malnutrition endemic and life spans were short. The modern world had made very little impact in these communities.

If the industrial revolution was about steam and simple machines replacing animal and human power, then by definition these rural Southern African villages were pre-industrial. And yet modern technological society existed in towns and white-owned farmhouses a few kilometres away. I watched children carrying heavy buckets of water from streams to their homes. The environment had been depleted of most sources of energy. There were no trees. I watched women struggling to cook on meagre fires built from twigs and dried cow dung. People ground sorghum by hand for hours on end. School kids did their homework by the light of dim flickering candles. I became obsessed with the desire to work on bringing technology into their lives.

I realised that simply introducing modern technology into these communities was not a viable solution. Yes, a petrol pump could easily bring water from the distant stream to the village, but where would the petrol come from? Who would fix the pump if it broke? Technology exists in an ecosystem of available skills and services. I had seen brand-new machinery standing unused in villages because no-one knew how to run and maintain it, or because the fuel was too expensive.

I became interested in technology known variously as intermediate, alternative or appropriate technology. For various ideological reasons, I preferred the latter label. The key idea was to devise technology that fitted within the constraints of the environment in which it was used, but drew on modern scientific theories, principles and materials. Engineers had, for example, designed waterwheels that used the flow of a river to pump water to storage tanks hundreds of meters away. While the design of the waterwheel components was based on the most cutting-edge fluid dynamics theories, the material used could be found in a rural hardware store. The pump could be understood, built, operated and maintained by someone with basic mechanical knowledge.

In the 1970s, appropriate technology became a popular field of interest around the world as development professionals and their organisations followed in the footsteps of what had largely begun as an outgrowth of the alternative lifestyle hippie movement of the 1960s and their search for simpler ways of living. I read extensively on the topic and collected files of designs for pumps, stoves, water filters and methane digesters. Wits University management gave SAVS permission to set up some test sites at Frankenwald, a farm on the northern fringe of Johannesburg, owned by the university. With some of my SAVS colleagues, I spent many weekends splashing around in the polluted Jukskei river struggling to get ram pumps and waterwheels to work. We installed some of our successful devices in rural villages. I also spent time working on appropriate technology projects with Neil Alcott, who ran rural development projects on his farm near Tugela Ferry in Natal.

Like most things technical, there was a huge gap between having something that worked at the Frankenwald farm and discovering if it made a significant impact on people's lives. I remember feeling hugely frustrated and disheartened when I returned to a village a few months after installing and demonstrating a very clever and effective ram pump. It seemed perfect – it was cheap, needed no maintenance, and was powered by the flow of water in the stream, plus I had trained a local handy man to prime it and keep it running. On returning to the village, I had expected to see it pumping away, refilling the huge plastic water tank we had installed. Instead, I found the pump unused, the water tank empty and women carrying buckets of water on their heads.

The paradox I faced is not uncommon because development is far more complex than setting up a pump and water tank in a village. I realised that technology alone, known as "technological determinism", doesn't change the world, but that social and economic factors are far more important. This important insight has stayed with me ever since and has become an important cornerstone in shaping my understanding of the world. Even today, as I write these words, the complex interplay between technology on the one side, and social, economic and political factors on the other, helps me to understand the so-called Fourth Industrial Revolution and the impact of the COVID-19 pandemic.

———

IN 1976, I REGISTERED FOR AN MSc IN ELECTRICAL engineering and in 1977 was allowed to convert it to a PhD. The research I chose had nothing to do with my interest in appropriate technology nor my broader political interests. My PhD was in a sub-discipline of electrical engineering, called control engineering, and dealt with a very interesting set of mathematical functions called Walsh Functions.

There was method in my choice since control theory lies at the heart of several engineering disciplines. Electrical, mechanical and chemical engineers are all interested in feedback systems. In fact, biological systems are jam-packed with feedback loops. Control theory deals with how to analyse and design feedback systems. In general, a system is something that transforms inputs into outputs. The simplest form of system has a single input and a single output which are connected via some simple linear relationship. A system that transforms a number (i.e. an input) into the square of that number (i.e. an output) is a very simple system. Most systems in the real world are far more complicated, linking several inputs to several outputs via complex relationships.

A feedback loop measures the output of a system and modifies some of the inputs to ensure that the output remains within a certain range of values. Suppose, for example, that the system is a motor car driving along a highway. Inputs are the accelerator and the brakes, which the driver can control, and external factors are such things as the gradient of the road and direction of the wind. Suppose also that the only output we are interested in is the speed of the car. If the driver wishes to drive at a constant speed, they would monitor the output, i.e. the speed displayed on the dashboard speedometer, and use the accelerator and brakes to constantly adjust the speed. This is a feedback loop controlled via the human driver. Most modern cars have a cruise-control system which automates this feedback system. Control theory is used by engineers to design and build such systems.

My PhD was within the field of control theory, but focused on a specific sub-area dealing with system identification. When designing a feedback control system, the engineer needs to have a mathematical model of the system. For complex systems, it is often too difficult to carry out the mathematical analysis leading to the definition of such a model. In this case, experimental methods are used to fit a model that would best describe the relationship between a set of measured inputs and outputs. This in a nutshell was what I was focusing on in system identification.

If a system is time-invariant, in other words it doesn't change over time, system identification experiments can be carried out once before the control system is designed. However, many real-world systems are time-variant which means that the mathematical model that describes it varies over time. In this case, it would be necessary to carry out system identification repeatedly in real time, in something called an adaptive control system, as system identification is an integral part of the control loop.

In 1976, when I began my research, system identification in digital control systems was based on a set of exponential functions which, via Euler's function, consist of sine and cosine functions. In principle, a set of sine functions with increasing frequencies was fed into the unknown system as inputs. Corresponding outputs were measured and then correlated with the inputs. Doing this analysis on a computer was very computationally intensive, requiring many multiplications to be performed. This stretched, and often exceeded, the capabilities of the computer hardware available at that time. We tend to forget that in the 1970s computer hardware was in its infancy.

In 1923, the mathematician Joseph L Walsh had devised a set of functions, called Walsh Functions, that had identical mathematical properties to the set of sine and cosine functions. The interesting thing about Walsh Functions is that they are binary. They are square waves that vary over time between the values of +1 and -1. Researchers in the 1970s had rediscovered Walsh Functions because they fitted so well into the binary world of digital computers. My supervisor, Professor John Flower, had been toying with the idea of using these Walsh Functions in digital control. Using them in system identification would mean that the many multiplications that the computer would be required to perform would become simple additions and subtractions. It was obvious that this would be far more computationally efficient.

Undertaking this research meant that I had to teach myself a substantial body of mathematics that had not been covered in my undergraduate courses. I also needed to write large and complex computer programs in Fortran. While I enjoyed the maths, I loved the computer programming! I seized every opportunity to stretch my programming skills as I implemented a very sophisticated digital adaptive control system based on Walsh functions.

My PhD research gave me the opportunity to publish papers in leading international engineering journals and to attend several international conferences. My thesis was well received by the examiners and I received my PhD at the end of 1979. I received great support from my supervisors, John Flowers, Ken Garner and Mike Dewe. The work, however, did not have the impact it might have had in the field of control engineering since developments in computer hardware were rapidly making it possible to carry out multiplications as efficiently as additions. The computational advantage of Walsh Functions soon disappeared.

———

Eddie Wes and Sue Goldstein. [Photo: Edwin Wes]

Crown Mines house. [Photo: Edwin Wes]

Moira Niehaus at Peacock Cottage in Crown Mines. [Photo: Edwin Wes]

Barry Dwolatzky

Group of friends with Eddie Webster and Luli Calignicos. [Photo: Edwin Wes]

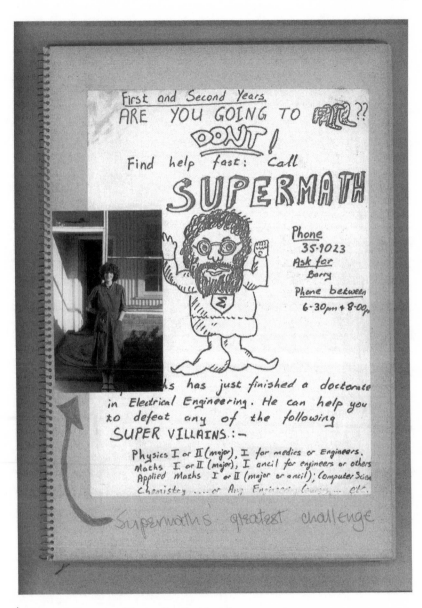

SuperMath poster. [Photo: Family Album]

chapter
six

PLANNING MY FUTURE

1979

I n the late 1970s, as my PhD neared completion, I became increasingly preoccupied with thoughts about my future. I had the prospect of being called up to army camps hanging over my head. For some of the people I knew, these call-ups were happening every year and they often involved active service in townships or on the border where, according to government propaganda, the SADF was 'defending South Africa from communists and revolutionary terrorists'. By 1978, the Apartheid regime had tightened its repressive grip in the wake of the June 1976 uprisings. My political conscientisation had brought me to the firm position that I was not prepared under any circumstances to serve again in the army, even if such service only required me to be a chef in an army kitchen.

As a full-time student, I had managed to avoid further

call-ups. I had hoped that the army would lose track of me as my address had changed several times and I had never informed them of these changes. This didn't help, however, as I, my parents and my housemates had received regular visits from the military police checking on my whereabouts. They warned me several times that I was required by law to keep the army informed of my current address. They also required evidence each time they tracked me down that I was still a full-time student, and showed no sign of losing interest in me.

Once I had finished my PhD, I would have two choices. Either I could refuse the call-up or leave the country. The former would mean going to prison, while leaving the country represented a huge leap into the unknown. There were others facing the same difficult decisions, but it was not easy to find them. Not only was it an imprisonable offence to refuse a call-up, but it was an even more serious offence to encourage others to refuse conscription. It was only several years later, in 1983, that an organisation called the End Conscription Campaign (ECC) was established to organise and support white South African "war resisters".

After a great deal of thought, discussions with my closest friends and much soul searching, I decided to go into voluntary exile.

I kept my decision secret, since I feared that the South African authorities might stop me from leaving. My next step was to work out what I would do and where I would go after leaving South Africa.

———

PIERS CROSS AND LINDA ALBERTYN LIVED IN THE TOP ROAD IN Crown Mines, opposite The Kremlin. They had an interesting house guest and late one evening dozens of Crown Miners crammed into the Kremlin's small lounge to hear him talk about his recent experiences. People squashed two or three to a chair, sat on laps, the floor, or stood against the walls and in the doorways. The room was full of cigarette smoke and excited chatter as we waited for the stranger to settle down in his chair. He had thick black hair, a neat beard and laughing eyes. He spoke with an interesting British accent and a friendly engaging tone. We all instantly liked him. My friend Melanie sat on the floor, entranced… her eyes locked on his face. Was this love at first sight? It definitely was as forty years later they're still married.

Neil Murtough was passing through Johannesburg on his return to London from Mozambique. He was a regional coordinator for IVS (International Voluntary Service) which was a sort of international version of SAVS. He spoke of his experiences working and living in one of Africa's newest independent states. He spoke about grass-roots democracy: street committees, block committees and district councils, and how they brought discussions about key issues of the day from the individual citizen to the highest decision-making bodies, and then back again. Everyone was involved in everything as a socialist economy was being built to replace Portugal's chaotic extractive colonialism. No longer would this huge African country be exploited to benefit a little slice of Western Europe.

But, as Neil explained, it wasn't all rosy in Mozambique. The anti-colonial war had ended but had morphed into a civil war between the ruling Frelimo party and Renamo. Neil spoke about how white mercenaries were in the country supporting Renamo and sabotaging efforts to develop the rural areas. Both western governments and South Africa were supplying arms and money to Renamo with the aim of destabilising the country and ensuring that Frelimo's socialist revolution would fail. The Soviet Union and its eastern bloc allies actively backed the new Mozambican government. It was a living example of the cold war in action on our doorstep.

As Neil spoke, many of us choked up with emotion and anger as he painted a picture of this new-born African democracy, full of hope and potential, being choked to death by western imperialism aided by the hated Apartheid regime.

Virtually since my arrival at Wits, I had been interested in Mozambique. One of the most colourful characters on the Wits campus in the 1970s was Carlos Cardoso, a white Mozambican who was studying at Wits. He had a wild beard, long hair, fiery eyes and an amazing oratorical gift. He looked like the poster of Che Guevara that many of us had on our bedroom walls. One of the regular activities outside the Students Union building at that time was the speakers' forum, an open platform for anyone to stand on a platform with a microphone in hand and say whatever they liked. Carlos was hands down our favourite speaker. He spoke about Portuguese colonialism, imperialism and Apartheid South Africa's support for it. One of his catch phrases that we adopted with enthusiasm was 'Everything is political! The very act of springing from your mother's womb is political'.

In 1974, the right-wing government in Portugal collapsed and the country's new left-leaning government rapidly moved towards granting independence to its colonies including Mozambique, Angola and Guinea-Bissau in Africa. Carlos, a staunch Frelimo supporter, was triumphant! He became the voice of Mozambique's liberation movement on Wits campus. He translated Frelimo statements from Portuguese to English and had them published in the student newspaper, Wits Student. In early 1975, he stood for election to the Wits SRC and won by a huge majority.

On 25th June 1975, Mozambique became independent with Samora Machel as its first president. This was a huge setback for the South African government, which saw our neighbouring countries, South West Africa (now Namibia), Angola, Botswana, Rhodesia (now Zimbabwe), Mozambique and Swaziland, as buffer states. This meant that they were the first line of defence between South Africa and the "communist onslaught". The loss of both Mozambique and Angola (which became independent on 11th November 1975) meant that the dreaded communists were now directly on the border. The ANC's armed wing, uMkhonto we Siswe, would now have direct access to South Africa's border.

In the eyes of the South African government and many of the large number of white Portuguese settlers who had moved from Mozambique to South Africa, Carlos Cardoso was a huge thorn in their side. He was articulate and popular and becoming the face and voice of Frelimo in South Africa. On 24th August 1975, he vanished. None of us knew what had happened to him. Carlos had simply disappeared. My friend, Gil Brokensha, who was a good friend of Carlos, launched a desperate search for him. We knew that white Portuguese vigilantes had threatened him. For three anxious days, everyone was convinced that he had been murdered. And then we found out that he was being detained by the Security Police. He was being held at the John Vorster Square police headquarters in central Johannesburg. This was still bad news, but better than him being murdered. The Minister of the Interior had decided that Carlos, a foreign national, would be deported from South Africa. In a final act of petty spitefulness, the government decided to put Carlos on a plane to Portugal, rather than send him over the border to his home country, Mozambique.

A few days later (on 1st September), about fifty of us gathered to see Carlos off at Jan Smuts Airport. Tears flowed and we sang as Carlos disappeared from our lives. I thought I would never see him again, but this proved not to be the case. He became a journalist in Mozambique, and in the early 1980s, when I was living in Manchester, Carlos was part of a delegation visiting the UK with Armando Guebuza, who was then the Mozambican Minister of Defence. The Manchester anti-Apartheid group, of which I was a member, hosted the delegation and organised a talk at the university. I had the chance to speak briefly to Carlos. I remember him being super optimistic about things in Mozambique. He shook his head in amazement and said, 'Whew! Mozambique! Every day is a miracle!'. The next, and last, time I saw Carlos was at a trade fair in Johannesburg in the late 1990s. He was again accompanying an official delegation as a journalist. His attitude towards the Mozambican situation had changed dramatically. He was very disillusioned. We spoke for a long time. I remember him asking me the question, 'Do you know what *kapenta* is?' I was a bit surprised by the question, but I did know the answer. 'It's a small fish, like a Mozambican sardine', I said. 'No', replied Carlos, 'It's a whale that's lived through three socialist transformations.' This was his cynical view of the Mozambican economy.

Carlos had become a highly respected and outspoken critic of the Mozambican political establishment. He worked as an investigative journalist in Maputo, exposing corruption and incompetence. On 22nd November 2000, he was being driven home from his office when a red Citi Golf pulled over in front of his car. The occupant raised an AK-47 and fired a volley of bullets which killed Carlos instantly. The assassin has never been caught and an adequate explanation for Carlos' murder has never been given. His funeral was addressed by the Mozambican President, Joaquim

Chissano, and attended by prominent figures from all walks of life. Mia Couto, one of Mozambique's best-known novelists, said at his funeral, 'We are not merely weeping for the death of a man. It wasn't just Carlos Cardoso who died. They didn't just kill a Mozambican journalist... a piece of the country has died, a part of us all.' Carlos was forty-nine years old.

Having known Carlos while he was at Wits, and been inspired by him, I had started reading everything I could find about Mozambique. I wondered about the possibility of working on appropriate technology projects in Mozambique. As I listened to Neil speaking in Crown Mines in 1978, I made the decision that not only would I leave South Africa as soon as I finished my PhD, but I would move to Mozambique to work as an appropriate technologist. The only question was to work out how to organise this.

I managed to speak to Neil alone for a few minutes before he left Crown Mines to catch his flight to London and informed him of my aim to work in Mozambique. He said that I would need to get clearance from the ANC-in-exile. The Mozambican government was very nervous about white South Africans coming into their country. Neil advised me to try to make contact with Ruth First, a prominent ANC leader living in exile in Maputo, to ask for her advice about clearance, and offered to get a letter to her when he next travelled to Mozambique.

Neil returned a few months later, *en route* to Mozambique, and I gave him a letter I had written to Ruth First. I told her about myself and about my desire to work in appropriate technology in Mozambique. Several months later, Neil brought me a response. Ruth suggested that I go to London and make contact with an organisation called the Mozambique, Angola and Guinea-Bissau Information Centre (MAGIC) who would help me with obtaining clearance and finding work in Mozambique. She also told me about T-BARN, an appropriate technology group at Maputo University. I felt both happy and excited that I now had a plan and a clear way to implement it.

Me with Neil Murtough near Manchester in 1980.
[Photo: Edwin Wes]

Barry Dwolatzky

16 June 1979

In reply to your letter of queries about working in M - for which
slow, late reply I am very sorry.. - there is no problem with
white southafricans working in M as long as (1) they are suitably
cleared a: suitable for the jobs for which they apply (2) they get
a political clearance. The latter can be difficult; in general
it is done by MAGIC (Mozambique Angola Guinea Information Centre :
34 Percy street London W1) when South Africans apply through London.
With MAGIC checking names etc with the ANC.
South Africans in Lusaka or Botswanawhere there are ANC offices
could try to have their clearances connected there.

Jobs themselves are notified to MAGIC in London, and other bodies
in other countries (USA Canada Holland etc where similar support bodies
are functioning). So a job list of various kinds is available from
MAGIC, which may supply on request, though they may not want to do
this direct to SA.

There are jobs in the University and some technical institutes.
There are rural development projects but these generally draw on
Mozambicans at the ground level, and a small number of rural
specialists in bodies in the capital; appointments depend on
experience. Fluent Portuguese is essential, of course.
There is a technology centre at the University (TBARN) which has
..ried to devise appoppiate technology for villages.
TBARN is part of IICM (The Institute for Scientific Investigation): you
might write MAGIC for information specifically about jobs here, and
if you can apply, send a copy of part of your thesis or other work.

Sorry I can'. be more helpful; it isn't easy at this distance.

R

| Letter to me from Ruth First.

104

chapter
seven

INTO VOLUNTARY EXILE

1979 to 1980

I stood at the centre of a noisy group of friends, fighting back tears. About thirty people had come to Jan Smuts Airport to see me off. I had planned on slipping out of the country quietly, but the Crown Miners would have none of that. Suzanna was the spokesperson. She made an impromptu speech and presented me with a fat envelope as a parting gift from my friends. I pushed it into my hand luggage. We stood around chatting, experiencing the difficult emotions departures into the unknown raise. We were all sad but expressed it differently. Some laughed and joked, others were serious, while a few simply choked up and wept. After a while, I looked at the clock, said a last good-bye, shared some final hugs and kisses and detached myself from the group. I headed towards the departure gate, beyond the sign that read "Passengers only". It was late December 1979.

Some of the friends left, while a few watched through the glass partition, smiling and waving as I presented my passport to the emigration official and then headed towards the doors into the departure area. And then two grey suited men appeared out of nowhere and instructed me to follow them into a small windowless office to the left of the departure area doors. I glanced back and saw the few remaining friends watching through the glass, smiles being replaced by looks of alarm. Inside the office, one of the grey suits asked where I was going.

'To London', I said.

'What is the purpose of your travels?' asked the other grey suit.

'Holiday', I lied.

'Are you carrying any prohibited items?' asked the first grey suit.

'I'm not sure what prohibited items are', I said.

'Put your bag on the table', he instructed.

I put my hand luggage bag on the table. I watched as he poured everything out of the bag onto the table. He picked up the envelope Suzanna had just given me.

'What is this?' he asked.

'A present from my friends', I said.

'Open it up', instructed the second grey suit.

There was a card signed by many of my friends, some photos, and a fat wad of money.

'Are you aware that it's illegal to take South African currency out of the country without permission?' he asked.

He picked up the card and pretended to read it. He then started counting the money. It was several hundred Rands, which was a lot of money at that time. My friends had been very generous. He held the money in his hand, looking at it thoughtfully.

'Will he confiscate it?' I thought.

The first grey suit stared at me. I kept calm and stared back.

'It's a present from my friends', I said.

These two Afrikaner officials symbolised for me the hated instructors in the army who had bullied me, the policemen I had faced in protests on Wits campus, and all the petty bureaucrats who had monitored and regulated my life since I was born. I stared into their faces and hoped that they saw the hate in my eyes.

'Take your stuff', said the grey suit returning my stare with a superior contemptuous sneer. He then threw the money down on the table. He dismissed me with his eyes, nodded to his partner and they both left the office. I pushed everything back into my bag and emerged, slightly shaken and certainly stirred. I saw relief replace panic on the faces of friends who had remained to watch. I gave a thumbs up and passed through the door into the departure area.

'Fuck Apartheid South Africa!' I thought as I prepared to leave it forever. I didn't know then that I would be back far sooner than I expected.

———

I FELT LIBERATED AND FREE WHEN I ARRIVED IN LONDON. Everything I owned in the world was packed into a 20kg backpack and a small steel trunk. The trunk was stored with friends in Crown Mines and the backpack accompanied me to London. It was only years later that I began to realise how much other baggage I carried with me, psychological baggage which I never left behind. It took me years to understand how powerfully it shaped my life in the subsequent decades.

The world I had just left was a vicious, authoritarian, repressive police state. As part of the white left, I had been sucked into an existence where distrust and paranoia were central. There were few people one could trust as even close friends could have been agents of the State spying and informing on one. The politically focused Special Branch (SB) of the police force was assumed to be everywhere, watching where you went, noting who you met, reading your letters and listening in on your phone calls. One spoke in code, never mentioning names. While these sinister forces were real, their by-product was an imaginary world of rumour and gossip. Innocent interactions could be distorted and be interpreted as suspicious. It was imperative to never lower one's guard. There were too many examples of people, some of them close friends, being detained, interrogated, and tortured.

We also knew, but had difficulty confirming, that the South African State apparatus spread way beyond the country's borders. It had spies all over the world who worked with their counterparts in Britain and other western countries.

This pervasive atmosphere of fear and paranoia manifested in a strange way for me while I lived in Crown Mines and continued when I moved to London. Not only did I distrust others, but I worried about how they perceived me. After all, on Wits campus, I was an engineering student spending my days with some of the most reactionary people around. Did people gossip about me behind my back? Were there discussions in Crown Mines houses about 'this Barry person... how do we know that he isn't a spy?' These thoughts became very toxic in my own imagination. If people were questioning my political credentials behind my back, how could I send out signals that I was authentic? My anxieties made my life more complicated than it needed to be, but they were nevertheless very real.

Soon after arriving in London, I made my way to the Mozambique, Angolan and Guinea-Bissau Information Centre (MAGIC) office in central London. I believed that the key to my entire future lay in their hands and I approached that first visit with a great deal of trepidation. MAGIC was a solidarity organisation providing information about those three ex-Portuguese colonies. My immediate aim was to work in Mozambique, and I would need information and support from MAGIC to make this happen as quickly as possible.

Clutching a folder of documents and a borrowed London A-Z, I set off to find the office on a wet and cold day. I expected something quite substantial and impressive. It was, after all, the public interface in London for three African countries. When I arrived at the address I had been given, I was convinced I had arrived at the wrong place. It was a nondescript closed door in a dingy back street. On the left-hand side of the door was a row of doorbell buttons with handwritten labels. Some had names, others were simply numbers. I studied the labels through the blur of my wet glasses. One of them read M.A.G.I.C in very small writing. I rang the bell. There was a buzzing sound inside the door and I heard the electric lock click. I let myself into a tiny corridor cluttered with a battered bicycle and damp rainwear hanging on hooks. At the end of the corridor was a steep flight of stairs. Somewhere from above, a man's voice shouted out 'Who's there?'

'I've come to see MAGIC', I shouted back.

'Where you from?' he asked.

'Can I come upstairs?', I shouted. 'I need to speak to someone at MAGIC.'

'We're on the third floor", he said. I detected – or thought I detected – a sudden chill in his voice.

'Had he picked up my South African accent?'. My invisible psychological baggage had kicked in. 'How do I convince him that I'm a "good" South African?' I thought.

In my dripping raincoat, I trudged up the three flights of stairs past several closed doors. I came to a door with the letters MAGIC neatly painted on a sign. It was half-open.

The voice I had heard earlier said 'Come in!' as I was about to knock.

He sat on a chair with an open box of books on the floor in front of him. The office I entered was small and cluttered with books everywhere. On the wall, there were posters advertising previous meetings and solidarity events. I recognised a large photograph of Mozambican President Samora Machel dressed in military fatigues smiling his familiar smile. The man on the chair had a neat beard, receding hairline, and bushy eyebrows, partly hidden by black-framed glasses. He was a few years older than me. He looked me up and down for a few seconds and then spoke, in a British accent.

'You should have left your wet raincoat on the hook downstairs.'

I started to remove my wet raincoat, feeling a bit stupid. He pointed to the door.

'Leave it on the landing outside,' he said.

'Not a good start,' I thought. He didn't introduce himself. He sat on his chair, obviously keen to get back to packing books in the box, watching me and waiting for me to explain why I was there.

This was the first time I met Paul Fauvet, who ran the MAGIC Office in London at that time. Although I saw him often over the next few years, I never felt comfortable in his presence.

This discomfort had more to do with me than with Paul. If I had been Paul, I would have been on my guard against anyone connected to South Africa – particularly an awkward white man, with a strong South African accent, who arrived unannounced in my office on a rainy January morning in 1980.

Having projected this imaginary distrust onto Paul, I set out to put his mind at rest by proving that I was not an agent of the South African government. I felt I needed to assure him that I could be trusted. The problem was that this interaction happened in my mind, while for all I knew Paul Fauvet was not thinking at all about white South African agents or finding me suspicious. All he wanted to do was get back to the job he was busy with.

I explained to Paul why I was there. He got up from his chair and rummaged through a drawer in a filing cabinet. He gave me a form and an information sheet with the heading "Applying to work in Mozambique". He didn't say much. I, by contrast, said too much, as I tried to put his real, or imagined, concerns about my authenticity at rest. He did explain, as I already knew, that I would need to get clearance from the ANC.

'This can take a long time,' he said. 'The last person who applied had to wait for more than a year. While the process is happening, you will have to be available for interviews. Will you be living in London?'

This question took me completely aback. I had imagined that the process of going to Mozambique would take a few weeks. I had been planning for a short stay in London and was squatting on the couch of my friend Eddie Wes and his sister, Diane. I had enough money to keep me going for a month or two but certainly hadn't planned to spend 'more than a year' in London.

I left the MAGIC office in a state of panic. My not-so carefully laid plans were in tatters. I would need to rethink things.

———

FIRST UP, I WOULD NEED A JOB. I HAD A BRAND-NEW PhD IN electrical engineering and I had become adept in computer programming. I knew I had a good chance of finding something. I bought some newspapers and read through the "Situations Vacant" section. I also visited an employment agency and registered with them. I sent off a number of job applications and waited for replies.

The stumbling block, however, was that I had entered the UK as a tourist, and I needed a work permit to enter paid employment. While I waited for responses to my job applications, I found casual work via a no-questions-asked agency appropriately called Banditoon. The way it worked was that you visited their office on a Friday. They gave you an address of where you should be on the following Monday morning. You reported at that address and would be put to work on some menial task, such as packing, filing, or washing dishes, for the week. Every Friday you returned to the Banditoon office where you would be paid (in cash) and receive an address for the following Monday. It was highly illegal.

Most of the people working through Banditoon were young Australians, Canadians and New Zealanders passing through London. Friday evenings at Banditoon's offices were party times. Beers, joints and snacks were available for a price and people spent a big slice of their week's earnings on getting intoxicated. I sometimes stayed for a beer and a packet of crisps, but no more as I needed the money and had a mission.

The jobs I did through Banditoon didn't earn me much money, but they brought me down to earth. One week, I reported to the address I was given, which was an anonymous door in a back street close to The Strand. I was shown into a scullery with a pair of huge sinks. Dirty pots and pans were pushed through a hatch on my left. I cleaned them in boiling hot soapy water until they shined, and then pushed them through a hatch on my right. At lunch time, a tray with food was pushed through the hatch on the left, and I was allowed to sit alone at a small table in my scullery to eat for thirty minutes. Throughout the week, I hardly saw a single person, and those I saw were other Banditoon casuals working in the kitchen at the other side of the hatches. I had no idea whose kitchen this was. It was only at the end of the week that I discovered that I was working in the staff canteen of the multinational corporation, Lever Brothers (now UniLever).

After a few weeks of doing this type of casual work, I received a reply to one of the many job applications I had sent off. The Control Systems Centre at the University of Manchester Institute of Science and Technology (UMIST) invited me to come for an interview.

MY FIRST IMPRESSION OF MANCHESTER WAS ONE OF DRAB, damp greyness. It was a short walk from the railway station to UMIST, where I met Professor Neil Munro and Dr Peter Wellstead. Prof Munro was the head of UMIST's Control Systems Centre (CSC). I had become familiar with his name while I was still at Wits as he was one of the pioneers of using computers to design control systems. Peter was head of a research team in the CSC doing work on what were called self-tuning control systems and was employing post-doctoral research associates to work on this project.

I arrived at the interview mentally psyched up to do my very best. I was desperate for a job and really wanted this particular job. Above all, I felt I needed to make a positive impression on both of them but bizarrely it soon became clear that they wanted to make a positive impression on me. Peter had read my CV and one of my published papers and had also spoken on the phone to Mike Dewe, my PhD supervisor at Wits. He came into the interview having already made the decision that he wanted me and was ready to convince me to work for him. Peter and I ended up spending an hour walking around some of the labs at UMIST and talking about the work I would be doing in his team. We then met some of my future colleagues at a pub for lunch. The one obstacle which remained was getting a work permit.

Peter left me with the person in the UMIST administration responsible for employment contracts, who sat pursing his lips as he paged through my passport. I had entered the UK on a tourist visa. He explained that for a foreigner to get a work permit in the UK they needed to apply for it *from their home country* and, once they had received it, they should then enter the UK not as a tourist, but as someone with permission to work in the UK. He advised me that if I wanted to take up the job offer from UMIST, I would need to return to South Africa and wait there until approval from the Home Office was received.

I was in a state of turmoil on the train back to London. On the one hand, I was really happy. My long-term plan had become more possible. I could support myself living legally in the UK for as long as I needed to while my application to work in Mozambique was processed. Furthermore, I wouldn't be doing menial or meaningless work. The job at UMIST seemed really exciting. On the other hand, I would have to return to South Africa a few weeks after 'leaving until Apartheid ended'. It felt like such a cop-out.

Back in London, I had a long discussion with Eddie and Di, weighing up the pros and cons. We spoke late into the night. Fortunately, I had a return ticket to South Africa, which was a prerequisite for entrance into the UK as a tourist. The following morning, I booked a return flight to Johannesburg. With my tail between my legs and feeling very embarrassed, I arrived back in Crown Mines in early February 1980.

———

WHILE I WAITED FOR A WORK PERMIT THAT WOULD ALLOW ME to return to the UK, I managed to arrange a short-term contract back in the Wits Department of Electrical Engineer-ing. I helped one of the lecturers, Ian McLeod, on some computer programming. It was reassuring that I had the ability to earn money wherever I found myself.

The following six weeks passed in a blur. I have retained very little memory of what I did and who I saw. It feels now almost as if it never happened. I had left South Africa forever in December 1979 and while I had physically returned a few weeks later, my mind had remained in the UK and was working on dealing with living far away.

Using the money I had earned working with Ian McLeod, I booked a one-way ticket to London and a few days after my work permit arrived, I slipped quietly out of Jan Smuts Airport. This time there was no crowd at the airport and no farewell tears. This time I knew for certain that I wouldn't be back for a long time. I was going into exile.

chapter
eight

MANCHESTER

1980 to 1982

Helicopters hovered overhead, sirens wailed, and the smell of burning wafted into our house. I sat with some of my housemates watching the scenes on ITV news that were being beamed live from a few hundred metres away from where we were sitting. We were gathered in our living room in Heald Place, Rusholme, an inner-city area in Manchester. An angry crowd was smashing shop windows, starting fires and setting up barricades in Wilmslow Road, our "high street". Most of the shops were owned by "Asians" – British citizens whose origins were in Bangladesh, Pakistan and India. These were the shops we visited every day. The local news agent where I bought the Guardian every morning, the shops that displayed towers of brightly coloured Indian sweetmeats in their windows and sold delicious gulab jamun, the hardware store which was packed with "thingamajigs" from floor to ceiling at which you could find anything as long as you knew what to ask for, the laundromat where you could warm yourself near the tumble dryers on a freezing Manchester evening, and the clothing shop with the headless mannequins modelling saris and khurtas in the windows. The angry crowd was largely composed of young black British citizens whose family origins were mostly West Indian. It was July 1981 and Britain was experiencing a widespread outbreak of racial tension fuelled by mass unemployment and a deepening economic recession. Young people from marginalised minority communities were venting their anger against police victimisation and economic exclusion. These were the early days of Thatcherism. It had begun in Brixton in London a few weeks earlier, and then spread to Handsworth in Birmingham, Southall in London, Toxteth in Liverpool and Moss Side and Rusholme in Manchester.

Some of the myths I had brought to Britain from my post-colonial South African upbringing were shattered that day. The myth of the fine upstanding British Bobby as a symbol of non-partisan law enforcement dedicated to keeping all citizens safe, the myth of the British media as a source of unbiased truth, the myth of racial equality: all of these were shattered over the next few days.

On a piece of open land between our house and Wilmslow Road, I had earlier that evening seen a large number of police vehicles, police horses and literally hundreds of policemen in riot gear. They were sitting around, waiting for action. As I watched events unfold on TV later that night, I saw some of the local shop keepers standing help-lessly watching as their businesses, their livelihoods, were smashed and looted. There was no one there to protect them. Where were the police? Why were they not deployed? After all, I knew that they were right there in numbers far larger than the rioting crowd. I had managed to tune my FM radio to the frequency the police were using for their internal communications. Listening to the chatter on that supposedly secure and private frequency, I heard a commander telling police on the ground to not do anything to stop the rioting. He said something like, 'Let them burn those Paki shops. I don't give a fuck if they kill each other.'

So the police did nothing as Asian businesses were destroyed. Their lack of intervention was again evident that night in Moss Side and Hulme, neighbouring areas of Manchester. However, when the angry crowd moved towards Manchester's city Centre, with its predominantly white-owned businesses, the full might of the police was unleashed to protect life and property.

The media were no better. I was shocked to read the newspapers the following morning telling a story of the police struggling to maintain order and protect property. They spun a yarn about how the police were outnumbered and were forced to withdraw while they waited for rein-forcements. I knew these were lies. The Prime Minister Maggie Thatcher and some of her ministers picked up on this theme in the following days. "Fake news" is not the invention of Donald Trump; It was alive and well in Britain in the 1980s.

I SETTLED DOWN QUICKLY WHEN I ARRIVED IN MANCHESTER IN March 1980 to take up my position as a postdoctoral researcher at UMIST. Apart from the work, the other factor that excited me about coming to Manchester was that one of my dearest friends, Melanie Pleaner, was already living there.

On the same evening that I had heard Neil Murtough talking about Mozambique in Crown Mines two years earlier, Melanie had also met him and fallen in love with him. After more than a year of negotiating a long-distance relationship, they had decided to live together in Neil's communal house in Heald Place in Manchester.

Situated in the Rusholme area to the south of Manchester's city centre, and only a ten-minute cycle ride away from UMIST, several terraced houses in Heald Place had been bought by some of Neil's friends. Together with others, they lived in these houses communally. Barry Munslow and Pauline Ong, Sue Mac and her partner Richard, Jane Rosser, Polly McAnaneny, Mark van Harmelen, Neil and Mel, and others were a wonderful group of really interesting people. All of them were socially conscious and politically progressive. It had the feeling of a mini-Crown Mines, complete with interpersonal intrigue and ample scope for endless gossip.

I moved into one of the houses in Heald Place and having Mel as a neighbour made settling down in Manchester so easy. I slotted in well and very quickly formed solid friendships with my housemates, Mark and Jane. Mark is also a South African originally from Cape Town, who, like me, left South Africa to avoid the army call-up. He worked as a researcher in the computer science department at the University of Manchester, so we had a great deal in common.

Soon after arriving back in Britain, now equipped with a work permit and a secure job, I went back to the MAGIC office in London to start the process of acquiring clearance from the ANC. I was very eager to get to Mozambique as soon as possible, but now knew that clearance could take a long time. I also visited the International Defence and Aid (IDAF) office in London to begin establishing connections with the South African exile community in Britain. IDAF was originally set up to raise funds to defend Nelson Mandela and his co-accused in the Rivonia Trial in the 1960s. After the trial, it transformed into an international anti-Apartheid solidarity organisation. Its London office employed a number of South African exiles and the events it organised were meeting places for the anti-Apartheid South African community in London. One of my school and university friends, Ian Robertson, worked at the IDAF offices. Another Wits friend still living in Johannesburg, Barbara Hogan, who I knew had unspecified connections to the ANC, had given me a letter before I left South Africa, asking Ian to assist me with my ANC clearance.

All of these encounters – visiting the IDAF office, meeting with Ian, handing over the letter from Barbara – were complicated for me by the burden I carried in my head. How can I convince these people to trust me? How can I show that I'm not an informer?

People at IDAF also introduced me to the Anti-Apartheid Group in Manchester. I remember attending my first meeting with them in a small room above a pub in Moss Side. Mel came with me. Frances Kelly was the coordinator and there were about fifteen people present, all of them British. Although none of them had been to South Africa, they had an amazing knowledge and depth of insight into the situation in South Africa. The agenda at this meeting covered issues such as uranium mining in Namibia and campaigns being waged in support of trade unions in South Africa. Frances and some of the other seasoned British anti-Apartheid activists voraciously read and analysed everything they could find about South Africa. They had contacts in South Africa who regularly sent them press cuttings and trade union newsletters. They demonstrated dedication and energy which bordered on religious zeal. They viewed Mel and I as new sources of information to be milked. After the meeting, we sat in the pub being grilled by them. They asked questions and mentioned names and incidents, desperate to glean more information, to connect more dots. I think that Mel and I were something of a disappointment as we didn't know details like the name of the FAWU shop steward who was arrested the week before in Port Elizabeth.

I found the Manchester Anti-Apartheid Group puzzling. What was the source of their intense interest in a struggle being waged on the tip of Africa thousands of miles away?

Yes, I understood the concept of international solidarity, and that all struggles throughout the world are part of the same struggle, and that British capitalism was hugely invested in South Africa. But why should someone like Frances Kelly in Manchester pick up the South African situation with such razor-sharp focus and such seriousness? I don't have an answer to this, except that British activism has a strong tradition of focusing on international solidarity. While I had tremendous respect and admiration for Frances and her comrades, I found them humourless and intimidating. I attended meetings and became peripherally involved in some of their campaigns, but British anti-Apartheid activity wasn't for me.

I also felt the need to not publicly align myself closely with any group so soon after leaving South Africa. I needed to first work on my own political education. I had also begun to sense the complex factionalism and intrigue in the British Left as well as South African exile circles.

———

THERE'S A WONDERFUL SCENE IN THE MONTY PYTHON MOVIE *The Life of Brian*, which was released in 1979. Set in Roman-ruled Judea two thousand years ago, the people of Judea are agitating against Roman imperialism and many anti-Roman political organisations have been formed. One of these organisations, which seems to have only four members, is sitting together in a Colosseum-type stadium. A food vendor asks them if they are the Judean Peoples'

Front (JPF). They're horrified by the mistake. They are the Peoples' Front of Judea (PFJ) and the JPF is their bitterest enemy! They also point out that they hate all other anti-Roman groups, such as the Judean Popular Peoples' Front, who are not to be confused with the Popular Front, whose only member is sitting alone nearby, mumbling to himself. This scene perfectly satirised the state of left-wing politics that I encountered when I arrived in Britain in 1980.

The mainstream left-leaning party of British politics was the Labour Party, which grew out of the trade union movement, represented by the powerful Trade Union Council (TUC). One of the oldest parties to the left of the Labour Party/TUC was the Communist Party of Great Britain (CPGB), which never gained the kind of electoral support that the communist parties in Italy or France had. The CPGB was strongly aligned with the Soviet Union (USSR) and was perceived as Stalinist. This referred to a major division which had opened up in the USSR's Communist Party between followers of Joseph Stalin and those of Leon Trotsky in the 1920s. The pro-Trotsky factions were purged from the USSR's Communist Party and other communist parties around the world and those that were purged formed new organisations which were seen as Trotskyist. The Socialist Workers Party (SWP) was one of the biggest Trotskyist parties in Britain. There was also a very small Maoist faction that aligned with the Chinese Communist Party, plus various anarchist groups. Over a period of time, for reasons of ideology and principle, factions had split off from all of these left-leaning parties so that, by the time I arrived in Britain, there were, to name but a few, a Revolutionary Communist Party (RCP), a Revolutionary Communist Group (RCG) and a Revolutionary Communist Tendency (RCT), all vehemently opposed to one another. It was obvious that Monty Python had a rich vein of comedic material to draw on, but it also confounded and made ANC politics in the UK rather complex.

The ANC in exile, strongly influenced by the South African Communist Party (SACP), was closely aligned with the Soviet Union and, in Britain, with the CPGB. Some of the South African exiles I met were strongly opposed to the SACP, which they labelled as Stalinist. They were actively involved in some of the British Trotskyist factions. I learnt that the RCG had split off from the RCP because of a disagreement about the RCP's position on South Africa. I never completely understood what exactly this position was.

In July 1980, a few months after I arrived in Britain and while I was struggling to understand who was who in both British politics and South African exile politics, Mel and I decided to attend an event called "The Communist University of London", or CUL, held at London University. It was attended by hundreds of people and was a fascinating week of talks, seminars and workshops that brought together almost the entire alphabet soup of British left-wing politics. We were able to hear the leadership of mainstream parties and some of the factions passionately expound on key issues of the day. These issues included the situation in Northern Ireland (or "the North of Ireland", as we learnt it should be called), nuclear disarmament, liberation theology in South America, neo-colonialism in Africa and the struggle against Apartheid. Maggie Thatcher had been in power for only a year, but people on the left were already starting to warn about what was to come. I sought out several talks and seminars on appropriate technology and found out about some of the groups based in Britain doing work in this field. I never lost sight of my intention to go to Mozambique where I planned to work on appropriate technology projects.

CUL was a rewarding experience. Both Mel and I gained many valuable insights and deepened our understanding of politics in different parts of the world. We also laughed a lot about the nature of factionalism in the British Left. We saw many real-life versions of the Monty Python sketch playing out as factions viciously attacked each other over what seemed to us to be obscure and minor issues.

A major topic of conversation at CUL and among the South African exile community was the suspension by the ANC of Martin Legassik, Paula Ensor, Dave Hemson and Rob Petersen, who had been accused of forming a faction within the ANC. Legassik was a well-known South African academic living in exile, employed at Warrick University. Ensor was one of the NUSAS-8, a group of student leaders banned by the South African Government in 1973. Hemson had been involved in the early 1970s with the setting up of trade unions in Durban and had also been served with a banning order. Rob Petersen was another prominent exile living and working in Britain. One of the reasons for their suspension and ultimate expulsion from the ANC was that these four tried to trigger a debate within the ANC around the role of the SACP in shaping the liberation movement's strategies. They were coming from a Trotskyist perspective and saw the SACP as a puppet of the Stalinists in Moscow. Legassik and the others had set up a group called the "Marxist Workers Tendency of the ANC" and produced a journal called *Inqaba yaBasebenzi* and a newspaper called *Congress Militant*. They set out to recruit members from the South African exile community in Britain. Their publications carried very well-written articles putting across views that were very different from the official line of the ANC and the British anti-Apartheid movement.

Mel and I became targets for various factions aiming to recruit us to their ranks. A fellow Manchester-based South African exile, named Denise, whom I had known vaguely at Wits in the early 1970s, had somehow obtained my phone number and called to invite me to meet her at a pub one evening. She spoke earnestly about the situation in South Africa and asked for my opinion on various issues. She stared intensely into my eyes as I spoke. In my naivety, I thought that she was flirting with me and making small talk while we got to know each other better.

We agreed to meet a few days later for dinner. Was it a date? She arrived at the dinner with a bulging shopping bag which she said was for me. 'So kind of her to bring me a gift', I thought. I peeked inside and saw that it was filled with old issues of the weekly newspapers sold by either the RCG or RCP (I can't remember which). She instructed me to read them and said that we should meet again a few days later to discuss the contents. It dawned on me that she had no intention of developing a romantic relationship but was focused on recruiting me as another warm body for her faction. I wasn't interested. We didn't meet again, but I often saw Denise standing outside Manchester's Piccadilly Station on a Friday afternoon selling her newspaper to commuters.

On another occasion, an earnest young man, called Leon, contacted me. He was the son of older South African exiles living near Manchester. We met and he set to work on trying to recruit me to the Legassik Militant faction. While I found some of the analyses in their publications very thought-provoking and interesting, I resisted Leon's very insistent attempts to recruit me. I couldn't imagine myself standing outside Piccadilly Station selling *Congress Militant* or *Socialist Worker* or the RCP or RCG or any other faction's newspaper.

I hadn't come to Britain to engage in British, or South African, factional politics. I was there to clear my way to get back to Southern Africa as quickly as possible, specifically to Mozambique where I intended applying all my energy to working at community level developing appropriate technology solutions. That was my mission!

———

MANCHESTER IN THE EARLY 1980S WAS NOT ONLY AN IDEAL place for me to settle into life in Britain, nurtured by communal living in Heald Place, and sharing my political education with Mel. It was also a great place to enter the world of work as a postdoctoral researcher.

I was ambivalent about my job at UMIST. I had taken it to sustain myself until I could leave for Mozambique. I knew that as soon as my ANC clearance came through, I would resign from UMIST and leave the UK. For obvious reasons, I hadn't shared this information with my boss, Peter Wellstead. While the job was merely a stopgap, it turned out to be a wonderful position in an excellent working environment.

Peter was a little older than me, and an up-and-coming researcher in the field of control engineering. His specific field of research was in something called self-tuning or adaptive control. Simply stated, he dealt with situations where the system being controlled was not linear and not time-invariant. When university students learn about control systems, they are usually told to make the simplifying assumption that all systems they deal with are both linear (they are modelled by a single continuous mathematical function) and time-invariant (the model of the system is not a function of time). Unfortunately, the real world is not so generous. Engineers tasked with developing control systems for real-world systems soon discover that most systems are nonlinear and time-variant.

Peter, together with his research students at UMIST and a number of collaborators at other universities, did research on developing the theory and techniques for dealing with such systems. He used digital control techniques, which were at that time at the cutting edge of control engineering practice. My doctoral research had dealt with something called "system identification", which was a critical step in developing a self-tuning control system. Peter wanted me to integrate my novel techniques, based on the so-called Walsh Transforms, into his system. I took to working with Peter and being part of his research group like a duck to water. It was both challenging and fun and was the first time I was part of a large research group. My post-grad research experience at Wits had been very solitary as I was the only person in my department working on my specific research topic. My only collaboration had been with a few researchers at universities around the world with whom I communicated via post in an era long before digital communications. It took literally weeks for letters to get from me to a collaborator and back again.

While working on developing algorithms for digital self-tuning control, I drew heavily on linear algebra. Implementing these algorithms in software required complicated manipulation of vectors and matrices. We used various programming languages, but I worked mostly in Pascal. Writing code to do this in Pascal is very tedious and error prone. In a conversation one day with Peter and some of our team members, I made the observation that we needed a specialised programming language to deal with the type of software we were writing. Half in jest, Peter said to me, 'invent that language.' I thought about it, and the more I thought, the more excited I became. It was agreed that this would become my primary task.

The language I invented was called PLASMA, which stands for Pascal Language Additions to Simplify Matrix Arithmetic. Steve Sanoff, who became a good friend, came up with this name. As the name suggests, PLASMA was to be an extension to the Pascal language. I decided to implement it by writing a "pre-processor". What this means is that a programme written using my newly defined language PLASMA would be translated into a standard Pascal programme. This translation would be done using a pre-processor which I would develop. The new language PLASMA would have built-in types called **Matrix** and **Vector**, greatly reducing the complexity of the software we were writing.

Developing the PLASMA pre-processor took me about six months of very hard work. It became a major obsession. Developing code for a pre-processor is as complex as writing a compiler (for those readers to whom any of this makes sense!). In doing so, I needed to teach myself substantially more formal computer science theory than I had previously encountered in my engineering studies. When I was finished and the PLASMA pre-processor had been thoroughly tested by Peter, Steve and some of our team, we were ready to go public with what I had produced.

We demonstrated PLASMA to other research groups at UMIST and to some of our collaborators at other universities. Everyone loved it. Peter and I had several discussions on what we should do with PLASMA. We could either give it away to anyone who wanted to use it, which today we would call open source, or we could try to sell it. We decided to do the latter. Peter had several other pieces of software that had come out of his research group. This was well before universities in the UK and elsewhere had any policies or restrictions, that I knew about, on who owned intellectual property developed in their labs. It was assumed in those days that a researcher owned anything they invented and if they found a way to commercialise it, good luck to them. Some of Peter's group's best software had been developed by one of his PhD students, Denis Prager, who had left UMIST a few months before I joined the research team. Denis had been in my class when I started at Wits in 1971. He was by far one of the smartest electrical engineering students to come out of Wits University and also happened to be an accomplished concert pianist.

Peter, Denis and I registered a company which we called Logical Research. It would sell PLASMA and other software developed by the three of us. PLASMA was our first product which would be sold on an 8-inch floppy disk together with a printed manual. The storage capacity of an 8-inch disk was 360KB, which is the same size as a Word file holding about fifty pages of text or two low-resolution images on a website. I'm amazed to reflect now on how small the PLASMA pre-processor was in kilobytes and how complex and powerful it was in functionality.

Logical research my first start-up business, although we certainly wouldn't have called it that. Silicon Valley, the home of the start-up revolution, was in its infancy at that time. Like all entrepreneurs, we had high expectations for the success of our small venture. We were convinced that the international control engineering community and others who had to deal with linear algebra in developing software applications would beat a path to our door. We advertised in engineering publications and at conferences and waited for the orders to flood in. And then, like all entrepreneurs, we had to deal with disappointment. As it turned out, we sold only about ten copies of PLASMA.

As brilliant an idea as we thought PLASMA was, others had also come up with the same or similar solutions. We landed up competing with others who had more experience in business, bigger marketing budgets and connections to established companies. The other software we tried to sell through Logical Research also failed to make much of a mark and, after about a year of trying, we closed our company down. It was, however, lots of fun and taught me many lessons that would prove valuable later in my life.

A final note about PLASMA was that the application I had developed was, in concept, something called object oriented programming (OOP). Although some of the concepts of what became known as OOP date back to the 1960s and the language SIMULA, it was only in the early 1980s that OOP entered the mainstream of computer science with the release of a public version of Smalltalk, the first programming language that was based fully on OOP. An important concept in OOP is the power it gives the programmer to very easily create "classes", which serve the same purpose as built-in types. PLASMA's Matrix and

Vector types are merely OOP classes. The concepts in PLASMA were textbook OOP, although such a textbook hadn't yet been written and I had no knowledge of OOP at the time. My incredibly difficult implementation as a fully-fledged pre-processor was superseded with the release of Smalltalk and later by C++ released in 1985. It was only at that time that I got to teach myself to use OOP.

––––––

THE PROCESS OF RECEIVING ANC CLEARANCE DRAGGED ON IN the background of my life in Heald Place and all the exciting computer work. From time to time, I travelled to London to attend MAGIC and anti-Apartheid events. I would seek out Paul Fauvet or Ian Robertson to ask if there had been any progress on my ANC clearance. The answer was always vague and non-committal. 'These things take time' or 'We'll let you know'. I felt very frustrated, because I deeply believed that I had skills and enthusiasm that could be used beneficially in Mozambique. I believed that the struggle (however one might define that) was in need of what I had to offer, and yet I was left kicking my heels in soggy cold Britain while some undefined bureaucratic process moved along at a snail's pace within the ANC. At the same time, I was reluctant to be too pushy. What if the delay was due to some gossip or unsubstantiated evidence that cast doubt on my authenticity? Were there people within the ANC's structures who suspected my motives? My strategy became one of convincing these invisible, and probably imaginary, "anti-Barry" forces that I was for real. How I should do this was never that clear, but it played out in all of my interactions with the exile community in London. I needed to prove that I could be trusted through my actions.

It became apparent to me that I should be living in London where I would be more engaged within South African circles. Although I loved living and working in Manchester, my sporadic appearances at weekend events in London weren't enough to demonstrate my commitment to the ANC. I began looking for a job in London.

One of Peter Wellstead's research collaborators at the time was Martin Zarrop, who had close ties to the control systems group at Imperial College in London. He introduced me to members of a very interesting research team working under Professor John Westcott. The group was called PROPE, which stood for Programme of Research into Optimal Policy Evaluation. This group was looking for a post-doc with my exact skillset and interests. Towards the end of 1981, I travelled to London to meet Prof Westcott and the PROPE group. As with my job interview at UMIST, it turned out that I had the job before I was even interviewed. And yet again, the issue of a work permit was the only obstacle preventing me from taking up the job offer. In Britain at the time, a work permit applied to a specific job. My permission to work in the UK was attached to my job at UMIST. Moving this permission to Imperial College took another very frustrating six weeks.

I had already discussed leaving UMIST with Peter and,

although he was sad to see me leave, he thought that the opportunity at Imperial was one I should take. The control engineering community at British universities was deeply interconnected, so moving to London was not severing ties with UMIST's Control Systems Centre. Peter and I hoped to continue collaborating on various projects, including the further development of PLASMA.

The final step in acquiring my new work permit turned out to be a wonderful lesson in how the old boys network operated in Britain. I had travelled to London from Manchester several times to meet with obstructive bureaucrats at the Home Office's headquarters in Lunar House in Croydon. Every visit turned out to be extremely frustrating and unproductive. I would spend hours queuing in the vast waiting room area only to be told that there was yet another hurdle I would need to jump. After several such visits, I went to Imperial College to meet with the person in their administration who dealt with work permits. He suggested that I should speak to John Westcott to see if he could help, which seemed unnecessary since this was an administrative issue that I was sure couldn't be solved by Westcott.

I took the administrator's advice, however, and met with Prof Westcott to explain the problem. He nodded and paged through his address book. He then reached over to his phone and dialled a number. John Westcott's side of the conversation went something like this:

'Hello Bunter, John Westcott here. How are the wife and children?'

Pause.

'She's doing well, thank you. We must meet up at the Lakes again soon. Let's get the wives onto that.'

Pause.

'So… the reason I'm calling is that I have a young chap here who we need to employ. He's in a bit of a tangle over his work permit.'

Pause. He points at the Imperial College folder, that I'm holding in my hands. The admin person had given it to me. I pass it to him and he flips through the pages inside.

'The name is Barry Dwolatzky.' He spells the surname. 'The application number is …'. He reads a number from the file.

Pause.

'Thank you, old chap. Regards to the wife.' He hangs up the phone.

To me, he says, 'If you go to Lunar House now, your work permit will be ready.'

It was as easy as that. I have no idea who "Bunter" was, but John Westcott's old boys' network certainly solved that problem quickly.

A few days later, I said my good-byes in Manchester and prepared to move to London.

Camping near Manchester with David Rees, Sue Goldstein, Neil Murtough and Mel Pleaner. [Photo: Edwin Wes]

Near Manchester. [Photo: Edwin Wes]

On a canal boat with Martin Rall. [Photo: Edwin Wes]

chapter
nine

THATCHER'S BRITAIN

1981 to 1986

I had never been part of such a huge crowd. The newspapers reported that over a quarter of a million people wound their way through the streets of Central London on that day in October 1981. I was now living in London and had joined my friends Charlotte Burke and Di Wes and some of their friends on my first huge London protest march. The mood was festive, and I was impressed by how self-disciplined this protest was. While the banners and placards displayed angry words raging against the government, and the crowd sang revolutionary songs, protestors stuck obediently to the designated route. Some marchers pushed babies in prams or old people in wheel-chairs. Others had bicycles that they wheeled along as they walked. There were people in fancy dress in among others, walking side by side, deep in political and ideological conversation. The police and marshals held up long ribbons of plastic tape to keep the crowd on one side of the road, so that traffic could still inch its way along on the other side.

We were marching in protest against nuclear weapons. It was also a protest against the increasingly close relationship developing between Maggie Thatcher's Britain and Ronald Reagan's America. The issue that had brought people out in their hundreds of thousands was Thatcher giving the Americans permission to station Tomahawk cruise missiles at Greenham Common, a British air force base in Berkshire, about 100 km west of London[1].

Nuclear weapons played a critical part in the so-called balance of terror that had kept the Cold War in a perpetual stalemate. Both the Soviet Union and the USA and their allies had accumulated large arsenals of nuclear weapons, enough to destroy life on earth several times over. The stalemate had the appropriate acronym of MAD (Mutually Assured Destruction).

Tomahawk cruise missiles represented a significant escalation in the nuclear stand-off, with a range of about 3000 km, which is roughly the distance from Greenham Common to Moscow. They carried an atomic warhead and could fly low enough to evade detection by radar. They were what are called first-strike weapons, meaning that they could be used to knock out key targets in the USSR before the Soviets had time to launch a counterattack. Once they had been developed and tested, the Americans needed to place them at sites close enough to key targets in the USSR. Most European countries were reluctant to allow the Americans to station these missiles in their territories. People in Britain feared that Greenham Common would become a prime target if tensions rose between the USSR and the USA. Given its location in the densely populated south of England and its proximity to London, a nuclear attack on Greenham Common would result in huge loss of life and destruction of property, hence the angry response to Thatcher inviting Reagan to place his missiles at Greenham Common.

The Campaign for Nuclear Disarmament (CND) had organised the protest. They had been campaigning since the 1950s for Britain to unilaterally give up its own nuclear weapons. Their reasoning was simple. If Britain had no nuclear weapons and refused to allow the USA and others to place these weapons on British territory, there would be no reason for the USSR to ever launch a nuclear strike on Britain.

Soon after word got out in 1981 that Thatcher had agreed to allow the Americans to station cruise missiles at Greenham Common, a group of women set up a Women's Peace Camp outside the air force base which became the site for continuous protest over the next nineteen years. Many of the women I knew in Britain in the early 1980s spent some period of time camping outside Greenham Common. Sometimes tens of thousands of women converged to join human chains surrounding the whole military base, or blocking roads and gates, or chaining themselves to the fence. Their resistance was a constant thorn in the side of Thatcher and her allies.

CND and my first huge protest march in London taught me about the nature of opposition politics in Britain. Marching was part of a long tradition and was one of the ways the British people expressed their views. Numbers were important especially as media coverage always attached great importance to how many people turned up. The numbers were always in dispute, with the police or government spokesperson under-reporting and the organisers and participants over-inflating. There were other forms of traditional British protest that I learnt about: writing angry letters to the press, signing petitions, or going to the House of Commons (i.e. the parliament) to lobby your own constituency's MP.

I participated in all of these polite forms of protest over the next few years in support of causes I believed in, although I was never fully convinced that any of them had much impact. There is no doubt, however, that it is a useful safety valve that allows the public to let off steam. For me, it was hard to beat the satisfying feeling of returning home exhausted after walking for miles through the streets of London with tens of thousands of others shouting slogans and waving banners, or seeing a letter you thoughtfully drafted printed in the Letters to the Editor pages in The Guardian. Summoning your elected MP to meet you in the lobby of the House of Commons to receive a letter demanding an end to the sale of British arms to the Apartheid regime was equally satisfying.

———

THATCHERISM WAS THE ALL-PERVASIVE BACKDROP TO MY LIFE IN Britain over the next eight years. There were three themes that summed up Margaret Thatcher and her Conservative Party government for me. The first was her turning Britain into an eager junior partner of the USA. She saw her relationship with America as much more important than her relationship with the rest of Europe. Secondly, she set out to destroy the British welfare state and the social contract that had shaped British politics since the end of the Second World War. Thirdly, working closely with Ronald Reagan, she set in motion the process of globalisation that saw the British and American economies move from being based on industry and manufacturing to a strong emphasis on the financial and services sector. We still see the ramifications of these shifts playing out today.

What was known as the special relationship between Britain and the USA certainly pre-dated Thatcher's government. However, Thatcher's eagerness to allow American cruise missiles to be based at Greenham Common indicated a new enthusiasm to make Britain's interests subservient to those of the USA. While the UK's European relationships were treated with suspicion and scorn, America was treated with blind trust. This manifested most clearly for me in the way Thatcher dealt with Africa in general and South Africa in particular. She enthusiastically followed America's lead.

In America's eyes, Africa was a subtext in the global narrative of the Cold War. Many newly independent African countries were aligned with either the USSR or China. America worked behind the scenes to undermine this alignment by setting up, funding, training and arming opposition factions such as Renamo in Mozambique and UNITA in Angola. There were frequent references in the press about waging a war for democracy against the spread of communism in Africa. South Africa became a proxy for America's covert involvement in these wars. At the same time, European countries sought to develop supportive post-colonial relationships with these newly formed African states, which meant that Europe and the USA found themselves aligned on opposing sides in many of these African conflicts. Britain, particularly under Thatcher, sided with American interests in Africa, rather than other European countries. I remember the time when Thatcher was forced by international and domestic pressure into imposing a new set of sanctions on South Africa. She appeared on TV emphasising how tiny and insignificant these sanctions were. Apartheid South Africa certainly had a pair of good friends in Thatcher and Reagan.

One of Thatcherism's primary objectives was to chip away at Britain's post-war social contract that gave rise to the welfare state. One of the key obstacles for her was the very powerful trade union movement. She and her fellow

Conservatives realised that they needed to defeat the unions if they wished to reshape the way Britain's economy worked. This became the top priority on Thatcher's agenda.

The big showdown came in 1984-85 when the government-controlled National Coal Board (NCB) announced the closure of a number of coal mines. Mining villages which were scattered across Wales, the North of England and Scotland were tight and cohesive communities with long histories. Working on the mine was the only major form of employment in these villages, which meant that the battle was for a way of life, a culture and a community, all of which was lost when a mine was shut down. The National Union of Mineworkers (NUM), led by Arthur Scargill, fought these closures by declaring a national strike. Thatcher's hand-picked chair of the NCB was the Scottish-American Ian McGregor, who adopted a particularly brutal attitude towards the NUM. It soon became clear that mine closure was being used as a pretext to take on and destroy the power of Britain's unions.

The mining communities were confronted by a well-coordinated police force, a well-oiled government propaganda machine, and the formation of a breakaway union. Thatcher and her ministers had prepared for the confrontation beforehand and used a mixture of dirty tricks and state resources, such as the intelligence agency MI-5. The strike continued for a year, but eventually the miners and their families could not sustain it any longer. The NUM led some of the miners back to work with brass bands and parades in the streets of their small mining villages. Many of us who had supported the miners by raising funds, collecting food and attending protest marches wept as we watched on TV as the defeated strikers tried to put on a brave face as they suffered a humiliating defeat at the hands of Thatcher. For her part, Thatcher gloated and boasted. She became, and remains, one of my most hated figures in world politics.

While the Miners' Strike certainly had a profound effect on me, it was a subsequent confrontation between Thatcher and the union movement that brings back the most vivid memories.

————

IT WAS A COLD WINDY DAY IN 1986 AND I WAS AGAIN PART OF a protest march. This one was heading from Central London to Wapping, east of the city centre. As protests go, this one wasn't that huge, maybe fifty thousand people. It felt to me, at first, like yet another typical London march which I had become accustomed to over the past five years with the usual mix of people and friendly London Bobbies keeping everyone in line. As we approached our destination, the brand new News International buildings in Wapping, I caught glimpses of very different types of police gathered down the side streets. These police were in full riot gear. There were also large numbers of mounted police. This puzzled me, given that everything seemed so peaceful.

As we came within sight of the News International buildings, barricaded behind barbed wire fences, I noticed that the Bobbies were no longer with us. I saw some of them heading down a side street away from the march. 'That's strange!' I thought. I was walking with a group of friends, and we were passing a park with high metal railings separating it from the road we were on. The crowd in front of us had stopped moving. They had reached the News International buildings. The crowd behind us was still marching forward. Then I heard shouting from behind. I spun around and saw people scattering. In the distance, I saw the most terrifying sight I had ever seen.

Charging through the crowd was a line of police horses. They rode abreast, filling the width of the road. The horses were fitted with protective padding making them look like medieval war machines. The riders were also wearing protective gear and were swinging long truncheons. They looked like medieval knights, lowering their lances as they galloped into battle. People scattered as they approached, but there was nowhere to go. I saw people falling as they were struck by truncheons or horses. The riders approached at speed, cutting through the crowd. People fell under horse hooves. They were screaming, bleeding and panicking. The line of horses was bearing down towards the part of the crowd I was in. People were pressing themselves against the park's metal railings, hoping to keep out of the path of the charging horses. I saw a side street across the road from me. I tried to run into it and then stopped. Rushing towards me was a huge platoon of riot police. I rushed back towards the park railing.

The horses had stopped about fifty metres from where I

stood. They stood in a menacing line, blocking the road and sealing off that escape route. We were trapped. The riot police were now among us. They weren't trying to arrest people or control the crowd. Their orders seemed to have been to spread panic and hurt people. They ploughed into the crowd swinging their heavy truncheons. People were lying on the ground injured, some had bleeding heads and bloody faces. I saw a woman clinging to the metal railing screaming as two policemen struck her back and legs. I saw a teenage boy trying to climb over the high railing so that he could escape into the park. He was pulled back and beaten. I also saw a policeman who had become separated from his squad being surrounded by a crowd who started kicking him and shouting abuse at him. He lay, curled up on the ground, whimpering. It was all so scary and almost unbelievable, until I remembered having seen similar scenes on TV in mining villages during the miners' strike.

I somehow avoided being beaten. I managed to push myself forward through the crowd towards the News International buildings. On a makeshift platform outside the building, I saw Tony Benn, the Labour MP, grab a microphone. He appealed to people to keep calm and suggested that everyone should sit down. He shouted at the police to stop, saying that he had witnessed with his own eyes what had happened. He appealed to the media present to film what they were seeing and to report it to the world. He promised to bring this outrage to Parliament and demand an explanation from Thatcher and her ministers. Gradually, things calmed down.

A few hours later, I found the friends I had been marching with. Luckily none of them were injured, but we were all very shaken and angry. One of those I was with was Francis McDonagh, my housemate. We went off together in search of a bus back to our house in Stoke Newington. When we arrived home, we poured stiff drinks and turned on the TV, in time to catch the 10pm news. The media had indeed filmed the events we had been part of in Wapping a few hours earlier and it was now the lead story on the national news. However, the story being told was very different from what we had experienced. The footage had been edited to support a statement made by the Head of the Metropolitan Police standing outside Scotland Yard. He reported that everything had been passing off peacefully until a number of Labour MPs and trade union leaders called on the crowd to attack the police. The news report showed a snippet of a speech that I knew was made *after* the police attack. The report then showed the policeman I had seen being kicked and abused by a crowd of protestors. The head of the Metropolitan Police said in his interview that it was only after the crowd had been provoked by the speakers to turn on the police, who were outnumbered and at great risk, that the commanders on the ground called in reinforcements to bring the rampaging, rioting mob under control. We knew that the situation had deteriorated *because* the police were deployed. The Head of Police blamed anarchists for inciting the crowd and added how grateful he was that only two police officers had been injured. He admitted that a handful of protesters had sustained 'slight injuries' and that 'unfortunately' one member of the public had suffered a heart attack and died. I had seen hundreds of people injured, many of them badly.

The story being spun by the police and the government a few hours after the incident was a complete fabrication and distortion of the facts. Tony Benn was interviewed over the next few days and gave an accurate account. Benn called it a police riot. He was mocked as a liar and opportunist. 'How dare he try to besmirch the reputation of the fine, upstanding Metropolitan Police!' shouted the media, claiming that 'There was actual footage that showed Benn was lying!'. Yes, there was footage, but it had been edited and taken out of context. It was a seminal lesson in how the media can be abused, which was ironic given that it was the power of the media that was at the heart of these very disturbing events.

The British press had, in my mind at least, a long and proud tradition of independence and quality. Some of the major newspapers had been in existence for centuries. The Times, for example, was first published in 1785. The Telegraph first appeared in 1855 and The Guardian, my favourite, started in 1821. Each major newspaper had a specific readership aligned with some social or political segment of Britain's very stratified society. One could literally sit in a tube train in London observing the newspapers people read and know where they lived and who they voted for. The Telegraph and The Times were both read by those who voted Conservative. The Telegraph was more upper-class and traditional. The Guardian was read by intellectuals who supported Labour. The Daily Mirror was read by blue-collar Labour supporters, and so on. Tens of newspapers were published each day attracting a loyal band of readers. Most people I knew had their chosen newspaper, in the same way that they had their favourite football team, to whom they remained loyal through thick and thin.

At the lower end of the market in the realm of credible journalism was The Sun, which featured naked breasts daily on page three and often made up news stories so as to make sensational front page headlines. My favourite was "Freddie Starr Ate My Hamster" from 1986. I never bought The Sun but loved reading the headlines on other people's papers as I rode on the tube. Even though it was rubbish, The Sun was one of the most popular papers in Britain at the time.

The importance of newspapers in British society can be measured in the statistics of the 1980s, when reportedly 80% of households bought a daily newspaper and 95% bought a Sunday paper. It was obvious that the press exercised considerable influence on the public. While most papers took great pride in ensuring editorial independence, this was not always uncontested. In the late 1960s, the right-wing Australian media tycoon, Rupert Murdoch, had entered the UK media scene when he bought The Sun. In 1981, he bought The Times. These two papers gave him, via the editors he appointed, huge influence over British public opinion. In 1985, he formed the company News International, which controlled newspapers in Australia, UK, USA and elsewhere.

Murdoch was a great supporter of Thatcher and her brand of politics, and throughout the miners' strike, his papers shamelessly pumped out Thatcher's version of the truth. Murdoch's papers certainly played a key role in the defeat of the NUM. However, the powerful trade unions in the British printing industry remained a major irritation for Murdoch. They stood in the way of him increasing his profits from the UK papers he owned. Following the defeat of the miners, Murdoch and Thatcher turned their attention to the print unions. This would both assist Murdoch's business and would allow Thatcher to bang another nail into the coffin of the trade union movement.

At that time, most national papers were edited and printed in Fleet Street, in central London. The printers' unions had tight control over who was employed and what they were paid. This was known as a closed shop. They were also able to block the introduction of new computer-based technology into the industry. Murdoch's News International started secretly to work on building new modern printing facilities in London, at Wapping, and in Glasgow. The technology being introduced would make many of the old printing skills redundant. About 90% of the jobs in his company would be lost. In January 1986, Murdoch announced that the printing of his newspapers would be moved to the new facilities in Wapping and Glasgow. He said that the new plants wouldn't operate a closed shop and he offered his Fleet Street workers a redundancy payment of a few thousand pounds.

In January 1986, the unions went on strike and Murdoch responded by firing six thousand workers. He moved production of his papers to the new facilities. The striking workers attempted to blockade Wapping to prevent newspapers leaving the site. Thatcher sent in huge numbers of police to prevent this from happening. The strike lasted fifty-four weeks and led to the defeat and destruction of some of Britain's most powerful unions. Murdoch's News International grew from strength to strength. It set up Sky TV in the UK and the Fox network in the USA. Fox News continues the Murdoch tradition of being a central influencer of right-wing public opinion, Donald Trump's major source of information and key mouthpiece for his brand of fake news.

I personally felt very ambivalent about the printers' strike. On the one hand, I believed it was important to resist Thatcher's onslaught against Britain's working class and the trade unions. This is what brought me out to march in support of the print unions in 1986. I also hated the fact that the likes of Rupert Murdoch were gaining influence and control over the media. On the other hand, the printing unions represented a group of over-paid workers who resisted the type of technological change and progress I believed was necessary.

Barry Dwolatzky

THATCHERISM AND THE DEFEAT OF THE TRADE UNIONS IN
Britain in the 1980s, together with similar developments in
the USA under Ronald Reagan, set the scene for a huge
change in how the global economy operated. Capitalism
stopped seeing itself as being anchored to individual countries. The concept of an international supply chain gained
momentum. Companies began moving the expensive,
labour-intensive parts of their manufacturing operations to
low-wage economies such as China, South Korea and India.
The countries of Europe and North America focused their
economic activities on the financial and services sectors. As
a result, manufacturing as a significant employer and
economic engine all but collapsed in the UK and USA. This
led to a further erosion of the working class in both of these
countries. This emergence of globalisation did much to
undermine the social contract and the welfare state that
characterised Britain between the Second World War and
the 1980s.

The consequences of this shift still lie at the heart of politics in the USA and the UK. It has also shaped many aspects
of post-Apartheid South Africa and most other countries in
the world.

Carlotte Burck on a Campaign for Nuclear
Disarmament protest march. [Photo: Edwin Wes]

Protest in London. [Photo: Edwin Wes]

1. *The air force base closed in 1997 and Greenham Common has now become a popular location for movie makers. The Star Wars films "The Force Awakens" (2015) and "The Last Jedi" (2017) were partially filmed at Greenham Common. I find this ironic, given what it was being used for in the 1980s.*

chapter
ten

THE TREASURY MUDDLE

1981 to 1985

They arrived on my London doorstep wrapped in bulky coats and woollen hats from the height of the South African summer. I helped them lug heavy suitcases and parcels and packages from the taxi that had brought them from Heathrow airport. I showed them to the spare room with its two double beds, clutter of excess furniture and other odds and ends. Once we had brought in all their luggage, the room looked over-full and felt claustrophobic. Khatija closed the heavy curtains and turned on the oil-filled fin heater, while Cas spoke in his booming voice about their flight and the ride from the airport. Their son Mohamed fished around in one of the bags looking for something. He eventually found what he needed, another scarf, which he wrapped around his neck as he perched on a chair close to the heater.

The Saloojee family were part of a seemingly never-ending stream of visitors to arrive at the house I shared in Evangelist Road, Kentish Town, with my housemate Francis McDonagh. Word had reached my friends in South Africa that I had a spare room in London. Friends, acquaintances and sometimes virtual strangers would contact me to ask if they could stay. I usually obliged unless the spare room was already being used.

A few days earlier, my friend Mel had phoned from Manchester to ask if her ex-boss and his family could stay in my house for a few days. Although I had never met him before, I knew that Cassim (Cas) Saloojee was a well-respected anti-Apartheid activist in South Africa and a veteran of the 1950s and 60s struggles. He ran an organisation called JISWA (Johannesburg Indian Social Welfare Agency) where Mel worked in the 1970s. In 1983, Cas had been centrally involved in the launch in South Africa of the ANC-aligned UDF (United Democratic Front) and had been elected treasurer.

When Cas and his family arrived at my house in Evangelist Road, I had no clue how large an impact their visit would have on the rest of my life, even though they barely emerged for five days. Although it wasn't very cold by London standards, they kept the oil heater on and the windows and curtains tightly shut. They only left their room to use the bathroom and eat meals with Francis and me in the kitchen. After a day or two, their bedroom was like a sauna, but they still insisted that they were so cold they needed to stay in their beds covered in blankets and warm clothes.

The major reason for their visit to London was to see their older son Riaz. He had left South Africa while still at school and went to live with family in Canada. Riaz was very mysterious. Even his name was a mystery. While his parents and brother called him Riaz, his wife called him Calvin (or Cal) Khan. He was married to Muff Andersson, the younger sister of Gavin Andersson who lived as a banned person in Crown Mines. I suspected that Riaz/Cal and Muff were somehow linked to the ANC underground but nobody said anything about this, and I certainly wasn't going to ask. While the Saloojee family were staying with us, Cal and Muff visited every day. When they visited, they would sit with their family in the spare room/sauna, with the door closed, speaking in whispers.

Francis was really intrigued by this interesting family and the cloak-and-dagger atmosphere that surrounded them. While I avoided asking them anything, Francis asked probing questions to which he received no answers.

Soon after the family visit, Cal and Muff asked me to meet them for lunch. We met and became very good friends. A few months later, they asked me to help them with "a project". I agreed, and almost without thinking about it, I was recruited into a secret world which I occupied for the next seven years.

———

IN 2019, MY WIFE RINA AND I VISITED ONE OF MY FAVOURITE places in London, the Science Museum in South Kensington. Although I had been there many times over the past forty years, I discovered an interesting exhibit that I had never seen before. It is a device built in 1949 by an electrical engineer-turned economist named Bill Phillips, who worked at the London School of Economics (LSE). This device uses water to model a national economy. It consists of pumps and tanks connected via pipes and valves. The water represents money as it flows through the economy. Various actions, such as increasing savings or reducing income taxes, can be modelled by opening and closing valves and by changing the speed of various pumps. Its purpose was to teach students key economic principles.

I found this particularly interesting because between 1981 and 1985 I had worked as part of a team at Imperial College, which is located adjacent to the Science Museum, using models of the British economy. These models were very different from the water-based one built by Bill Phillips in 1949. Ours were large computer models.

The team I joined at Imperial College after I moved from Manchester to London in mid-1981 was within the Department of Electrical Engineering. The head of Electrical Engineering at that time was Professor David Q Maine, a Wits University alumnus. There were many links in those days between Wits and Imperial College.

The research team I joined was called PROPE (Programme of Research into Optimal Policy Evaluation). We were investigating ways of using control methods, usually used to automate electro-mechanical systems, to develop rational economic policies. Consider the following scenario: the British Chancellor of the Exchequer is making his budget speech in the House of Commons. He says that he is planning to reduce unemployment by 5% and grow GDP by 2% and will achieve this by raising taxes and spending more on certain export incentives. How does he know this? In preparing his budget, a team of economists and other experts at Her Majesty's Treasury (HMT) simulate hundreds of scenarios using a large macroeconomic model run on a powerful computer. In today's age, the age of the Fourth Industrial Revolution, we would call this a digital twin. In the early 1980s, it was simply called the Treasury Model (or the Treasury Muddle, as some of my friends called it). It was massive, containing thousands of equations and variables. The coefficients of these equations were set using huge amounts of historical and current data.

PROPE used the Treasury Model, and another huge multi-country econometric model developed by the OECD (Organisation for Economic Cooperation and Development), to implement optimal feedback loops around these models. PROPE's theory was that, by using modern control theory, the Chancellor could simply work backwards by specifying his targets for the national economy and our software would come back with a list of budgetary measures he would need to announce to achieve these targets. It seems too good to be true – and unfortunately *was* too good to be true. A problem was that although the models we used were the best available, they were still filled with numerous simplifying assumptions and approximations. The other, more philosophical, problem was that these econometric models did not account for human behaviour and reactions. Humans change their behaviour in response to government announcements and the models we used weren't able to deal adequately with this, although we did venture into game theory to seek more accurate approaches.

The PROPE group was led by Professor John Westcott and had three other members. Berc Rustem was the control theorist in the team. He was of Turkish-Armenian descent and had a great sense of humour and a fiery temper. Elias Karakitsos was the team's economist, born and raised in Greece. He also had a great sense of humour and an equally fiery temper. The third member of the team was Robin Becker. He was one of the best software developers I've ever met, and I don't bestow this honour lightly because I've met many amazing software developers in my time. Robin was British and had such a dry sense of humour it was almost no sense of humour, and, like Berc and Elias, a fiery temper.

My role in the team was to bolster its software development capacity, which meant working closely with Robin. I was also there to act as a bridge between Berc and Robin. With a PhD in control engineering, I certainly understood the concepts Berc dealt with, and with my growing expertise in software development, I knew how to translate these concepts into working software. I thought of myself as the glue in the group, helping to combine and amplify the efforts of these three remarkable specialists.

The dynamics in our group were interesting and sometimes terrifying, mainly because of the fiery tempers of the other team members. We would often gather in our team office in front of a blackboard to discuss some detailed problem. In no time at all, the quiet discussion would become louder as Berc and Elias raised their voices to emphasise the points they were making, at which stage the shouting would start, followed by slamming of fists and throwing of blackboard dusters. No sooner had Berc and Elias reached consensus on how to solve a particular problem than Robin would step in and stir things up again. He loved playing devil's advocate and would find some reason why the solution being proposed was impossible to implement in software. More shouting would follow as Berc and Elias ganged up against Robin. Eventually, sometimes after several hours of open warfare, a way forward would be agreed, and we would all return to work. This was the mode of operation within the PROPE group, and the creative energy it released led to some excellent research papers.

I barely featured at all in these loud and emotional exchanges. I don't have much of a temper, fiery or otherwise. I hardly ever shout and never throw things or bang my fists. I avoid conflict at all costs and prefer to compromise and seek a middle path. Compared to Berc, Elias and Robin, my personality was a complete mismatch. I sometimes tried to intervene to calm things down, but they would cut me short and all three would unite against me. After a while, I realised that they loved arguing and yelling.

It was their thing and eventually I simply enjoyed the spectacle.

We shared our part of the building with other researchers who would often tentatively peep into our office to see who was being murdered. David Maine and John Westcott frequently received complaints about the disruptions caused by the PROPE group.

The interesting thing was that after hours of shouting, which often descended into personal insults and name-calling, the four of us would set off for a walk in nearby Hyde Park, and within no time they were all the best of friends again, laughing and joking as if the past few hours had never happened.

The work PROPE did was not purely academic. We worked with the policy team at HMT and with a parliamentary committee headed by the Labour MP Jeremy Bray. Our work often helped to inform economic debate both in parliament and outside. This was the early 1980s and Maggie Thatcher and Ronald Reagan were trying to convince the world that economic policy-making was simple. All governments had to do, they said, was control money supply and set the market free.

My work at PROPE also included a huge software maintenance task. I converted the poorly documented and dauntingly massive Treasury Muddle from FORTRAN 4 to FORTRAN 7 so that it could be moved off the mainframe computer to be run on a more user-friendly workstation. If one really wants to learn about software engineering, doing this kind of maintenance work on a large legacy program does the trick! My conversion of the Treasury Model was completed successfully and for many years I would listen to the UK budget speech with the warm satisfaction that my version of the Treasury Model had been used to develop the detailed assumptions. As far as I know, it might still be in use today. It's quite possible that it was used by civil servants to develop scenarios for Brexit. Who knows?

———

WHEN I FIRST CAME TO LONDON IN 1980, I MET CHARLOTTE Burke who lived in the same block of flats, called Albert Mansions in Crouch Hill, as my friend Eddie Wes and his sister Diane (Di). Albert Mansions became my refuge in London and Di and Charlotte became my proxy family. When I moved to London from Manchester in 1981, I shared a house with a South African friend, Isabel Hofmeyr, who was studying in London. When she completed her studies and returned to South Africa, I needed to find a new home. I was beginning to feel quite anxious about my living arrangements when Charlotte invited me for Sunday lunch where I met her friends Colin Davies and Liz Wickett, who lived in Egypt. Colin ran a language school in Cairo and Liz carried out social anthropology research in various parts of Egypt. When the conversation turned to my living arrangements, they told me about the big, almost empty, house they owned in Kentish Town. Their friend, Francis McDonagh, looked after the house for them. They only visited London and stayed in the house once or twice a year. They suggested that I move into their house to help Francis look after it. Later that day I met Francis and he agreed to this arrangement.

Francis was a few years older than me. He was of Irish descent but had always lived in England. He was slightly built with sharp features and penetrating eyes. He was impressively knowledgeable on a wide variety of topics, softly spoken and rather intense. His only form of transport was his bicycle which he rode through the streets of London whatever the weather, the time of day, or distance he had to travel. He worked for an organisation called the Catholic Institute for International Relations (CIIR), which was an NGO that produced publications and organised events with the aim of informing the public about underdeveloped countries with large Catholic communities. It adopted a progressive perspective within a Christian context. This meant that CIIR often took a line that was opposed to official Vatican policy and was more aligned with liberation theology, which was an important force in South and Central American politics at that time. Francis worked as an editor at CIIR and was fluent in several languages including Spanish and French. He had a deep interest in Africa and South America.

The house we shared became my first real London home, and Francis became my housemate for the rest of the time I lived in the UK. We became very good friends. He had previously been married and had a pre-teen daughter, Grace, who spent some weekends and holidays with us, which added to the sense of it as a home.

As we had spare rooms in our house, we had a stream of house guests, including the Saloojees and many others equally as interesting. They ranged from people associated with Francis' work to my network of random South Africans passing through London. One distinguished visitor was Cardinal Jaime Sin of the Philippines who was in London for a CIIR event. Another was South African Black Consciousness leader and liberation theologist Rev Frank Chikane, who was also in London on CIIR business. We also hosted prominent members of the Nicaraguan Sandinista National Liberation Front who were both socialist freedom fighters and ordained Catholic priests, some of whom had been excommunicated by the conservative Vatican-aligned leaders of the church. Francis also had a wide variety of fascinating friends living in the UK who came for meals. I recall many interesting discussions around our kitchen table with house guests and friends telling remarkable stories about their lives and the things they did.

My South African visitors were as interesting and Francis was as intrigued by them as I was by his visitors. One was Auret van Heerden, who had been detained with Neil Aggett in 1981. Neil had died in detention after being tortured by the South African security police and Auret had been one of the last people to see him alive. He gave evidence at the Aggett inquest in 1982 and then came to London to try to recover from his traumatic ordeal. He stayed with us for several weeks and we gave him space and a quiet place away from spying eyes and vicious gossip. Francis cooked him special meals but he hardly ate anything and seemed to never sleep. Late at night and early in the morning, we would hear him pacing and prowling around the house.

Another visitor I remember well was Mama Lydia Kompe, who, like Cas Saloojee, was a veteran of the anti-Apartheid struggles of the 1950s and 60s. She had lived in Crown Mines at the same time as me in the 1970s where she masqueraded as a domestic worker and lived in the back room of one of the houses. In the mid-1980s, she was working for the Metal and Allied Workers Union (MAWU) and played a significant role in the formation of South Africa's trade union movement. She fought many battles in support of female workers. She had been invited to a trade union event in London, which was her first journey outside of South Africa, and came to stay with us in Kentish Town. I became her tour guide as we visited some of London's many sights. I also accompanied her to the BBC and sat in the studio with her, providing her with moral support, as she gave a live radio interview. I always enjoyed seeing London, my new home city, through the eyes of visitors who were seeing it for the first time. Mama Lydia went on to serve as a longstanding ANC MP in South Africa's post-1994 national parliament.

———

WHILE I FILLED MY LIFE QUITE HAPPILY WORKING AT IMPERIAL College and running my free guesthouse in Kentish Town, my primary purpose for being in London remained getting myself out of London and back to Africa to Mozambique. In late 1981, I had a meeting with Paul Fauvet at MAGIC and later with some of my ANC contacts to see whether any of them could help to speed up the process of getting ANC clearance. I had been patiently waiting without any feedback for more than a year.

Ian Robinson, my friend working at IDAF (International Defence and Aid Fund), made some enquiries on my behalf at the ANC's London office. The information he received at the end of 1981 was that my papers were waiting in Lusaka for arrangements to be made to courier them back to London. This sounded promising, although the wait was increasingly frustrating. I felt my life was in limbo while this process dragged on. What really frustrated me was the fact that I was ready and willing to leave for Mozambique at a moment's notice, and everything I read confirmed that someone with my skills and qualifications was definitely needed in Mozambique. I could be doing useful work there rather than biding my time in London.

I began to contact MAGIC every week. I attended all of their events and met up with other white South Africans requiring ANC clearance so they could work in Mozambique. Two of these, Martin Rall and his wife Colleen, had already received clearance and were making final arrangements to relocate to Mozambique. I also began attending Portuguese lessons at an adult education centre in Kentish Town.

In the first week of March 1982, I received a message

from MAGIC to say that I would be required to attend an interview at the ANC offices in Islington. My papers had arrived back in London and the purpose of the interview was to finalise my application for ANC clearance. The date for the interview was set for late in March. It looked, at last, as though my grand plan was progressing, and I would soon be able to undertake my move to Mozambique. I let some close friends know that I would soon be leaving London.

———

THE PHONE IN THE LOUNGE OF OUR HOUSE RANG EARLY IN THE morning on Sunday 14th March 1982. I was asleep, but the ringing woke me. I heard Francis answer the phone. He came upstairs and knocked on my door.

'Someone needs to speak to you urgently', he said.

I pulled on my dressing gown and went downstairs. I picked up the phone.

It was my friend Russell Caplan. 'Did you hear the news?' he asked.

'I've just woken up', I said. 'What's happened?'

'The ANC office in Islington has been bombed!' he said. 'No one was injured but it's a mess.'

An image flashed before my eyes. My long-awaited clearance papers scattered randomly among the wreckage of the ANC office. Lost forever.

In the days that followed, this image proved to be real. Most of the documentation in the ANC office had been destroyed. The message I received was that my clearance process would probably need to start again from scratch.

Years later, several members of the South African security police owned up at the Truth and Reconciliation Commission (TRC) to the bombing of the ANC's London Office.

I remained hopeful that the clearance process would move more quickly the second time around. I heard that some documentation relating to me remained intact in Lusaka. But a year after the London bombing, my Mozambique dream finally ended. On 16th March 1984, the South African Prime Minister, PW Botha, and Mozambican President, Samora Machel, signed the Nkomati Accord. This was a "non-aggression pact" between the two governments. It was also an admission by Mozambique's government that South Africa's covert war against it had become too costly to resist. Nkomati's major thrust was to stop Mozambican support for the ANC. All ANC members and supporters would have to leave Mozambique. Suddenly ANC approval of my application to work in Mozambique was the last thing I needed.

After nearly six years of seeing my life in Britain as a short-term arrangement, I was forced to accept an uncomfortable truth. This grey and depressing island in the northern hemisphere was destined to be my home for the rest of my life. My Mozambican dream had evaporated, and I couldn't see myself being anywhere else in Africa other than South Africa. At that time, the mid-1980s, Apartheid South Africa seemed invincible. Bolstered by a huge war machine and supported by Thatcher and Reagan, PW Botha's hard-line government had a firm grip on power. Despite rising resistance both inside and outside the country, I didn't believe things would change any time soon. I decided that all I could do was to whole-heartedly offer my support to the struggle against Apartheid, while I accepted that I was now permanently living in Britain.

Based on this mental re-alignment, I decided to change my job, buy a house, become a British citizen, and join the struggle against Apartheid as an underground operative.

Dianne Wes and Charlotte Burck with her son Ben in Albert Mansions, London. [Photo: Edwin Wes]

Charlotte Burck at Albert Mansions, London. [Photo: Edwin Wes]

Barry Dwolatzky

Birthday Celebration in London with Christopher Warburton,
Roderick Rischen and Eddie Wes. [Photo: Edwin Wes]

chapter
eleven

LIVING IN THE SHADOWS

1985 to 1987

Without drawing attention to myself, I scanned the other arriving passengers as we queued at passport control at Johannesburg's Jan Smuts Airport. I was relieved to see no familiar faces. If someone had recognised me, things would have become far more complicated. The queue slowly inched forward towards the immigration officer checking and stamping passports. He was a stereotypical Apartheid-era white South African government official. Young, smartly dressed in his well-pressed uniform, his lips set in an arrogant sneer under his neatly trimmed thin moustache.

It was my turn to step forward. Although my heart pounded, and my palms felt clammy, I did as I had been trained to do. I looked directly at his face. I would only speak if he spoke first. I had prepared short and clear answers to any questions he might ask. My carefully constructed and rehearsed cover story was that I was a South African-born British citizen visiting South Africa on a short business trip. I would only be in the country for a few days. I worked in the research department of a large company, GEC-Marconi (this was true), and I had to attend a few meetings with academic researchers in Johannesburg and Cape Town. The purpose of these meetings was to discuss possible collaboration on confidential research projects (this was not true).

I tried to look irritated by the delay. As I handed over my brand-new British passport, I focused on listening calmly to anything the immigration officer might say. Without a word, he flipped through the passport stopping at the page with my photo. He looked at it and then looked up and met my gaze, paused for a second, and then stared again at my photo. He reached for something hidden from my view on a low desk in front of him. Was it a list of names? He paused, scanned whatever it was in front of him, and looked again at my passport. I concentrated hard on keeping my eyes steady and my facial expression unchanged. Without looking at me again he reached for a rubber stamp, flipped to a random page in my passport, stamped it loudly, closed it, and slid it across the desk towards me. He hadn't said a word. As I picked it up, he was already beckoning to the next person in the queue to step forward. Was that it, or was I on his list? Was he giving an invisible signal to security branch policemen lurking in the shadows? Would they let me through and then pounce on me as I left the airport? Or would they follow me to see what I did and who I met? I had no way of knowing.

After an absence of seven years, I was back in South Africa. It was early on a Monday morning in May 1987. When I was last at Jan Smuts Airport, it had been 1980 and I had been on my way into exile. I had solemnly promised myself that I would not come back to South Africa until Apartheid had ended, something that seemed unlikely to happen any time soon. I didn't know then that seven years later I would be flying into Johannesburg on a secret mission.

My decision to leave South Africa in 1980 had been openly discussed with some of my close friends. My return in 1987 was very different. Nobody knew that I was back in the country. My greatest worry, in fact, was that I would bump into someone who recognised me.

My mission was very specific. I was bringing information and a large amount of cash to someone I had never met. I only knew her as "Sandy". She was in Cape Town, so my first task was to buy a ticket to Cape Town. With my briefcase in one hand and a small overnight suitcase in the other, I walked over to the South African Airways ticket counter and bought a return ticket to Cape Town. The next flight departed in forty-five minutes which was perfect as I wanted to get out of Johannesburg as quickly as I could. The longer I stayed, the higher the probability of being recognised by someone who knew me.

A few hours later, I was at DF Malan Airport in Cape Town. I took a taxi from the airport to the main railway station and sat on a bench in the station concourse observing the passing crowd, trying to make certain that no one was watching me. After about half an hour, I walked a few blocks to Loop Street looking for a medium-priced hotel. There were a few to choose from and I popped into the nearest one. I asked for a room, paid cash in advance and went up to my room. I hadn't slept a wink since leaving London. It was mid-afternoon. I locked the door, closed the curtains and lay down, still in my business clothes, on the bed. I fell into a deep sleep.

I woke at 7pm with a sudden feeling of fear, realising where I was and what I was doing. The political situation in South Africa was on a knife edge. It was late May 1987. Many believed that the country was edging closer to civil war. A few weeks earlier, white voters had participated in a general election. There had been a distinct shift to the far right, which was about as right as one could get. While PW Botha's ruling National Party (Nats) remained comfortably in power, the newly formed Conservative Party (CP) had replaced the middle of the road Progressive Federal Party as the official parliamentary opposition. Andries Treurnicht, the Deputy Minister of Education at the time of the 1976 Soweto Uprising, had split from the mainstream to lead an ultra-right political party. At the same time, opposition to Apartheid was growing stronger by the day. Inside the country, the UDF and trade unions were gaining strength and confidence. Internationally, the ANC, supported by a broad anti-Apartheid alliance, was isolating and demonising the South African regime.

A State of Emergency was in force, giving Botha and his securocrats sweeping powers to arrest, detain, torture and kill opponents. My secret mission was such that if I was caught, arrest, detention, torture and possible death were very real possibilities.

It was early evening. I changed into casual clothes. I removed a parcel from my briefcase and hid it under some blankets in the cupboard in my hotel room. I then stepped out of the hotel in search of something to eat as well as to carry out a test run of my route for the following morning.

I would be meeting Sandy at 10:20am the following day in the foyer of the five-star Mount Nelson Hotel. I walked from my hotel and meandered through the city centre. I had been trained to check whether I was being followed. I zig-zagged along, stopping to look at items in shop windows. I observed people and vehicles around me. I went into a small nondescript café that served toasted sandwiches over the counter and ordered a toasted cheese and tomato, which I ate standing on the pavement, keeping an eye on everyone and everything around me.

I strolled into the Gardens and paused to look at the Parliament building. I sat on a bench and watched people coming and going. It was early autumn and a little cold and windy. There weren't many people out and about. There was no hint that I was being followed, although one can never be certain.

I then stood up and stared for a few minutes at the Parliament building in front of me. This was the place where the legal framework of Apartheid had been enacted and white rule solidified. Standing near that place and thinking about what it symbolised, I was overcome by a wave of anger. I thought about some of the heroes and martyrs of The Struggle, not only the iconic figures that we all knew about but had never met, like Mandela, Sisulu and Hector Peterson, but particularly those who had been my personal friends and acquaintances, like Neil Aggett (tortured and dead in detention), Barbara Hogan (languishing in prison) and Jeanette Curtis (killed with her child by a parcel bomb). Thinking about the South African parliament and the evil it had created was an important moment to sharpen my focus and ramp up my resolve for the task that lay ahead over the next day or two.

I walked into the Mount Nelson and stood in the foyer pretending to be waiting for someone. I seemed to successfully blend in. None of the staff members approached me or paid any attention to me.

I walked slowly back to my hotel, making sure as I went that I was not being followed or watched. I went back to my room, locked the door, climbed into bed, and then tossed and turned all night. I knew I should sleep so that I would feel calm and rested the next morning, but I couldn't sleep a wink. My brain was buzzing in anticipation for the meeting with Sandy at 10:20 the following morning.

———

I GAVE MYSELF AN HOUR TO GET FROM MY HOTEL TO THE Mount Nelson on that Tuesday morning. I was dressed in a dark grey business suit and carried a leather briefcase. In the case was a parcel containing tens of thousands of Rands in cash. I walked in a direction away from the Mount Nelson for about twenty minutes and then doubled back and walked towards it. I constantly checked and re-checked that I was not being followed.

At 10:10am, I walked into the Mount Nelson foyer with a confident look firmly fixed on my face. My cover story was that I was a businessman from the UK waiting to be collected for a meeting. I made a point of looking at my watch and then stood in the foyer where I could see people entering the main door. At 10:14am, a short dark-haired man wearing a blue jacket with some sort of badge sewn on the breast pocket approached me.

'Are you Horst?' he asked.

'Sorry. Wrong person,' I said with a forced smile, my heart beating loudly.

'Okay,' he said with a nod and walked off towards the reception desk.

I moved further from the main door and carried on waiting, watching the clock on the wall to my right. It was 10:22am and Sandy had not yet arrived.

My instructions from Muff had been clear. If Sandy didn't arrive by 10:25am, I was to leave the Mount Nelson immediately. There was a backup plan with a different meeting place at a different time for the following day.

At 10:24am, a tall, smartly dressed woman with short brown hair entered the hotel foyer and walked towards me.

'Hello, you must be Pete,' she said.

'Are you Sandy?' I asked.

'Yes. Good to meet you. How was the weather in London?' she asked.

'Surprisingly mild for May,' I answered.

'My car's outside. I will drive you to the meeting,' she said.

Every word in that conversation had been scripted by Muff. I had practised it with her before I left London. If a single word was left out, changed or added on either side of the conversation, the meeting was to be aborted. It would be a sign that something had gone wrong and I was to get out of South Africa as quickly as possible.

The interchange, however, had been word-perfect and both Sandy and I were comfortable to move to the next step of the plan. Without saying anything further – Muff had insisted that there must be 'No small talk' – I followed Sandy to a light blue Datsun parked outside. We drove off in silence.

I watched as Sandy drove through the streets of Cape Town. I noted that she was turning often and watching her mirrors. She was making sure that we weren't being followed. After about twenty minutes of aimless driving, she headed out of the city centre towards Sea Point. My head was full of questions, as I'm sure hers was too, but we continued to drive in silence. She drove through Sea Point and then on to Victoria Road towards Clifton. She pulled into a car park area above Second Beach and stopped. There was nobody around. We sat in the car for about five minutes, silently watching Victoria Road and waiting to see whether anything suspicious happened, such as a car driving past in one direction and then coming back in the other direction. Everything seemed fine and Sandy relaxed.

'I think we're okay,' she said. 'Let's get out of the car and walk over to that spot over there. People often park here and get out to admire the view. Leave your briefcase in the car.'

We left the car and walked over to the scenic vantage spot where we sat on a low wall. Sandy was carrying an artist's sketch pad. She opened it to a blank page and started to doodle. This was my cue to deliver the detailed briefing I had been sent to give her.

For more than a month before I had left London, I had sat for hours and hours memorising many pages of information. One page had been details of recent changes in leadership positions in the ANC Executive Committee and the command structure of MK (uMkhonto we Sizwe – the ANC's military wing). My instruction from Muff was that I needed to remember every single detail from this page perfectly. Although Muff had never explained this, I suspected that Sandy had also memorised the information on this page and that any errors would alert Sandy that I was not to be trusted. The other information I had needed to commit to memory was several pages of descriptions of boxes. For example, one box was 890mm by 50mm by 260mm. It was made of ¾ inch thick plywood and lined with aluminium sheeting. It had one of its 890mm by 260mm sides fixed into place by self-tapping screws.

As I spoke from memory, Sandy carefully wrote all I

said in her sketch book. At the end of each description, she read back to me what she had written so that I could confirm it was correct. After about three quarters of an hour, everything Muff and Cal had given to me in London and that I had memorised had been accurately captured in Sandy's sketch book. We stood up and walked slowly back to her car. As I climbed into the passenger seat, she opened the boot. I heard some scraping and scratching. When she slipped into the driver's seat, the sketch book was nowhere to be seen, obviously safely hidden in the boot of her car. As we pulled off, she told me to hide the parcel of money I had in my briefcase under my seat so that she could recover it later.

We drove on in silence. In Sea Point, she stopped on the side of the road.

'You can get out here,' she said.

As I opened the door, she looked at me and smiled warmly. 'Well done comrade! I hope you get back home safely. Greet Muff from me.'

'Good luck to you,' I said as I closed the door. The light blue Datsun joined the traffic and disappeared from view.

––––––

AFTER GETTING BACK TO MY HOTEL IN LOOP STREET, I TOOK A few minutes to change into more casual clothes, grabbed my overnight bag and immediately checked out. I walked to the front of another hotel around the corner and asked the porter outside to get me a taxi to the airport. I caught the first flight back to Jan Smuts Airport and checked into the airport hotel. It was late on Tuesday afternoon. I had been in South Africa for just over a day. My return flight to London was booked for 8am on Wednesday morning. I bought a toasted sandwich and coke from the hotel snack bar and holed up in my room until it was time, early on Wednesday morning, to return to the airport concourse.

I don't remember much about those hours waiting to get out of South Africa, but I do recall having a sudden panic attack. What if Sandy was a security police agent? Or what if she had been detained after we met and the cops now knew about me? Or what if Muff's cell was infiltrated by an agent and I had been set up? Would the cops arrive soon and burst into my room? Would they detain me as I arrived to board my flight to London? I went through all of my pockets. I found a receipt for the hotel in Cape Town, my boarding pass from Cape Town to Joburg, a receipt from my taxi. I scrunched them all into a tight ball and flushed it down the toilet. I couldn't sleep that night as I waited until it was time to leave for the airport.

It was only once the British Airways flight to London lifted off from Jan Smuts Airport that I relaxed. It was clear that none of my fears had materialised. I looked out of the window as we gained height over Johannesburg. I could now look calmly at my home city. As I had done seven years earlier, I wondered when I would return. I was exhausted and fell into a deep sleep.

———

Successful undercover missions depend on keeping all the elements separate. In my secret trip to South Africa in May 1987, I only knew as much as I needed to know to ensure that my part of the mission could be carried out. My job was to deliver money and information to Sandy. Her job was to do something with this money and information. Neither of us knew anything more about one another. The information I brought was very detailed and very specific, but I had no larger context about how this information would be used. Nor did either of us know about other parts of the plan and how these parts fitted into a bigger project. If either of us had been captured by the security police, there was very little we could tell them, even if they tortured us for days.

It was only years later that I learnt about the "bigger project" and how I had played a critical part, albeit a very small part in its overall success.

In the late 1980s, the leadership of the exiled ANC made a strategic decision to step up the armed struggle within the borders of South Africa. Increasing numbers of trained MK soldiers were infiltrating into the country from across its borders and were linking up with internal structures. While the government maintained a façade of military invincibility and control over all aspects of life in the country, huge cracks were beginning to appear. Each daring operation executed by MK operatives inside the country struck fear into the hearts of white South Africans and encouraged black South Africans and those forces ranged against the Apartheid regime.

Stepping up MK's capacity to operate within South Africa's borders required the setting up of supply lines for arms, ammunition and explosives. Equipment had to be smuggled into the country and hidden at strategic locations. Since arms caches were frequently discovered by the Apartheid authorities, a large number of small caches had to be established throughout the country.

A pair of MK operatives in exile, Muff Andersonn and "Calvin Khan" (I was one of the few people who knew his real name was Riaz Saloojee), were given the task of setting up and running the supply chain bringing military equipment and supplies from Zambia into South Africa. Working with others, they developed a scheme in which a tour company, called Africa Hinterland, was established by ANC members in the UK. It sold over-land trips through Africa to adventurous travellers, mostly young people from Europe, Australia and the USA. A big Bedford truck was bought and specially fitted out. Unbeknown to any of the travellers, secret compartments were built into the chassis of the vehicle. When a tour stopped in Lusaka, arms and ammunition were hidden in these compartments. After loading up in Zambia, the truck continued its journey south, passing through border checks into South Africa. The truck was driven by young anti-Apartheid volunteers from the UK and Netherlands. Only the driver knew about the cargo he was carrying.

When the tour arrived in Johannesburg and Cape Town, the truck parked at camp sites where the cargo was secretly transferred to specially-made boxes which were concealed in cars and small pickup trucks (known locally as "bakkies") and transported to different parts of the country. Arms caches were established in many locations. MK operatives requiring ordinance for a mission would be given the location of an appropriate cache.

I knew nothing about any of this. My mission in 1987 was to bring money and detailed instructions to one of the cells receiving the ordinance being brought to Cape Town. The detailed dimensions I gave to Sandy would be used to make some of these specially-designed boxes. The money was probably used to buy one of the bakkies.

Over a seven-year period (1986-1993), about forty trips were made by the Africa Hinterland Bedford bringing about thirty tonnes of weapons, ammunition and explosives into South Africa without a single mishap. Several small arms caches were, however, discovered by the security police. Finding these caches filled the Apartheid regime with fear because they realised they were up against a well-organised, well-trained and well-equipped adversary. Some of those involved in the struggle now believe that the success of this operation and the psychological impact it had on the South African government played a significant part in hastening the end of Apartheid.

———

I HAD BECOME FRIENDS WITH MUFF AND RIAZ EARLY IN 1985, when his family had stayed with us in Kentish Town. At first, we spoke very little about ourselves, or, more accurately, they spoke very little about themselves. I had no idea what it was that they did, although I knew that they were somehow involved in the ANC's underground structures, but nothing more. I never asked questions, even though I was dying to find out more. They would disappear from London for long periods of time without ever giving a clue about where they were going or where they had been. They often asked me pointed questions about my past and what I was doing in London. They were very curious about who I had known in South Africa and who my current friends and acquaintances were. I constantly felt that I was being assessed.

I also became involved in more normal interactions with some of the other South African exiles in London at that time. Through Neil and Mel, my friends in Manchester, I met Paul Jourdan, a South African geologist who had worked in Mozambique where he had met Neil and some of the people I lived with in Heald Place in Manchester. Paul was a dedicated and energetic member of the above-ground ANC and was studying in Leeds. He introduced me to a group of ANC members in London who were carrying out research on environmental issues related to Apartheid. The coordinator of this group was Frene Ginwala, Head of the ANC's Policy Research Department and a very prominent figure in ANC exile circles. She would later become the Speaker of South Africa's first democratic parliament in 1994. I agreed to write a section on water supply for a report they were compiling. I used my academic position at Imperial College to write to several government departments and research institutes in South Africa asking for unpublished statistics and reports on water supply. I pretended to be doing an engineering study on water in Southern Africa. I received a mountain of really useful information which I turned into a long and detailed analysis of how Apartheid's policies affected the quality of water and access to fresh water both in South Africa and the frontline states. I was very proud of this piece of work. I think, although I haven't been able to find it, that the overall report, including my section on water, formed part of the ANC's submissions to an international conference.

Another member of the exile community I met in the mid-80s was Lynn Danzig, who worked for Gill Marcus in the ANC's Department of Information and Publicity (DIP) in London. Lynn and I became good friends. She was a wonderful example of the dedicated, hardworking, and resourceful young South Africans working for the ANC in London. She received a small stipend that covered little more than the cost of basic needs and worked long hours, days on end. Lynn and many other ANC comrades in London remain some of the unsung and under-appreciated heroes of The Struggle.

In 1986, Lynn introduced me to her flatmate, Tim Jenkin, who worked in some capacity for IDAF. She hadn't told me anything about Tim before I met him, except that he 'was interested in computers'. Although I should have recognised his name, I didn't and had no idea who I was meeting.

As I remember it now, our first meeting was quite

awkward. My old habit of assuming that people would be suspicious of me, a white South African man hanging around the fringes of the ANC in exile, leading me to over-compensate by trying too hard to prove my authenticity, might have kicked in. Tim didn't say much, while I blabbed on about the work I was doing with computers hoping to impress him.

I also remember that I completely misread Tim at that first meeting. I saw a slightly built man, about my age, with a thin face and serious eyes behind thick glasses. He had a bookish, academic appearance and seemed very much a soft-spoken backroom operator. As I read him, Tim was definitely not going to be found close to the action. I could imagine him happily tucked away in some corner doing great work analysing documents or writing computer programs.

It was only after that first meeting that Lynn and others reminded me who Tim Jenkin was. In 1978, while I was a PhD student at Wits, we heard about the arrest of Stephen Lee, whose mother worked at Wits. Stephen had been arrested in Cape Town for producing and distributing pamphlets in Johannesburg and Cape Town in support of the ANC and SACP. Stephen was detained with another young white activist who was none other than Tim Jenkin. They had set off dozens of leaflet bombs in Cape Town. At their trial, Lee and Jenkin were sentenced to eight and twelve years respectively. They were sent to Pretoria Central Prison to serve these ridiculously long and unfair sentences. However, just over a year later, Jenkin, Lee and a third political prisoner, Alex Moumbaris, were again in the news. They had escaped from South Africa's maximum-security prison. The South African media accused a prison warder of helping them.

It was only later when I read the book Tim wrote called *Escape from Pretoria*, published in 1987, that I fully appreciated how amazing their escape had been. They had not received any help from a warder; that was merely a fabrication by the prison authorities to hide their embarrassment. I also fully appreciated Tim's bravery and genius. He had managed to make thirteen keys out of wood to open all the doors between their cells and the outside world. He had made the keys by staring for hours at each key on the prison warder's bunch, memorising every minute detail. Then, by trial and error, he got each wooden key to work.

I had completely underestimated Tim. The work I went on to do with him raised him even higher in my esteem. He is one of the most remarkable people I've ever known.

Tim Jenkins

chapter
twelve

PARALLEL UNIVERSES

1986

I had an important rendezvous in central London that morning, and whatever happened, Tim Jenkin couldn't know about it. I knew he was following me. I would need to avoid him.

As I exited the Oxford Circus tube station turnstiles, my suspicion about Tim spying on me proved to be correct. I spotted him pretending to read the timetable on the wall close to the ticket office. I had seen him, but had he seen me? I walked quickly to the stairs leading up to street level. At the top of the stairs, I walked over to a shop window and pretended to read a poster in the window advertising holidays in Thailand, while using the window as a mirror to watch the stairs I had just climbed. I waited for two minutes. No sign of him. I walked casually away from Oxford Circus along Regent Street, heading towards

Piccadilly Circus. I stopped a few minutes later and bent down on the side of the broad pavement to tie my shoelace. It was late on Sunday morning and while there were a fair number of pedestrians around, this busy part of London wasn't nearly as busy as it could be. While tying my lace, I had a good chance to look in all directions. There was certainly no sign of Tim. Had I given him the slip? From the corner of my eye, I thought I saw someone ducking behind a phone box. Could that be him?

I went into the Liberty's store and ducked behind a rail of coats, watching the entrance. Nobody had followed me in. I hurried through the shop toward an exit on the opposite end and slipped out into Carnaby Street where there was absolutely no sign of Tim. I walked rapidly and purposefully, turning left, then right. I turned a corner and stopped, did a U-turn and then retraced my steps, all the time scanning the pavements and shop entrances. I was confident I had lost Tim.

Ten minutes later, I entered The Queen's Head Pub in Denman Street. This was where I needed to be for my important rendezvous. Unless he had followed me, Tim couldn't know this, and I was absolutely certain that he hadn't followed me. I tried to attract the barman's attention.

'Half a bitter,' I said when I caught his eye.

'Make that two,' said a voice to my left. I spun round. Tim Jenkin was standing next to me, a broad smile on his face.

———

EVERY WEEKEND FOR TWO OR THREE MONTHS, TIM WOULD teach me tradecraft. These are the techniques, methods and technologies used in modern espionage. Tim had several books and manuals, together with notes he had written himself. We went through these in great detail. We practised following a person without being seen. We practised avoiding being followed. We walked around London following random pedestrians, whispering into tiny two-way radios. He taught me about dead letter boxes and codes, about invisible inks and disguises. We would practice and then discuss what we had practised. I became better at it, but was never as good as Tim.

How did I come to be recruited into this shadowy world? A week after I first met him at the flat he shared with Lynn Danzig, Tim had sent me a message asking me to meet him for a beer at a pub in Islington. When we met, he cut straight to the point. He had discussed me with some of his superiors and had been given permission to ask me if I would work with him on a certain project.

This left me with a dilemma because a few months earlier I had had a similar discussion in a pub in another part of London with Muff. She had also asked me to work with her and Riaz on a secret project to which I had agreed.

'Can I be recruited twice?' I wondered as I sat with Tim. 'Did Tim and his superiors know about Muff recruiting me? Was I allowed to tell Tim that I had already been recruited?' I was sure I wasn't. Muff had made it clear that all conversations between her and me were ABSOLUTELY TOP SECRET. All these questions ran through my head.

All I said to Tim was something like, 'Thanks for asking, but I need some time to think about this. Can we meet again next week?'

A day or two later, I met with Muff and told her about Tim's approach. She was irritated but said she would 'speak to someone' and then get back to me. 'In the meantime, avoid speaking to Tim,' she said.

I've no idea what happened behind the scenes, but Muff contacted me a few days later to say that 'it had been agreed' that I would work on both Muff's project and on Tim's. She said that this was very unusual since people only ever worked with a small number of others in a single cell. Working across cells was very risky, but nevertheless, it had been decided that an exception would be made in my case. She also said that Tim would train me in tradecraft. Muff had started to train me, but we hadn't yet progressed very far.

The tasks Muff initially gave me relied on the fact that my connection to the ANC was not obvious to those within the South African exile community in London. Even among those who knew me, I was seen as someone who had left South Africa to avoid conscription and who worked as a researcher at some university. It was known that I occasionally attended anti-Apartheid meetings and rallies, but that was all. Muff also relied on the fact that I was dependable, disciplined and able to follow instructions meticulously. The jobs she gave me mostly involved meeting with strangers in various parts of London, checking them out via carefully rehearsed pass phrases and silent signals, and then discretely slipping them a parcel or a note. As far as I knew, such parcels usually contained large amounts of cash, so Muff needed someone she could trust completely.

My work with Tim was much more exciting and significant.

―――――

ON 16TH DECEMBER 1961, THE ANNIVERSARY OF THE INFAMOUS Battle of Blood River, celebrated by white South Africans as the Day of the Covenant, the ANC initiated armed struggle against South Africa's Apartheid regime. On that day, it launched its armed wing, Umkhonto we Sizwe (or MK), with the bombing of an electricity sub-station and other government targets, carefully chosen so that no lives were lost. Nelson Mandela was named as the Commander-in-Chief of MK. It was a real David and Goliath situation, given the relative size and sophistication of South Africa's military and security forces.

From its very inception, MK struggled with communications. Many of its setbacks could be traced back to the way in which messages were passed between those coordinating its actions and those tasked with carrying them out. Communication is one of the most critical issues in any type of warfare, as is the need to communicate in a way that cannot be intercepted and understood by the enemy. Over 2000 years ago, the Roman Emperor, Julius Caesar, invented one of the first schemes for writing messages in code. This is called the Caesar Cipher, which is a shift cipher. These are very easy to break. By the time of the Second World War (1939-1945), the science of cryptography had become far more sophisticated. The Germans invented a cryptographic machine, called Enigma, which produced coded messages that were unbreakable, or so they thought until the British mathematician Alan Turing managed to find a way of cracking it. With the advent of computers and digital communications, cryptography became far more effective. As I write this in the third decade of the 21st Century, cryptography and related disciplines have reached unbelievably high levels of complexity and sophistication.

Between the founding of MK in 1961 and the 1980s, the ANC's underground operations depended on very primitive communications. Messages were written using invisible ink on a piece of paper. An innocent letter was then written on the same piece of paper in normal ink and sent via the regular postal services into and out of South Africa. Messages were also smuggled in and out of the country sewn into the seams of people's clothes or hidden in other ways. Often these messages weren't encrypted at all, or when they were encrypted, very simple ciphers, like the Caesar Cipher, were used. By the 1980s, the Apartheid security machinery was huge. Almost every piece of mail coming into and going out of South Africa was opened and inspected. They were aware of most of the ANC underground's communications methods, and often intercepted and decrypted secret communications. They gathered huge amounts of intelligence in this way, and used it to detain, torture and kill MK operatives.

Tim Jenkin, working with a small group of other comrades, organised as a technical support group in London, struggled to convince the ANC leadership to take secure communications seriously. Several years later, in 1995, he wrote a series of fascinating articles describing in detail how this group went about developing a computer-based communication system in the late 1980s[1]. Eventually, this ingenious do-it-yourself system, developed by a group of enthusiastic amateurs on a shoe-string budget, was deployed. It proved to be sufficiently secure and sophisticated to operate without being detected by the experts working in the expensively equipped security agencies of Apartheid South Africa and their western allies.

Given my background in engineering and computer programming, Tim brought me in as an advisor to help him solve some of the technical problems he struggled with. I was only ever in touch with Tim, never meeting other members of the technical support team. Tim had a vast collection of electronic devices spread over several tables in his bedroom in Islington. Wires hung out of most of them and his soldering iron was always close by. Although I have a PhD degree in electrical engineering, I soon realised that, although he was self-taught, Tim had a far deeper knowledge of the practical nuts and bolts of the specific technologies he was working with than I did. I helped where I could, and hopefully filled some of the gaps in his theoretical knowledge.

Early in 1989, Tim asked me whether I would be willing to return to South Africa to work on a very important project for him. It was only several years later, when I read Tim's articles on operation Vula, that I completely understood what this important project was.

———

IN THE MID- TO LATE-1980S, I LIVED SEVERAL SEPARATE parallel lives which I kept tightly sealed from each other. It was schizophrenic and very stressful.

While my underground activism continued in two mutually exclusive compartments, one directed by Muff and Riaz, and the other by Tim, the rest of my life proceeded on a relatively calm and conventional trajectory.

As it turned out, the year 1986 was a very significant turning point in my life for many reasons. It was the year when the ANC's presence in Mozambique was removed and my intention to return to Africa and work in Mozambique ended. I no longer saw my life in the UK as temporary and began to come to terms with the unhappy fact that this would be where I lived for the foreseeable future.

I was eligible to apply for British citizenship which became a priority, since travelling on a South African passport while international sanctions against Apartheid grew became more and more difficult. Having a respectable academic job as a highly qualified white male meant that acquiring UK citizenship was a mere formality. I soon found myself in a lawyer's office with one hand raised asserting, rather than swearing (I was given a choice), allegiance to Her Majesty the Queen and All Her Heirs. Soon afterward, I was in possession of a Certificate of Naturalisation and a brand-new British Passport.

With my eyes now set on a long-term stay in Britain, I had started to think afresh about where I worked and where I lived.

The house I lived in in Kentish Town with Francis McDonagh was to be sold as the owners were divorcing. Over the previous years, Francis and I had got on really well. We were each busy and self-sufficient in our own circles of friends and activities, while we had enough in common to be compatible house mates. When we found out that we would need to move out of the Kentish Town house, we agreed to combine resources and buy a house together. In 1986, after months of house-hunting around London, we found a really great house in Lavers Street in Stoke Newington. We bought this with each of us owning half of the property. It was the first valuable asset I had ever owned.

The other change I made in that same year was to look for a permanent job. My work at Imperial College, which I really enjoyed, depended on the research group I was part of receiving research grants. There were many uncertain times when one grant was about to run out and the next grant hadn't yet been secured. This was a typical situation in academic research jobs at the time but I really longed for stability. Having a house of my own gave me some of that, but also created the need to have a dependable income.

I had kept in touch with Steve Sannoff, who had been a PhD student at UMIST in Manchester while I was there.

Steve and I had become good friends. In 1986, as everything else was falling into place for me, Steve contacted me to ask if I was interested in applying for a job at the company he was working for. After completing his PhD, he had gone to work for GEC, a very large British company, not to be confused with the American multi-national GE.

The job I applied for was a permanent post as a Research Associate at one of GEC's research facilities, the GEC-Marconi Research Centre situated in Great Baddow, just outside Chelmsford in Essex. The Great Baddow site has a very important place in the history of technology. It was established in the 1930s by the company founded by the Italian-British inventor Guglielmo Marconi, the pioneer of radio communications. The company had begun operations in a building in Hall Street in central Chelmsford but needed a large site away from the centre of a busy town where electromagnetic interference caused by motors, transformers and other electrical equipment adversely affected their ongoing research. When it originally opened, the Marconi Research Centre in Great Baddow was out in the countryside, and even in 1986 it felt rural.

In the 1930s and 40s, the Marconi Research Centre was the focal point of research into radio-based communications and radar. Many of the world's leading scientists and engineers in radio-related fields worked at, or had some association with, the Marconi Research Centre. One of its biggest claims to fame was the part it played in the development and testing of radar during the Second World War. When I went to work there, people proudly pointed to an ugly

110m tall tower which had been part of the Chain Home radar system that gave the Royal Air Force early warnings of approaching German bombers during the war.

In the 1980s, the GEC-Marconi Research Centre, as it was then called, was involved in a broad range of research programmes covering both top-secret military research and commercially-oriented industrial research. I applied for a job in the Industrial Automation Division (IAD) working under Ian Powell, the team leader, and alongside Steve Sanoff and about ten other scientists, engineers and technicians.

As had happened at both UMIST and Imperial College, the process of getting the job proved to be very easy. I arrived on the morning of my job interview psyched up and ready to sell myself, only to find that Ian Powell and his boss had already agreed between themselves to employ me based on my CV and references. I met with them briefly, spoke about the weather, as one usually does in Britain, and the history of the Great Baddow research site, and was then handed over to someone from the personnel department who presented me with a contract and other information. The only potential obstacle to me getting the job was that I had to be given security clearance by the British Ministry of Defence and I would have to sign the Official Secrets Act. I wondered whether my support for the ANC or my participation in various anti-Thatcher protest actions had come to the attention of the authorities, but no concerns were raised. I received a letter of appointment a few weeks later asking me to confirm my starting date.

My colleagues at Imperial College were sad when I resigned but understood my need to find something more secure than the short-term contract that they could offer. We parted on the very best of terms and agreed to stay in touch.

Francis and I were in the process of moving out of the house in Kentish Town and had not yet finalised the purchase of our new house in Stoke Newington. I decided to move to Chelmsford temporarily and I found a rented room in a house owned by a couple named Barry and Beryl, in a council-housing development near Great Baddow. When I agreed to take the job at GEC-Marconi, I had made it clear that I would live in London and commute to Chelmsford. My few months living as a lodger in suburban Chelmsford absolutely convinced me that my decision to live in London was the right one.

As soon as Francis and I were able to move into our new home, I began my life as a long-distance commuter. Chelmsford is the capital of Essex and, as the crow flies, is about 50 km from central London. My journey from Stoke Newington to Great Baddow took nearly two hours and involved a train and two buses. This meant that I spent about four hours each day commuting. I imagined myself using that time to do productive work like reading and writing. As it turned out, this was wishful thinking. I either dozed, day-dreamed or felt frustrated and irritated because the train was delayed, or the bus came late, or my fellow commuters spoke too loudly or misbehaved.

This became the gruelling pattern of my life for the next three years.

———

WHEN I JOINED THE INDUSTRIAL AUTOMATION DIVISION (IAD) at the GEC-Marconi Research Centre, one of its major research projects was a large international collaboration involving research groups from Spain, France, the Netherlands and Germany. It was a five-year project which was just entering its second year. The project was partially funded by the European Union through a programme called ESPRIT. Our project (number 384) had the title "Integrated Information Processing for the Design, Planning and Control of Assembly".

The context of the project was small-batch assembly. This is almost the opposite of mass production invented by Henry Ford and others in the early 1900s. Ford's innovation centred around an assembly-line that had the objective of producing large numbers of identical products as quickly and cheaply as possible. Ford is often quoted as saying that 'the customer can have any colour Model-T, as long as it's black.' While this quote may be apocryphal, the message was plain. Ford's manufacturing system was definitely not about flexibility and variety.

Our project aimed to do the opposite. It was focused on automating the production of small quantities of products while still achieving some of the benefits of mass production such as speed, low cost and uniform quality. To do this, we would need very special smart robots. The scenario we imagined was as follows:

Suppose I want to make a small product such as an electric toaster. It is made by assembling a collection of components, some of which are sub-assemblies (that is, they are made up of components that have been previously assembled). To build the toaster, we need to bring the components together in a specific order. We will also need to use various tools.

There are various ways to make the toaster. At one extreme, we can assemble each toaster by hand: a skilled operator is given a box of all the required components and sub-assemblies, together with a set of instructions and access to the tools required. At the other extreme, we can automate the assembly of the toaster on a mass production assembly line equipped with specially designed machines carrying out each step in the prescribed order.

Suppose now that we are not making hundreds of thousands of identical toasters, but that we are making similar but different toasters. Each toaster is customised in some way. One toaster might be red on the outside with slots for three slices of thin bread. The next might be green with only two slots, one for a thin slice and one for a thick slice. One can imagine tens of variants of the same basic toaster. Suppose, in addition, that we make these variants of our toaster as people order them. We would need to decide dynamically how many of each variant we need. Mass production on a fixed assembly line is not suited to this small batch assembly scenario. It would be more appropriate, but far more expensive, to manually assemble each toaster.

The other alternative would be to have robots that are intelligent and flexible enough to assemble any variant of our toaster. This would be the best of both worlds.

Our ESPRIT project was to look at the information requirements to design, plan and control a flexible assembly system in which artificial intelligence (AI) and flexible robotics were used. A number of interesting and important new technologies were emerging at that time.

The focus of AI in the late 1980s was rule-based expert systems. These systems consist of a number of rules which encapsulate all of the necessary knowledge about the domain of interest, and an inference engine or semantic reasoner which receives inputs and then infers information from the rules. These are then turned into outputs.

The flexible assembly robot which was used in our project was a brilliant piece of equipment invented in our own laboratory and was called the Tetrabot. It was far more accurate and stable than the conventional mechanical arms that were popular at that time.

The other emerging technology we engaged with was object-oriented (OO) programming (OOP) and design (OOD). It was that same concept that had interested me at UMIST five years earlier when I developed the language PLASMA. Whereas PLASMA had required the development of a complex pre-processor, there were now OOP languages like Smalltalk that made using these concepts very easy to implement.

The most wonderful thing about working in the IAD at

GEC-Marconi Research was that we had access to all the latest, most expensive equipment. We had a Symbolics 3600 Lisp Machine, which was specially designed for dealing with rule-based expert systems. We had UNIX-based workstations, on which I could run Smalltalk. We also had some IBM PCs and the recently released Apple Macintosh.

I became the OO expert in the group and spent many hours reading about OO and developing a deep understanding of the concepts that lay at its heart. I became very good at teaching OO to my team members and to our ESPRIT partners. I also worked hard at bringing OO concepts into the information models we were developing for our flexible assembly system.

EVERY RESEARCHER HAS ONE OR TWO "EUREKA!" MOMENTS IN their career. I had one in mid-1987. Our ESPRIT project had hit a huge problem. The information model we had built for our flexible and intelligent small batch assembly system was simply too unwieldy. It was so big and complex that it would never be practically useful. Our international partners met every two months to review progress. Our partners were AEG in Frankfurt, Fraunhofer Institute for Production and Systems Design (IPK) in Berlin, TNO in Apeldoorn in the Netherlands, Telemecanique in Paris and Investronica in Madrid. At our meeting in Paris in April 1987, we reached the conclusion that our project might never produce useful results. Our

GEC-Marconi team were feeling really depressed as we flew back to the UK.

I felt certain that OO was the way forward, but I couldn't come up with a suitable design. Everything I tried led to the same dead-end. As often happened, my Eureka moment occurred when I was doing something else. I can remember it clearly. I was at home, flopped down in front of the TV at the end of a long and exhausting day. I was watching the World Snooker Championships and although I wasn't working, my head was full of work-related thoughts. Suddenly, the solution to our information model problem was so obvious. I abandoned the snooker and my half-eaten plate of food and rushed to my desk where I scribbled pages and pages of words and diagrams late into the night.

The next day, I didn't tell anyone what I had been thinking, but spent all of that day and the next developing a proof of concept in Smalltalk. I went home and wrote it up in a short report. Once everything was ready, I asked everyone in our team to gather around as I explained my idea and demonstrated the proof of concept. Everyone agreed that my idea solved the problem we had been sitting with. It was nearly lunchtime and we headed off to celebrate at our favourite pub. We drank all afternoon.

What was this great idea? Our original information model focused on the intelligence of the assembly robot. As each product was being assembled, our system would have to bring information about the product and how to build it to the robot. This included hundreds, even thousands, of rules, together with three-dimensional models of the product and its components. It was an information overload. My idea was to shift the focus from the robot to the product. I called it product-centred control. An intelligent product, implemented using OO principles, would instruct a dumb robot what to do in assembling it. This change in focus, supported by a good OO design, dramatically reduced the amount of information that had to be moved around our flexible assembly system.

Steve and I wrote a paper on this work[2] which Steve presented in Japan, as by that time I had returned to South Africa. Steve presented another paper in London a few weeks later[3].

An interesting footnote to this is that in 2019, I was reading an article about Industrie 4.0, the German precursor to the "4th Industrial Revolution" [4]. The authors wrote that one of the key principles at the heart of Industrie 4.0 are 'smart products' that 'know their production history, their current and target state, and actively steer themselves through the production process by instructing machines to perform the required manufacturing tasks.'

'Good grief!' I thought when I read this. 'My Eureka moment in 1987 gave rise to the 4th Industrial Revolution!'

---

1. See "Talking to Vula" by Tim Jenkin
2. B Dwolatzky and S P Sanoff, "A Product-centred Controller for Flexible Assembly Cells", Proc. of the 10th Int. Conference on Assembly Automation, 23-25 October, Kanazawa, Japan. 1989.

3. SP Sanoff "An object-oriented controller for flexible assembly cells" IEE Colloquium on Applications of Object-Oriented Programming, 16 November, London, 1989

4. Marco Herman, et. al. "Design Principles for Industry 4.0", Working paper 01/2015, Technische Universität Dortmund, 2015.

chapter
thirteen

A HOLY COVENANT

1987 to 1990

My schizophrenic life became even more complicated when I was diagnosed with hairy cell leukaemia in 1987. Following my diagnosis, my spleen was removed as the first step to save my life. The doctors were very frank with me. My chances of survival were slim. The splenectomy was a major operation and that came with its own risks. I had a long incision down my belly which felt like I had been ripped apart and sewn together again. In spite of being given large doses of morphine, the pain was excruciating. I was being fed intravenously and needed regular blood transfusions. At some point, I was given an infusion of platelets. For some reason, my body started to shake violently and nurses and doctors came running to jab huge syringes into my arm.

As I lay in hospital in a dazed and drugged state, friends

visited as often as they were allowed. There were very strict visiting hours in the ward. One of these friends, Russel Caplan, took on the role of social secretary, organising who visited when, so that I always had visitors but was never overwhelmed. Mel and Sue Mac came all the way from Manchester so they could sit next to me for an hour. Sue brought a teddy bear from her son Joe, which I still have today. Steve Sanoff, Ian Powell and other work colleagues brought a huge get well card signed by people I had never met. My London proxy family, Di and Charlotte, and house-mate Francis, visited often. I really felt supported and loved.

Between visiting hours, I thought a lot about this unex-pected sinkhole that had opened up in the path of my life's journey. I wasn't nearly as afraid as I should have been. My over-riding emotion was sadness. Sadness at the thought that my life might end too soon. There was still so much I felt I had to do. I was only beginning to feel self-assured and confident in my ability to get things done, to contribute to those things I cared about, and to reach my potential. It couldn't all end so abruptly.

Although I'm not religious, I spoke a lot to God at that time. I asked if I could make a deal. The deal was about South Africa. I accepted that I was going to die, but I at least wanted a chance to do something more with my life before I died. I wanted some additional time to contribute more significantly to a better South Africa. I had no idea then what this significant contribution might be, but I at least wanted more time to find out. Lying in my hospital bed in the haematology oncology ward of St Bartholomew Hospital in London, with tubes and monitors attached to my body, I entered into a Holy Covenant. My own secret deal with God.

People have often asked what made me decide to leave a comfortable life in Britain, where I had a great job, a house of my own and a growing circle of friends, to return to Apartheid South Africa in July 1989. At that time, South Africa was in a state of emergency. Many people spoke about the prospect of a bloody civil war. I have usually fudged the answer to this question. This is the first time I'm telling the absolute truth. I came back to South Africa because I made a deal with a God who I might not even believe exists.

My recovery from the splenectomy took almost two months. As soon as I was out of hospital and able to travel, I went to my family in Israel. My parents were living with my younger brother, Hilton, and his family in Efrat, close to Bethlehem. Family is what I desired most at that time. I needed my mother to fuss over me and fatten me up with her wonderful home-cooking, and my father, who, although dealing with his own physical and mental health issues, was a solid anchor in my life and a source of great comfort. I also wanted Hilton, my sister-in-law Shelley, and their wonderful children to fill my world with their energy and warmth.

My friend, Di Wes, took me to Heathrow airport, and since I was still feeling weak and fragile, she arranged a porter and a wheelchair. As the porter wheeled me towards the check-in counters, Di walked beside us making sure that I was well taken care of. The porter spoke to Di about me as though I wasn't actually there.

'What time is his flight?' he asked Di.

'Has he got a British passport?' he asked Di.

'Will he need to go to the bathroom?' he asked Di.

At this, she snapped. Di was never one to avoid confrontation.

'He's in a wheelchair because he's not comfortable walking, but he is certainly capable of speaking for himself and answering your fucking questions! If you want to know anything, ask him!' she shouted to the bemusement of everyone in earshot.

I certainly had a tiny taste of what people in wheelchairs face throughout their lives.

I was wheeled to my seat on the plane by the now surly porter. Many inquisitive heads turned to watch me being deposited in my seat. When we arrived at Ben Gurion Airport in Israel, the flight crew announced that anyone needing assistance should stay in their seat until everyone else had disembarked. 'Screw this', I thought to myself as I gathered my things and walked off the plane with everyone else.

As I stood waiting for my luggage, one of my fellow passengers sidled over and said with a sardonic sneer, 'Another miracle cure in the Holy Land. Baruch Hashem (Blessed be God)!'

WHEN I RETURNED TO WORK IN MARCH 1988, I HAD MADE A number of important decisions. One of these was to lead a healthier life, another was to get back to South Africa as soon as possible.

Living a healthier life was a natural response to finding out that I had what might be a terminal disease. The doctors had assured me that the form of leukaemia I had was not the result of lifestyle factors. It wasn't caused by smoking, eating the wrong food, drinking too much beer or not exercising enough, all of which I did. The causes of hairy cell leukaemia were unknown at that time. Thirty years later, the causes are still unknown. There is, however, some unsubstantiated evidence that it may be caused by exposure to radiation or certain agricultural and industrial chemicals. When I read this, I remembered that in early May 1986, about 18 months before I was diagnosed, I had gone on holiday in Scotland with my friends David Cooper and Monique Vajifdar. Two weeks before that, on 26th April 1986, the Chernobyl nuclear power station in Ukraine had blown up sending a huge plume of radioactive particles into the atmosphere. So much radiation was detected in Scotland in the weeks after Chernobyl that the consumption of Scottish mutton and lamb was banned. This ban was only lifted twenty-four years after I left Scotland! I have no way of knowing if there is any connection between the Chernobyl disaster and my leukaemia, but it certainly makes for a good conspiracy theory.

In spite of the fact that there was no causal relationship between my admittedly unhealthy lifestyle and my cancer diagnosis, I stopped smoking the day I went into hospital and began to exercise more and live more healthily. Although one can always do better, I've certainly continued to try my best to honour this decision.

My other resolution about returning to South Africa as soon as possible was something that took much more planning. In my mind, it was not just about getting on a plane and flying to Johannesburg. It required me to go back with a plan, preferably as part of the ANC's underground struggle with a specific job to do.

I thought about asking Muff and Riaz to send me back into South Africa to do the kind of work that the mysterious Sandy and others were doing as part of their secret operation, although I knew very little about their operation at that time. However, the more I thought about this, the less I liked the idea. Although I was more than willing to take risks and work actively underground, I didn't think I would be particularly effective in the kind of work they were doing.

My other option was to work with Tim on his increasingly sophisticated secure communication system inside South Africa. When I discussed this with him, he was very keen. He definitely needed people with strong technical skills working at the other end of his communication channel. His biggest risk was that people using his system in South Africa would make mistakes because they didn't understand the technology. Such mistakes might lead to the South African security police finding out about the system and how it worked.

Tim had also started working on a more advanced communication system using computers and online bulletin boards, but this would require operators on the South African side with much more knowledge. It would certainly benefit his work to have someone like me working with him from inside South Africa. We agreed to start working on getting me back into South Africa as his secret agent.

While I was looking optimistically into the future, I still had to deal with my hairy cell leukaemia diagnosis. When I returned from Israel, having recuperated from the splenectomy, I returned to Barts Hospital for a consultation with Professor Andrew Lister. He mapped out the path ahead, not pulling any punches. Statistically, my chances of survival beyond a year or two were small. Hairy cell leukaemia is a rare cancer of the blood. The disease causes one's bone marrow to produce an excess of abnormal white cells which look hairy under a microscope, hence the name. These hairy cells interfere with the production of normal cells, resulting in too few red cells (which carry oxygen), normal white cells (which fight infection) and platelets (which support clotting) in the blood stream. One of the immediate effects is that the spleen becomes enlarged as it tries to absorb the hairy cells. Having low blood counts results in extreme fatigue, an inability to fight infections, and bleeding. Unless the production of hairy cells can be stopped or controlled, this condition eventually results in death.

In 1988, there were very few treatment options. The first was to remove the spleen. In a very small number of cases, for reasons not entirely understood, this significantly reduced the production of hairy cells and resulted in the patient going into remission, sometimes for many years. If the splenectomy didn't have this outcome, the next step in treatment was to use alpha-interferon. My layman's understanding is that interferon is produced naturally in the human body as part of its mechanism to fight infection. Before the white cells go into battle against the infection, interferon is released to trigger this attack. When one has flu, for example, interferon is released to alert the white cells that the flu virus has entered the body. Classic flu symptoms such as a high temperature, sore joints and headaches are our response to interferon rather than the flu virus.

When the idea of using interferon as a treatment for certain conditions first emerged, the only source of interferon was the human body. Interferon was harvested from human donors, with tiny quantities coming from each individual donor. This made it extremely expensive as a therapy. Other ways were developed to extract interferon from animals, such as pigs, and then to produce synthetic interferon in a laboratory. This brought the cost down and made it more commonly used in treating certain conditions, including hairy cell leukaemia.

Professor Lister told me that should there still be a high level of production of hairy cells in my bone marrow following the splenectomy, he would put me onto interferon. The problem was that interferon only had the desired effect in a small number of patients. Even if it worked, it wasn't a cure. It would just reduce the production of hairy cells to an acceptable level for an unknown period of time. If interferon didn't work, or stopped working, he told me that there were other drugs, still in an experimental stage, that could be tried.

He tested my blood, examined me, and said it was still too soon after the splenectomy to assess whether I needed interferon and asked me to return six weeks later.

I visited Barts Hospital every six weeks for the rest of 1988. While Professor Lister and his team were careful not to give me false hope, they seemed very happy with my condition. While hairy cells were still present in my bone marrow, the levels of white cells, red cells and platelets in my blood stream were in the "normal" range. I felt better than I had in years. The possibility of being healthy enough to leave Britain and return to South Africa became real.

———

EARLY IN 1989, I WENT ON A SHORT HOLIDAY IN GREECE WITH my friend Mel Pleaner and her baby daughter Amanda. Mel is one of my oldest and dearest friends and had been an important part of my life since the early 1970s when we had met on a SAVS camp in Lesotho. I was in the throes of making my decision to return to South Africa to work on Tim's clandestine project. I trusted Mel completely and it would have been both natural and affirming to tell her all about my secret life and the work I was planning to do on my return.

Before going to Greece, I had decided to confide in Mel and ask for her advice. Once we were there, however, I decided to not speak to her about my plans. At the time, I justified this to myself by remembering the instructions I had been given by Tim. He said that to safeguard myself and others, I must keep my planned mission in South Africa absolutely secret. I took this obligation seriously and also didn't want to burden Mel with the responsibility of keeping this secret. Reflecting on this much later, I believe that there was another more authentic reason for not confiding in her. Looked at objectively, the mission being proposed by Tim seemed to be somewhat crazy. It was full of risk and uncertainty for me, while the benefits to the ANC were hard to see. I was afraid that Mel, who cared deeply about me and my well-being, would help me see these risks objectively and that she would persuade me not to go through with this plan. There was a big part of me that wanted to undertake this mission whatever the risks and uncertainties.

———

THE BEST COVER STORY IS ONE THAT'S MOSTLY TRUE. I BEGAN TO develop a cover story that would get me back to South Africa working on Tim's project without raising any suspicion.

I began to tell friends and my colleagues at work that I had decided to return to South Africa because my health issues had made me feel desperate to go home. My primary reason for having left South Africa was no longer an issue since I would definitely now be able to get medical exemption from the army. I emphasised how I was tired of the wet and cold British weather while downplaying politics. I stopped attending public protests and anti-Apartheid events. Without saying so, I tried to create the impression that I was done with politics. I didn't care any more about what Thatcher was doing in Britain and what PW Botha was doing in South Africa. All I wanted to do was to sit on a beautiful South African beach with the blue African sky overhead and the hot African sun on my back.

Some of those in my British circle of friends were mildly critical that I had gone soft on politics, but most were sympathetic, given the state of my health. The general feeling I picked up was 'Poor Barry is going off to die in South Africa, and who can blame him?'

That was the cover story. Behind the scenes, Tim and I worked hard to set me up so that I could support his work once I was back in South Africa. We agreed that the best cover for me would be working with computers and telecommunications in a university. This wouldn't raise any red flags with the South African authorities. It would be completely plausible for me to have a computer at home, connected via a modem to a telephone line. It was also legitimate for me to be dialling through to numbers in Britain or anywhere else in the world and going onto various online bulletin boards. In addition, working at a university would give me access to cutting-edge technology and much useful information.

Another huge advantage I had in undertaking this mission was that I was "clean", in that I had never been overtly and publicly engaged in militant anti-Apartheid and ANC activities in Britain. Yes, I had mixed in those circles and had joined in from time to time, but I had (hopefully) never done enough to alert the South African or British intelligence agencies that I was worthy of their attention.

BY JANUARY 1989, IT WAS BECOMING CLEAR THAT MY HAIRY cell leukaemia was in remission without me needing to go onto interferon. My plans to move back to South Africa began to take shape. As I was aiming to work at a university, my first choice was obviously to go back to Wits. I wrote to Professor Hu Hanrahan, who had taught me in the 1970s and was then the Head of the Department of Electrical Engineering. I asked him if there was a post available in his department. I also told him about my health issues. He wrote back to say that he would like to offer me a job as a senior lecturer, but that it seemed unlikely that Wits' medical aid would cover me. I was so keen to get back and to work there that I wrote back saying that I would take the job whether I had medical cover or not. Luckily for me, he was far more cautious. He had asked colleagues in the medical faculty about the cost in South Africa of treating hairy cell leukaemia. Through a private hospital, interferon was extremely expensive. I would never be able to afford it.

He arranged that Wits would give me medical aid coverage on condition that, should I need it, my leukaemia would be treated at the Johannesburg General Hospital, which was one of Wits' public teaching hospitals.

It was agreed that I would start my job in the second academic term of 1989.

Tim cleared his plan to send me as his agent into South Africa with Ronnie Kasrils and Joe Slovo. Joe was at that time the Secretary General of the South African Communist Party (SACP) and a member of the ANC's national executive (NEC) and revolutionary councils. He was also a founder of MK and had only recently stepped down as its Chief of Staff. Ronnie was also an NEC member and carried responsibility for the secret communications work that Tim was involved in. As far as I knew, no one else in ANC structures was aware of me and my secret mission. Tim also managed to get money from Ronnie to buy me a brand-new computer. It was a clone of the IBM AT 286 and came with all of the most cutting-edge features at that time. Tim and I spent many evenings configuring and setting up the communication system we would use once I was back in South Africa.

I resigned from my dream job at GEC-Marconi Research and made arrangements to fly back to South Africa.

———

IT WAS A HOT SUMMER NIGHT EARLY IN JANUARY 1990. I SAT alone in my flat in Hillbrow, the high-density inner city area of Johannesburg. I was on the eighth floor of a block called Highveld on the corner of Twist and Caroline Streets. As I did every night, I sat at my ANC-owned computer connected via my US Robotics modem to a SAPO (SA Post Office) telephone line. The modem communicated at 4800 baud, which meant that I could theoretically send or receive 4,800 bits per second. In practice, it was much slower than that[1]. I was connected, via a telephone number in South Africa, to a system called BT Gold in London. This system, run by British Telecom, offered a very early and very primitive form of email, long before the invention of the Internet.

Tim, using the name "Mike", and me, using the name "Pete", pretended to be playing a game of chess. We left each other tiny encrypted files accompanied by messages that went something like this:

Mike: 'Great move, Pete. I didn't see that my bishop was being threatened by your knight. My response attached'.

Pete: 'I think you missed something else! Look what my queen was up to. Check!'

Mike: 'Clever move, Pete, but not clever enough. Sorry to take your queen!'

And so it went. Each message was accompanied by a small file. If someone tried to open these files, all they would find is a string of seemingly random bits. What we wanted anyone snooping on us to believe was that these small files could be read into some unspecified chess playing programme.

On this particular January night, Tim (or "Mike") had sent me five different moves. We played a number of games simultaneously. I downloaded them and then used Tim's decryption system to turn them into recognisable text. I assembled these into one longer document, and then read it. Loaded there on my computer was one of the ANC's most important documents of that time. It was the "Annual 8 January 1990" statement. In it, the ANC went public for the first time with the terms and conditions for the secret negotiations that were then underway between the ANC and the De Klerk Government. This statement had just entered South Africa via my computer. Wearing gloves, I printed the text of the statement out on my Epson dot-matrix home printer and deleted everything from my computer. I carefully put the printed pages into an envelope on which I wrote a name, not a real name, which Tim had sent me. I then hid the envelope in a secret compartment in the lid of my briefcase.

I hardly slept that night. I was so excited at the hugely important job I had been given to do. As I arrived on Wits campus at 7:30 the next morning, I made a detour through Central Block. I stopped at the pigeonholes in a deserted corridor on the second floor. These pigeonholes were used to return student assignments. I quickly slipped on gloves and removed the envelope from my briefcase. I popped it into the pigeonhole that corresponded to the initial letter of the name I had written on the envelope. I then walked quickly out of Central Block and over to my office in the Chamber of Mines Building on West Campus. Three days later, the document was released in South Africa. Other ANC underground operatives had retyped the text I had delivered and had laid it out and formatted it. They had turned it into tens of thousands of printed leaflets that were distributed via grassroots networks in townships and work-places all over South Africa. Remember that at this time the ANC was still banned and even possessing one of these leaflets would land you in police detention and prison.

This was only one of several such jobs I had been given. I felt that I was at last playing a role, even if it was only a small role, in moving the ANC's struggle forward. A liberation struggle is waged in tiny steps that come together to have big outcomes. Maybe it is these tiny steps that count as much as big flashy acts of heroism.

God had given me a little more life and I had used it to begin making a significant contribution to achieving a better South Africa. My Holy Covenant had worked.

---

1. The fibre optic broadband connection I have at home today operates at 50 million bits per second, or more than 10 million times faster.

part two

chapter
fourteen

TO MY GOOD HEALTH

Wearing the yellow and blue colours of the Varsity Kudus, the Wits University alumni running club, I accelerated as the finishing line came into view. I broke away from the bunch of runners I had been with for most of the morning and sprinted across the line to the enthusiastic cheers of some of the other Kudus who had finished earlier. It felt good to be acknowledged by The Herd, as members of the running club called themselves. I looked at the time on the big electronic display board mounted on the roof of a car parked to the left of the finishing line. The display read 3:56. I had finished my first marathon in just under four hours. It was March 1992. I was thinner and fitter than I had ever been in my life. I was no longer on Interferon and I felt GREAT.

I had taken up running about a year before as a way to lose weight, something I have always struggled to do. I joined a programme called Walk for Life and progressed quite quickly to the stage where I could easily run 5km. I had never tried running before. I thought of myself as a sedentary inactive blob who avoided active exercise as something completely alien to my personality. My friend Helen Struthers, in whose cottage I had then been living, encouraged me to join her on her morning runs through the streets of Norwood and surrounding areas of northern Johannesburg. I found that I absolutely loved running and was soon joining Helen and her friends on regular weekend runs. I became aware of Johannesburg's huge road running subculture, with a multitude of running clubs that organised races almost every weekend. I competed in regular 10km and half-marathon races and found that, while I wasn't in the serious runners' league, I could certainly hold my own among the weekend plodders. At that time, I was injecting Interferon into my body three times a week and running seemed to ease the side-effects.

When I progressed from jogging a few kilometres twice a week with Helen to running in races, I set my target to run a marathon before I turned forty and I achieved this five weeks before my birthday. A few weeks later, I ran my second marathon, the recently introduced Soweto Marathon, which, although I finished, I didn't enjoy. I couldn't see the point of running such a long race. I never tried another marathon, but I continued to train and run shorter races whenever I could.

Being a runner, not smoking, drinking very little alcohol and trying to eat the right foods had helped to reshape my self-image from that of a sick person to being a healthy person. I believe that this powerful use of mind over body in some way accounted for my twenty-six years of good health between 1992 and 2018.

————

THE DATE WAS 24TH FEBRUARY 2019. TWENTY-FIRST CENTURY warfare was about to be launched. The weapon of mass destruction lay on a silver tray in a bulging transparent plastic bag. It looked like a litre of innocuous clear liquid.

I was in the Treatment Room at Olivedale Clinic, comfortably reclining in a huge Lazy-Boy chair, a bag of saline solution and other pre-meds dripping into my arm via a thin plastic tube. In an uncomfortable-looking upright chair next to me, my 22-year-old daughter, Jodie, sat calmly watching, ready to support me in any way she could. Sister V slowly read out the list of possible side-effects in a sing-song Afrikaans accent.

'You may experience nausea and headaches. If you feel pain in your chest or arms, or if you start coughing or shiv-ering, call us immediately and we will stop the treatment. The anti-histamine we're giving you now,' she said pointing to one of the small bags attached to my drip, 'may make you sleepy.'

I nodded attentively but was only half listening. I was happy to see that Jodie was taking it all in. My brain was coming to terms with the fact that my body was about to become a battlefield for high-tech biological warfare. I felt a little nervous, but was mostly calm, even a little excited.

This battle could well lead to the final victory over the hairy cell leukaemia that had lurked in my bone marrow for more than thirty years.

The Sister's briefing ended. I signed the consent form, and the bulging plastic bag was attached to my drip. A few seconds later, the Rituximab entered my bloodstream. I could feel it flowing into the vein in my arm.

I had tried a few days earlier to understand what this Rituximab was. The simple explanation I had managed to piece together from Googling around on the Internet was that it is a monoclonal antibody, hence the abbreviation "mab" at the end of its name. It had been extracted in some way from mice and would attach itself to the cancerous hairy cells deep within my bones. This would cause my body's own immune system to seek out and destroy the hairy cells. As I understood it, Rituximab was first approved for use in the 1990s when it was developed as an innovation in the rapidly evolving field of drug therapy.

I had searched the Internet for more detailed information so that I could really understand the biology behind all of this, but all I could find were pages of hypertext links. The World Wide Web really is a spider web of information and I was soon lost in endless sub-threads that took me further and further away from my main quest. I gave up, promising myself to spend more time in the future on this search for a better understanding of the science behind monoclonal antibodies.

As the big fat bag of clear liquid drained into my body, my eyelids grew heavy and the sleepiness Sister V had warned me about took over. I fell into a gentle sleep, while deep within my body the good-guy white cells targeted and destroyed the bad-guy hairy cells.

A set of three numbers had dominated my thoughts since July 2018, when my hairy cell leukaemia reappeared after decades of lying dormant in my body. Each set of three numbers was associated with a date. These numbers provide a quick summary of the state of my blood cells. They represent my level of haemoglobin, platelets and neutrophils, which is associated with white cells. Between October 2018 and March 2019, these measures improved dramatically:

	Normal Range	1st Oct 2018	15th March 2019
Haemoglobin	13.8 to 18.8	8.6	14.8
Platelets	150 to 450	119	291
Neutrophils	2.0 to 7.5	0.73	2.11

Since 1992, these numbers had been checked regularly by my GP. In early 2018, he had noticed them slowly edging down and in July of that year had sent me to Dr Phillipa Ashmore, a haematologist. I hadn't been feeling well, but I never imagined that my leukaemia might have recurred. Dr Ashmore confirmed that it had after sending me for a bone marrow biopsy. The good news, she said, was that since my first diagnosis, hairy cell leukaemia had become highly treatable. She explained that there were now several very effective treatment options. In October 2018, I received my first of five weekly doses of the chemotherapy drug called

Cladribine. This was followed a few months later with the biological Rituximab. By March 2019, my blood was back to normal, and I felt so much better. It remains to be seen whether this is a temporary remission, like the previous one, or whether Cladribine and Rituximab have resulted in a cure.

———

BEFORE I LEFT THE UK IN JULY 1989 TO RETURN TO SOUTH Africa on my "secret mission", my health had taken centre stage in my life's journey. The diagnosis I received at the end of 1987 hung over me and had put the possibility, or even the high probability, of imminent death firmly on the table. Having a splenectomy had halted the progression of the leukaemia, but I was told it would, in all probability, only be temporary. Every six weeks, I visited Barts Hospital in London for a blood test and examination, filled with dread that my blood counts would again be on a downward trend. To the surprise of the doctors treating me, my blood counts remained within the normal range. At my last Barts appointment in early July 1989, Professor Lister handed me a fat sealed envelope and advised me to seek out a good haematologist in Johannesburg. A few weeks later, I had my first appointment with Professor Werner Bezwoda at the Johannesburg General Hospital (now called Charlotte Maxeke Hospital).

Perched on top of the Parktown Ridge, Joburg Gen, as the Johannesburg General Hospital was commonly known, commands one of the best views of the city's northern suburbs and beyond. From its windows on a clear day, one can see the Magaliesberg, a range of hills, 60km away. I love looking out over Johannesburg's leafy suburbs. One of my favourite pieces of trivia is that Joburg is one of the largest man-made forests in the world, with tens of thousands of large gardens, tree-lined streets and sprawling municipal parks all contributing a rich variety of mostly alien trees. While Joburg Gen provides a vantage point for those wanting to admire the beautiful and affluent side of the city, it is itself an eyesore. Looking up at the once-beautiful Park-town Ridge from anywhere in the northern suburbs, one is confronted with the huge ugly concrete block structure of the Joburg Gen, a prime example of Apartheid architecture at its worst.

Sitting in the waiting area of the Haematology Oncology Department at 7am on a chilly August morning in 1989, I was not admiring the view. I was observing the other outpatients waiting to see a doctor. The health system was segregated both by race and class. A private medical care system operated in parallel to the public health system. For those who could afford private care, mostly those on private medical aid schemes, there were world-class private hospitals and clinics. Medical insurance came as part of the package for those in salaried employment, most of whom were white. For those who were not white or for poorer whites, there was the public health system consisting of clinics and hospitals run by local and provincial government departments. These, like all other amenities in

Apartheid South Africa, were racially segregated. There were white facilities that were usually well resourced, and then there were under-resourced and over-crowded facilities for other races. In cities and towns with universities that had medical schools, these public hospitals were used for teaching and research.

Wits University's Medical School had a number of teaching hospitals. The two largest were Joburg Gen, a white hospital, and Baragwanath Hospital (now Chris Hani Baragwanath) in Soweto, a black hospital. The doctors in these hospitals were mostly academics and students at Wits. Given Wits' standing as a top international university, some of these doctors were world renowned. The doctor I was waiting to meet, Professor Bezwoda, was the head of the Wits Department of Haematology and Oncology and all the people sitting with me that morning were dealing with one of the blood-related cancers.

I had only been back in South Africa for less than a month and was hyper-sensitive to the racial segregation I had once hardly noticed. My fellow outpatients were of all ages and were all white, apart from the elderly Indian man who sat at the far end of the broad passageway that connected the main waiting area to the fire-escape door. He had a drip attached to his arm and spoke quietly to a woman, probably his wife, sitting next to him. Most of the people around me seemed to know each other. They spoke loudly in Afrikaans, a language I had not heard for nearly a decade. They eyed me curiously, but no one spoke to me. Over the next few years, I got to know some of them on my regular visits to this waiting area. From visit to visit, I witnessed many of these people change from chubby, pink-skinned extroverts to sickly bags of bones with paper-white skins who struggled to whisper a greeting. Very often a familiar face was not there. People noted that "Oom X" or "Tannie Y" had passed away since we were last in the waiting area. There followed a few moments of silent head shaking and tongue clicking before a return to the light-hearted banter.

I was at the hospital waiting for my first appointment at which I would hand my case over to Professor Bezwoda. I was not there for treatment, I reminded myself. But some-where in my mind I found myself thinking, 'Was this the trajectory I would soon be on?'

After a four hour wait, my name was called. A nurse pointed to a door and I entered. Professor Werner Bezwoda sat at a desk reading the form I had filled in at reception. A young woman dressed in a white coat with a stethoscope around her neck, probably one of his registrars, stood next to him. She was speaking softly, reading numbers from a piece of paper. I guessed that these were the lab results of the blood that had been taken when I arrived early that morning. Bezwoda was an overweight man with small piggy eyes hidden behind glasses, brown hair and a dour expression. When he spoke to the registrar, I detected an unfamiliar accent. I found out later that he was originally from somewhere in South America.

I walked over to the desk waiting for him to speak. He didn't look up, but carried on reading the information on the form. I put the fat sealed envelope on his desk and said, with a hint of pride in my voice, 'Professor Andrew Lister from St Bartholomew's Hospital in London said I should give this to you.' I expected him to say something like, 'Oh! Andrew Lister! You were treated by the famous Andrew Lister!' or something similar. Instead, he passed the unopened envelope to the registrar.

He looked up at me for a brief second and said, 'Get undressed and lie there', pointing to a high bed in the corner of the room. He carried on reading my form and speaking softly to the woman.

She spoke to me, 'You just need to take off your shirt and your socks and shoes.'

I did so and sat on the high bed, waiting. As Bezwoda stood up, I noticed that the registrar had opened the envelope from Barts. Bezwoda stood up and walked over to stand beside me.

'Lie down,' he said. I did so.

He had pulled on rubber gloves and ran his fingers around my neck and into my armpits, feeling for something. He felt my ankles and then put his stethoscope on my chest. He shone a small bright light into my eyes and leaned in close. He didn't say anything.

He finished examining me and went back to his desk where he started sifting through the paperwork Lister had sent with very little interest. I doubt if he ever read any of the detailed case history and test results sent to him from London. He said something to the registrar and then left the room.

She said, 'I need to take a bone marrow sample. We can book you another appointment or I can do it now.'

My heart skipped a few beats. I had had several bone marrow biopsies at Barts. They had been horrible. It involved pushing a big needle into my hip bone and then using a syringe or some sort of drill to extract a sample of my marrow. Although they had given me a local anaesthetic, I had experienced it as a lot of pushing, pulling and pricking and had also been left with a lot of bruising and pain after the anaesthetic had worn off. My heart also skipped a beat because I started to worry about why they wanted to check my marrow. What had my blood test told them?

'Do the bone marrow now,' I said.

She went to the door and called over one of the nurses who came back with an assortment of instruments and test tubes. Assisted by the nurse, the registrar set to work extracting some of my bone marrow. It was as horrible an experience as I feared. When she had finished, I waited for some explanation. She said nothing.

I asked, 'Are my blood counts low?'

Whereas Andrew Lister and his team had always shared numbers with me and explained what they meant, this was obviously not the way that Bezwoda's team worked.

The nameless registrar didn't answer my question but said, 'You can get dressed now. Book an appointment for next week.'

After an anxious week, I returned to the Joburg Gen for my appointment. This time I didn't wait long. The anonymous registrar appeared and asked me to follow her into a small consulting room.

Bezwoda was nowhere to be seen, but she announced, 'Professor Bezwoda has decided that we should put you onto Interferon. He believes that the sooner we start treatment, the better. Interferon is proving to be relatively effective in the treatment of your condition. You can either come in here three times a week for an injection or we can show you how to inject yourself.'

I was shocked! I had somehow expected that the temporary all clear I had been given when I had my final appointment at Barts would last for at least a year or two. Instead, here I was, a mere five weeks later, being told I would need to start treatment. There was so much I should have asked at that moment, but I hardly said anything. One thing I definitely should have asked, but didn't, was about my blood counts. Had they dropped so significantly between my last blood test at Barts and my first one at Joburg Gen? I remember feeling like a passive cog in the huge machine of clinical medicine. I remember the registrar saying something about me being only the second case of hairy cell leukaemia that they had seen. I'm still not sure who she was referring to. Was it the registrar and her fellow team members, was it Bezwoda, or was it the Wits Haematology Oncology Department? Somewhere inside my head, I hoped that they knew what they were doing, but I didn't say that.

I said that I would prefer to inject myself. A nurse was called in to show me how to deal with the plastic syringes, needles, distilled water and precious vials of Interferon. Since I was being treated in a public hospital, it was free, but I knew that in private hospitals this drug would be costing me or my medical aid a great deal of money. The nurse and the registrar touched only briefly on the issue of side effects. I was told that I could take Panado (i.e. paracetamol) if I "felt bad", but I had no idea about how it would affect me.

As it turned out, I was on Interferon from August 1989 until early in 1992. Towards the end of that period, the dose decreased and so did the side effects, but for almost three years I injected myself with Interferon three times a week and experienced constant flu symptoms. I only took Panado when I felt really bad. These were the times that my head and joints hurt so badly that I struggled to get up in the morning. As far as I can remember, however, I soldiered on and didn't miss a single day of work, although I was sometimes tempted to do so.

Over this period, I became a regular fixture in the Haematology and Oncology outpatient department at Joburg Gen. Every six to eight weeks, I arrived before 7am for a blood test and then sat in the waiting area until my name was called. Sometimes I was called after an hour or so. Other times it was only mid-afternoon. I greeted my fellow outpatients and got to know some of their names. At first, they were all white, but as time passed a handful of coloured and Indian patients appeared. At that time, as Apartheid began to rapidly unwind, there was a huge push by activists to remove segregation in hospitals. I brought things to do while I waited and used these as a shield to keep me separate from the other patients. It allowed me to get away with a smile on arrival and a few short words, rather than sitting for hours on end gossiping and sharing views on the momentous changes that were happening in South Africa at that time.

White South Africans, particularly poor white South Africans who were being treated for cancer in public hospital, were full of fear both for themselves and for the society they were part of. The conversations around me always anchored on the news of the day before deteriorating into racist rants about what would happen when "they" took over. I didn't have the physical or emotional energy to engage in such talk, so I hid behind my work and listened attentively. I was also reluctant to interact with my fellow patients because so many of them were far sicker than I was. It broke my heart to see their suffering and rapid deterioration. I protected myself from the pain of it by limiting the amount I knew about each of them and their circumstances. I secretly saw myself and my possible future in each of them.

My interactions with Professor Werner Bezwoda and his team were also frustrating. I very seldom had the opportunity to speak to Bezwoda himself. I usually caught sight of him as he rushed through the waiting area clutching files. He completely ignored the greetings from patients and nurses as he raced past with one or more registrars in tow. My consultations were mostly with members of his team, some of whom were really nice. From these interactions, it was clear that Bezwoda was actively involved and interested in my case. On the rare occasions when he examined me and engaged with me, he had very little to say. He spoke about me to team members in the third person as though I wasn't in the room. He ignored my questions or answered in monosyllables. I found his attitude particularly irksome because we were actually colleagues – fellow Wits academics. While I always addressed him with respect as a senior academic colleague, he never reciprocated.

I sometimes spoke about Bezwoda to people who knew him and was generally told that he was a fantastic clinician and medical researcher and that I was very lucky to be under his care. Everyone agreed, however, that he scored a zero for people skills. I would have put it far more strongly than that.

In early 1992, I was taken off the Interferon treatment. Again, very little quantitative information was ever shared with me, but I assume that my blood counts were comfortably in the normal range. One of the registrars knew my GP, Dr Martin Connell, and suggested that I could start going to him for regular check-ups rather than coming to Joburg Gen. Martin would send me back to Bezwoda and his team at Joburg Gen if anything changed. It wasn't until 2018 that something changed and I again needed to see a haematologist.

I've thought a lot about why I was so fortunate after being diagnosed with a condition which, at the time, seemed certain to dramatically shorten my life, yet stayed in remission for thirty years. I was able to achieve so much and find great happiness and fulfilment in these bonus years. Was it my positive attitude and healthy lifestyle I spoke about earlier, or was this good fortune due to Bezwoda's decision to put me onto Interferon when he did, or was it my Holy Covenant with God and he was keeping his side of the deal I entered into? Who knows?[1]

---

1. An interesting footnote to this part of my story occurred in March 2000 when Werner Bezwoda became one of the very few senior academics to ever be fired by Wits University. This was not because of his incredibly bad bedside manner, but because of a scandal involving some of his research. He had conducted research using very high doses of a chemotherapy drug to treat patients with breast cancer. He claimed that he had conclusive evidence based on extensive research that his treatment significantly improved the probability of the patient surviving. His research was published and, based on his results, thousands of women around the world received this high dose therapy. Some of his international peers were suspicious of his results and conducted an audit of his published research. They found that his claims were fraudulent. Wits responded by dismissing him. He was not, however, stripped of his medical licence and he continues to run a large oncology practice in Johannesburg.

Before this scandal broke, he treated my mother, who was visiting us in Johannesburg in 1999 when the cancer she was being treated for in Israel made a dramatic and aggressive reappearance.

chapter
fifteen

UNDERGROUND SPECIAL AGENT

I t was an unseasonably warm night in July 1990. I sat alone in my flat in Hillbrow, Johannesburg, uncertain what to do. Should I stay or should I go? Before I left London, Tim had given me training on how to make a quick escape. My escape bag was hidden behind a sleeping bag and some blankets on the top shelf of the linen cupboard in the passageway. Inside it was cash (both Pounds and Rands), my British passport, my British credit card, and a change of clothes. I had returned to South Africa on my South African passport and the authorities knew nothing about my British one. I had also packed a few syringes and needles for my Interferon, which I stored in the fridge. I had an icepack in the freezer and a small cooler bag ready if I needed it.

I had already checked that there were no incriminating disks, printouts or scraps of paper anywhere in the flat. It was something I was always very careful about, even when I wasn't thinking about a quick escape.

My escape strategy was simple and depended on speed. I would have to be on a plane out of South Africa before the security police had time to initiate an airport watch list. When the time came, I would only take my escape bag and the Interferon from the fridge. I would leave my green Toyota Avante parked in its bay in the building's underground garage and walk to the metered taxi rank around the corner and get the driver to drop me at the domestic departures area at Jan Smuts Airport. I would then walk to the international departure area, check which flights were departing soon and pay cash for a ticket to anywhere on the first plane available.

I sat at my computer, waiting for a follow-up message from Tim on the bulletin board system we used. About two hours previously, I had received an encrypted message from him in which he had sounded the alarm. When I decoded the message, it said that there had been a major breach in our communication system. People had been arrested in Durban and Tim assumed that a large amount of detail had been discovered about how our system worked. None of this should affect me, but there was no way of being certain. I knew that there was no connection between my communication system with him and the one being used in Natal. Tim and I used a far more sophisticated and still experimental system; however, both the team in Durban and I had links to Tim. If the security police spotlight was on him, they could discover that he was also communicating with me.

I checked for the hundredth time. Still no message. I imagined Tim and his comrades in London frantically switching over to new passwords, new numbers, backup systems, covering tracks and setting up new lines of communication. There would be much to do. My safety wasn't their top priority, but having me on the ground could prove useful in dealing with the crisis. For this reason, I thought that it might be best for me to stay. However, what was the point of me being arrested? If I was going to escape, I should do so now, I thought to myself. The longer I stayed, the more time I gave the security police to cut off my departure. Was there already someone stationed outside the building ready to detain me or follow me when I emerged?

Another hour passed. Still no message. I made the decision to stay. I unplugged the modem and turned off my computer. I switched off all of the lights in my flat and checked again that the front door was locked. I climbed into bed and tried to sleep a bit, but my ears strained to pick up every sound. The lift door opening, footsteps in the corridor, sirens mixed into the traffic sounds in the busy Hillbrow streets.

I only heard from Tim about three days later in a brief message saying that, as far as we were concerned, things were back to normal. During those three days and for weeks afterwards, the newspapers and radio news were filled with stories about the arrests in Durban. The information that came out was as much of a revelation to me as it was to everyone else in South Africa and elsewhere in the world. Although I was part of what was playing out, I had only been allowed to see a few pixels in a far bigger picture.

I heard the name Operation Vula for the first time. The comrades arrested in Durban were said by the local press to be a Vula Cell responsible for establishing arms caches, running a secret sophisticated communications system, and undertaking unspecified terrorist actions. The security police rounded up about forty ANC and SACP members in raids around the country. On 11th July 1990, Siphiwe Nyanda was arrested after being followed from a safe house near Durban called The Knoll. Pravin Gordhan and others were arrested later that same day at The Knoll. Mac Maharaj and Billy Nair were arrested separately a few days later. I had never met Mac Maharaj, but I knew him as a senior ANC/SACP leader who I had heard on public platforms at Anti-Apartheid events in London. Some of those arrested were returned exiles who had been granted immunity from prosecution a few months earlier as part of the process that was unfolding following the release of Nelson Mandela and the unbanning of the ANC and SACP in February.

President FW De Klerk spoke about 'a major ANC plot, code named Operation Vula, which was entirely at odds with the organisation's undertakings in the Groote Schuur Minute and its professed commitment to a peaceful and negotiated constitutional settlement. In terms of the plot,' he said, 'the ANC had infiltrated key operatives into South

Africa including Mac Maharaj and Siphiwe Nyanda in 1988 and Ronnie Kasrils in 1990 to organize an underground network to prepare for revolution.' Ronnie Kasrils was one of the few people who knew about my mission in South Africa. He was not arrested with the others in July, presumably because he hadn't been located. The security police issued a statement declaring Ronnie, Janet Love, Charles Ndaba and Christopher Manye as dangerous terrorists. Descriptions and photographs were shown on TV and in the newspapers and they were said to be "armed and extremely dangerous". A reward was offered for information leading to their arrest. I was surprised to see Janet Love on that list since I had known her at Wits in the 1970s and knew that she had left South Africa. It was generally known in my circle of friends that she was involved in some way with the ANC in exile, but I had no idea she was back in South Africa and had no clue about how she was linked to Vula.

When the members of the Vula Cell appeared in court, I read the press reports with great interest and much frustration. They had completely screwed up and had broken all the rules and procedures that Tim had meticulously put in place. They were captured with computer disks and printouts containing both coded messages and decrypted "clear text". These were kept together with the disk containing the actual encryption program and unused "one-time pad" keys on another disk. Their ill-discipline had put many people at risk and had compromised the entire Vula operation.

Another fact that emerged in the media reports after the arrests helped me understand the reason for the secret mission I had undertaken for Muff and Riaz when I had flown to South Africa to bring a large amount of cash and construction plans to "Sandy" in Cape Town. I read that Vula operatives were accused of 'arranging for the transfer of large sums of money from outside (of South Africa) to finance the project's activities ... including the modification of vehicles to facilitate the clandestine importation of arms and explosives.' Obviously, my mission had been part of laying the groundwork for Vula.

In March 1991, as part of the ongoing negotiation process, the charges against the Vula operatives who had been arrested were dropped and they were all given indemnity from prosecution. Ronnie and Janet had to remain in hiding for three more months before receiving indemnity in June 1991, when they emerged without anyone seeming to notice that these armed and dangerous terrorists were now out in the open. [1]

———

WHEN I WAS SENT ON MY SECRET MISSION BACK TO SOUTH Africa in July 1989, the actual details of what I would be doing were very vague. The primary reason was for me to be inside South Africa at the other end of a secure communications link with Tim and his comrades in London. Tim was constantly innovating and refining his system and he needed someone who could work with him. Unlike the relatively primitive, but very effective, communication system being used by Vula operatives, Tim and I were exploring ways of making greater use of technologies that would over the next few years become the Internet. The other purpose was for me to gather intelligence using computers and to find ways to hack into key government computers. We weren't quite sure as to how I would do this, but the thought was that I would use my knowledge and access to computers to search for information stored in computers that might be useful to the ANC.

It is interesting to read how Tim perceived my involvement. The following is an extract from a series of six articles written by him and published in the ANC's monthly journal Mayibuye from May 1995 to October 1995 under the title "Talking with Vula":

All the while we knew that we would ultimately have to move over to a regular electronic mail service as our existing system had definite limitations. But this brought us back to the original problem: it was too dangerous to communicate from a known telephone line. Our whole quirky system had been designed to get around this inescapable fact. But what if the person who used the phone was someone who would normally communicate by computer and had no known affiliation with any political organisation? Surely this would not attract attention. Even using encryption should not raise eyebrows for businesses used it all the time to protect their information and it was built into ordinary programs such as word processors. In any case, did the enemy have the capacity to determine which of the thousands of messages leaving the country every day was a 'suspicious' one?

The only way to test out this hypothesis was to try it, and that's what we did.

During the preceding months I had been training an 'agent' whom the ANC was going to send back to South Africa in order to penetrate critical computer networks. The 'agent' was a South African who had been living abroad for many years and had worked as a computer programmer for major British electronics companies. He was also 'clean', having never been involved in exile politics.

In order to report on his activities he would need to be able to communicate abroad in much the same way as Vula. But because he would not be 'underground' in the same sense as the Vula operatives we decided to use an open, commercial electronic-mail service rather than our 'in-house' Vula system. This would serve both as an efficient, secret communications channel for his own work and as a test for Vula.

Later in the year the agent was sent in. He had already secured a position that was an excellent launching pad for his 'career'.

Immediately on arrival in South Africa he started communicating. This was a most normal thing for a person in his position to do. His training revealed no surveillance so we quickly realised that this was the way forward for Vula - find someone who would normally use a computer for communicating abroad and get that person to handle the communications. This would remove the constraints of the current system and allow the channel to be opened up for much greater things.

We explained to Mac how the system used by our 'secret agent' worked. If Vula could move over to a similar system, Mac suggested, it would not only allow more information to flow but it would also serve as a coordinating tool. It would link everyone internally and eliminate the need to travel around the country all the time. Also, because it was an error-free system, external machineries could produce fully-formatted propaganda material and send it in. Mac was convinced that they could find suitable people to do the comms. So many people and structures had been linked to Vula that it was now necessary to look at secret communications in an entirely different way.

I was this 'secret agent' in Tim's account and my cover was that I had a job as a Senior Lecturer in the Department of Electrical Engineering at Wits University.

I set to work with great enthusiasm and dedication soon after my arrival in July 1989. Although my primary research and teaching interest at Wits was in software engineering, I developed a close relationship with colleagues and post graduate students in the telecommunications group. I volunteered to serve on faculty and university committees dealing with issues around computing and computer networks. I also took as much interest as possible in professional and industry groups that focused on such topics. It must be said that in 1989 and 1990, before the age of the Internet, very few people had much interest in computers and computer-to-computer communication. It was just another area of technical specialisation. Apart from a small group of enthusiasts, most people had no interest in it at all.

I remember hosting a lunchtime workshop at Wits in 1990 aimed at introducing the concept of e-Mail to academics in all disciplines and to administrative staff. Only about 12 people showed up and the consensus among those who attended was that 'this e-Mail thing will never catch on at Wits.' At that time, we communicated with each other on campus via telephone or by sending internal mail. Wits ran its own huge post offices system using thousands of reusable brown envelopes circulated around the campuses. Each department employed at least one messenger, and there was a large central mail sorting room in Central Block. To communicate more widely, we used the national and international postal service and telephones. Why change this system that worked so well?

Between my arrival in July 1989 and December of that year, I made good progress in positioning myself to begin understanding who in South Africa used computers, for what purpose, and how these computers were connected.

I sent Tim regular reports which he forwarded to ANC headquarters in Lusaka. These reports contained information I had gleaned as I snooped around the local computing community. I don't remember much of what I sent, apart from one very juicy piece of intelligence I gathered in late

1989. Through the South African Institute of Electrical Engineers (SAIEE), of which I had become a very active member, I went on a tour to Airforce Headquarters in Pretoria. Our party of white male engineers was shown the air defence operations control room. From this facility, all air traffic along South Africa's borders with neighbouring countries was monitored around the clock. If an unauthorised plane was spotted, fighter jets could be scrambled from one of several bases to intercept it. The officer showing us around let us into a little secret.

'The system monitoring most of the Botswana border hasn't been operational for months,' he said, pointing to one of the displays. 'Don't tell anyone, but if I was the ANC or one of those terrorist groups, I would be sending planeloads of stuff over that border now.'

My fellow engineers all laughed, but I pricked up my ears. As soon as I was back in my flat in Hillbrow, I sent an urgent report to the still-banned ANC via Tim. Although I didn't know it at the time, the ANC was significantly preoccupied with discussions leading up to its unbanning and the release of Mandela. In all probability, my report was never read, and certainly was never acted upon.

As 1989 drew to a close, I was settling down for the long haul, and then everything changed.

————

ON 15ᵀᴴ OCTOBER 1989, THE GOVERNMENT OF FW DE KLERK released all of the Rivonia Trialists from prison, apart from

Nelson Mandela. After twenty-six years in prison, Walter Sisulu, Ahmed Kathrada, Andrew Mlangeni, Elias Motsoaledi, Raymond Mhlaba and Wilton Mkwayi all walked free. There were rumours of secret negotiations between de Klerk's government and Mandela, who was in communication with the ANC leadership in Lusaka. At the same time, the ANC was still banned and a state of near civil war existed in many of the townships around the country. In its 1990 "January 8th Statement", which I helped release within South Africa, the ANC set out its conditions for formal negotiations with the Apartheid government.

In spite of all of these signals, I was still surprised, and overjoyed, when on 2nd February 1990, at the official opening of the white parliament in Cape Town, FW de Klerk announced that Nelson Mandela would be unconditionally released on 11th February and that the ANC, SACP and PAC would be unbanned. Not only did this have a profound effect on South Africa, but it made a huge difference for me and my underground status in South Africa.

I asked Tim whether my mission had changed and whether I was still required to simply gather intelligence and penetrate systems, or whether I would now be doing something more specific. He tried to put me in direct communication with someone in Lusaka, but this didn't happen. He then said that it had been decided that I should meet with someone from the ANC leadership who was legally in South Africa and involved in negotiations. I was sent very complex and detailed instructions on where, when and how this clandestine meeting would take place.

———

IT WAS JUNE 1990, JUST BEFORE SUNSET. I PARKED MY CAR AT Bruma Lake shopping centre in the eastern suburbs of Johannesburg. I took a leisurely stroll around the shopping area, making sure that I wasn't being followed. I then set off on foot to the nearby Eastgate shopping mall. I bought some groceries at Pick n Pay supermarket and walked towards one of the exits carrying the plastic bag from Pick n Pay. I was wearing a blue sweater. The shopping bag and sweater would identify me. I got to the exit at exactly 6:45pm. A young white man also wearing a blue sweater came up to me.

'Hi Pete!' he said in a loud voice.

'Great to see you, Johnny!' I responded to the stranger.

These were our pass phrases. So far so good.

He pointed towards the car park and we walked out together, chatting like long-time friends. We climbed inside his car and drove off. He said softly in a very serious voice, 'I'll drop you at number 27. Walk into the gate and turn left before the garage. You'll see a small gate that connects to the yard of number 29. Go through the gate and into the cottage that'll be in front of you. The door is unlocked. Wait there.'

We drove on for two or three minutes in silence. I was pleased to see that he was being very careful to check that we weren't being followed. He made a few turns. Slowed down. Stopped.

'Not here,' he said.

We sat silently parked on the side of the quiet suburban road for about five minutes. We both watched for any sign of someone watching us. Everything seemed fine. He pulled off and drove for a few more minutes. We were in Kensington. He pulled into a very quiet tree-lined street, stopped and repeated the instructions about what to do next.

'Take your Pick n Pay bag and hold it so people can see what it is. I'll pick you up here after your meeting.'

He drove off and I made my way to the cottage at number 29 via the gate connecting it to the driveway of number 27. I had the sense of someone watching me from the shadows, but I wasn't certain.

The cottage smelled musty. I was sure that nobody lived there. The room I stood in as I came through the unlocked door had a large dining room table surrounded by eight chairs. There were also some tatty armchairs and a large sofa. The curtains were tightly drawn and there was a small lamp in the corner which provided a pool of light.

'Hello!' I called out.

There was no response and no sound from behind the closed door to my right. I pulled one of the dining room chairs away from the table and sat facing the door I had come through. I sat there almost afraid to breathe. I was very nervous. Who was the "senior ANC leader" I was about to meet? What would he or she know about me? What should I ask? What should I say? This whole secret meeting suddenly felt so silly. Here we were at a critical moment in history when the future of South Africa was being negotiated, and here I was, a mere foot soldier, wanting to meet one of those busy senior leaders. I felt like getting up and leaving before I made a complete idiot of myself.

I heard footsteps on the gravel pathway outside and voices speaking softly. I stood up and faced the door, my heart in my mouth. Suddenly the door opened, and in walked Joe Slovo.

He smiled and held out a hand. We shook hands.

It was amazing to think that I was in a secluded garden cottage in suburban Johannesburg meeting with one of the most admired and most hated white South Africans of our generation. In exile circles, he was universally referred to as JS, and to those of us who supported the struggle, he was a hero who was seen as one of the major strategists in the ANC's collective leadership. On the other side of the political divide, Slovo was seen as the devil incarnate. Because Apartheid propagandists found it hard to attribute competent leadership and strategic thinking to Black South Africans, they did all they could to emphasise Slovo's role and blame him for all ANC successes. They also emphasised his links to communism and the Soviet Union. If the communist threat to South Africa needed a name, it was that of Joe Slovo.

'Let's sit there,' he said, pointing to the armchairs. 'I believe we call you Pete,' he said. 'You don't look like a Pete,' he said with a broad smile. 'If you want, you can tell me your real name,' he said.

We then spent about twenty minutes talking about

where my surname originated from and where I grew up and went to school. We both had Lithuanian Jewish roots. He was born in Lithuania a year after my mother. Both he and my mother came to South Africa in the 1930s as children to escape the racial persecution and ultimate massacre of Lithuania's Jews. He asked me about my time at Wits and why I had gone to live in England. I could see that he had detected my initial nervousness and was trying to put me at ease. Very soon, he felt like a long-lost uncle who I had bumped into by chance.

I don't remember exactly what we spoke about when the conversation grew more serious. I recall that he admitted to not knowing anything about computers but that he knew it was important for someone to keep track of how they were being used in South Africa and how the ANC could get information out of them. He seemed to know something about the work I was doing and he thanked me for the reports I had been sending, although I was pretty certain that he himself hadn't seen any of these reports. He then spent a long time talking about the state of negotiations between the ANC and de Klerk and his government. He spoke about how little he trusted de Klerk and those around him and stressed that everyone working covertly should carry on doing so. This was the crux of our conversation. He was saying 'Carry on doing what you've been doing until instructed to do otherwise.'

At some point, I told him about my earlier dream to work in appropriate technology projects in Mozambique. I mentioned that his late wife, Ruth First, had sent me a letter advising me on how I could get into Mozambique. He asked if I still wanted to work in Mozambique and said that there would be great need for me to work in technology and development in South Africa after Apartheid ended.

After about forty-five minutes, during which time he did most of the talking, he stood up, thanked me for what I was doing and left the cottage. An unfamiliar voice from outside called out, through the half-open door.

'Give us ten minutes and then you can leave.'

I waited as instructed then left clutching my Pick n Pay bag. The car that had dropped me was waiting and the young man in the blue sweater drove me without saying a word back to Eastgate. I treated myself to a steak dinner, and then walked back to Bruma Lake to fetch my car. I drove around for about an hour making sure that I wasn't being followed.

———

A FEW WEEKS AFTER THIS CLANDESTINE MEETING, MY FRIENDS David and Monique invited me for lunch to their house on a small-holding near Walkerville, south of Johannesburg. There was quite a large gathering. I walked into their house and saw a group of people gathered around someone seated in a chair in their lounge. They were engaged in a very intense conversation. I walked over and, to my absolute surprise, saw Joe Slovo seated in the chair.

It turned out that Joe's wife, Helena Dolny, worked with David on agriculture-related projects. When Joe saw me, I noticed a momentary look of surprise and confusion cross his face. I'm sure he had seen the same look on my face. When there was a lull in the discussion, I introduced myself to him. We both pretended that this was the first time we had laid eyes on each other.

I saw him a few more times at Monique and David. We sometimes chatted, but never about my secret mission and our first clandestine encounter. In 1991, after one of these social occasions, he called me aside and suggested we take a stroll in the garden.

'Monique told me that you have leukaemia and that you are on some form of treatment,' he said.

'Yes,' I said, 'but I'm coping really well.'

'What treatment are you on?' he asked.

I told him about the Interferon and its side-effects. Just then, a few other people joined us and the conversation shifted to other topics.

A few days after that, I heard from Monique that Joe had been diagnosed with bone-marrow cancer and she had suggested that he ask me about my experience with Interferon.

In 1994, he became Minister of Housing in Nelson Mandela's first cabinet. We still bumped into each other from time to time, and I was sad to see that his health was rapidly fading. He died in January 1995 at the age of 68.

———

MY SECRET MEETING WITH JOE SLOVO IN 1990 WAS THE LAST official command I received from the ANC. I have never received a formal instruction to end my mission. I sometimes feel a bit like the Japanese soldiers found hiding out on remote Pacific islands years after the end of the Second World War. Nobody had officially told them that the war had ended, so they continued to fight on alone.

---

1. In the new post-Apartheid South Africa, Mac Maharaj, Ronnie Kasrils and Pravin Gordhan all served as cabinet ministers, Siphiwe Nyanda became Head of the South African Defence Force, and Billy Nair and Janet Love served as Members of Parliament. Charles Ndaba and another Vula operative, Mbuso Shabalala, were murdered by the security police shortly after being arrested in 1990. The truth about what happened to them has never been fully disclosed. Janet Love is currently Vice Chairperson of the Independent Electoral Commission (IEC).

chapter
sixteen

MY FAMILY

I t was the happiest wedding I've ever been to. It was
structured around the intricate sequence of activities
laid down in religious practice and tradition stretching back
centuries into the Jewish communities of my ancestors scattered across the shtetls (villages) and cities of Lithuania,
Russia, Latvia, Poland and other parts of Eastern Europe.
The most dramatic moment of the ceremony comes when
the groom, standing next to the bride under the ceremonial
canopy, called the chuppah, stamps his foot onto a glass.
The crunch of the breaking glass is followed by a loud cry
of 'Mazeltov!' from all present. The marriage is sealed. The
bride and groom are now a couple. The bride's veil is lifted.
The couple drinks wine from the same goblet. They kiss.
They smile. There is singing and dancing.

Rina Joy King and I were married on Thursday, 17th
December 1992, at a hotel in Herzliya Pituah, just north of
Tel Aviv in Israel. The entire occasion felt like an out-of-

body experience. I was both one of the central players and also an observer watching the elaborate and unfamiliar prescribed sequence of events unfold for the first time. I hadn't been to many traditional Jewish weddings and I found myself waiting in anticipation to discover what would happen next.

My brother Hilton, known in Israel by his Hebrew name Tzvi, was my best man and guided me through the steps. Before the ceremony, Rina and I were in separate rooms. I was in the main hall with the chuppah and rows of chairs set up at one end. Guests arrived and milled about. I drifted among them, smiling and shaking hands. Many of the guests were strangers to me, or people I knew vaguely from infrequent visits to Israel. There was a long delay before we could start. This was not dictated by tradition, but by the weather. There had been heavy rains and flooding in parts of Israel and the Rabbi who would be marrying us had not yet arrived.

When he arrived, the men gathered near the chuppah and stood in a cluster facing in the direction of Jerusalem to recite the evening prayers. Someone thrust a siddur (prayer book) into my hands, showing me the page to silently read from. I saw the familiar Hebrew words but forgot how to read them. I watched the others from the corner of my eye, moving my lips and turning pages when I saw others doing so.

We were now ready to deal with the paperwork, signing the ketubah, the traditional marriage contract. It's a standard ornate document written in the ancient Aramaic language which sets out the roles and responsibilities of the husband and wife as defined by Jewish custom. I sat with Hilton, Rina's brother Michael and the Rabbi at a table, surrounded by the official witnesses and others. The Rabbi filled in the blanks explaining and asking questions as he did so. My Hebrew name, Benzion ben Josef Kalman, and Rina's Hebrew name, Rina bat Eliezer Dov. The prespecified amount I promised to pay Rina in the event of a divorce? Someone suggested a number which was the standard amount. Someone else suggested a much larger number. I nodded. When it was my turn to sign the ketubah, the Rabbi did something very odd. He stood up and took his tallit (prayer shawl) out of its bag. 'This is for you,' he said. I was confused but very grateful. I fingered it, wondering what I would do with it as I already had one, and wondering why he was being so generous. He then showed me where to sign. The witnesses signed and then the Rabbi reached over and took his tallit back. 'What the heck!' I thought. I still don't completely understand what that was all about.

The next act was to make certain that I would be marrying Rina, and not some imposter hiding behind her veil. The Rabbi, Hilton, Michael, and some of the other men led me in a small procession to the room where the women were gathered. Rina sat on a chair surrounded by our mothers and other family members. I stood in front of her as someone lifted her almost transparent veil. I'm sure she winked. 'Is this your bride?' asked the Rabbi. 'Yes it is!' I said. Satisfied that there was to be no trickery, our procession returned to the main hall.

Four men designated as pole holders stood at the four corners of the chuppah. My parents, with my dad in a wheelchair, accompanied me to stand underneath it. A choir of men from the community in Efrat where Hilton, his family and my parents lived sang a familiar song as Rina, accompanied by her mother Ilana and her brother Michael, entered the hall. Rina joined me under the chuppah, where she walked around me seven times before standing at my side.

Mike Shine, the husband of Rina's cousin, was a semi-professional chazzan, the person who leads the congregation in prayer in Jewish religious ceremonies. He stood facing us next to the Rabbi and sang in his beautiful voice, accompanied by the Efrat choir. Rina smiled a lot. I thought that I smiled just as much, although when I later watched the video, I seemed to be very serious-faced most of the time. The Rabbi spoke the prescribed words, made a short speech and read the ketubah. I stamped hard on the glass, which was wrapped in tin foil so as not to leave a mess. 'Mazeltov!' resounded loudly through the universe. We sipped wine, exchanged rings, kissed, and we were married. Rina noted later that her only role in the ceremony had been to extend her finger so that I could slip the ring onto it. Orthodox Judaism certainly doesn't give much prominence to women in its ceremonies and traditions.

As the guests made their way into the banquet hall, Rina and I were escorted into the yehud, the seclusion room, where, in terms of Jewish tradition, we were alone in a room together for the first time ever. What did we get up to? We used the quiet time to report back on what had been happening and gobble down some food and drink. I was absolutely starving.

After about thirty minutes, we joined the guests in the banquet hall where the party was in full swing. A loud and joyful multi-piece band filled the room with a steady stream of Israeli wedding/bar mitzvah music. People danced with the men on one side and the women on the other, although there weren't the segregated dancing areas seen at some religious Jewish weddings. I was hoisted onto the shoulders of Akiva, a gentle giant of a man, and Rina was lifted as she sat in a chair. We were bounced around as the dancing grew almost feverish. At some point in time, we sat with my parents and Rina's mom on a row of chairs as men danced around us. Some of them did circus stunts to entertain us. Akiva balanced things on his nose and chin, Ronnie Wolfson did a head stand, while others performed acrobatic dances. When the dancing stopped, an endless procession of servers emerged from the kitchen carrying plates of delicious food, and disappeared into the kitchen carrying empty plates and spoons licked clean. Rina and I circulated, posing for photos at each table. There were a few happy speeches followed by more dancing and eating.

After seeing off the last of the guests, Rina and I made our way to our room in the hotel, ready to collapse into an exhausted sleep. As we opened the door, there was another surprise. Rina's cousins, Gabi, Mandy, Ilan, Yoni and her aunt Toots (Sylvia), had filled the room with balloons and streamers. Toots and family sat on the bed surrounded by all of the presents we had received. We spent the next few hours opening presents and recounting tales of the wedding.

———

IN APRIL 1992, MY OLD FRIEND FROM UNIVERSITY DAYS, CLIVE Kahn, invited me to have dinner with him and his wife Aviva at their home in Sydenham, Johannesburg. He made it clear that he was trying to 'set me up' with someone. I was reluctant to go. My life was so busy and complicated. I was busy with my underground work for the ANC, battling to deal with my regular doses of Interferon, and teaching, supervision and research at Wits. My life was already too full. In addition, Clive had become religious in recent years and I imagined the person he had in mind for me was a religious Jewish woman with an overbearing family and a lifestyle far removed from mine.

I asked who it was and he said that it was Rina King. He had introduced us once before, but on that occasion she had seemed distracted and not very interested in getting to know me. I didn't realise then that at that time her father had been seriously ill. Nothing had come of that first meeting, but I accepted the invitation.

I was thirty-nine years old and had never had a long-term serious relationship. Over the years, there had been a few women who were more attracted to me than I was to them, and a few with whom the reverse was true. Nothing had come of any of these relationships. I had always been too busy with my work or engaged in social and other activities. I had a few very good friendships, many of them with women, and never felt particularly lonely. I did find the idea of a life companion and a family of my own attractive, but it always felt like a future objective. I had also become very comfortable with my lifestyle as a single. I know that my parents worried about my single status and me being alone in the world. All my mother wanted for me was that I should settle down.

Rina is seven years younger than me. She grew up in Savoy, which is a neighbouring suburb to Highlands North where I grew up. She went to high school at Waverly Girls, the sister school of my school, Highlands North Boys High. Her mother shopped at my parents' drapery shop. Rina was much closer in age to my younger brother Hilton, and she knew him well through the Jewish youth organisation Bnei Akiva in which they were both very active. Rina had also studied at Wits, where she qualified as a chemical engineer. Our paths had meandered through the same terrain but, due to our age difference, had never crossed.

As we chatted at Clive and Aviva's dinner table in April 1992, we realised how much we had in common, apart from our family and Wits connections. After spending a few years in the early 1980s working as an engineer at the Caltex refinery in Cape Town, Rina had joined an NGO called TAG (Technical Advisory Group) in Johannesburg. TAG worked with trade unions on technology-related issues. In the 1970s, before leaving South Africa to live in Britain, I had been involved in setting up the organisation at Wits that grew into TAG. Rina and I also knew a lot of people in common in the White Left. As we sat at Clive's table talking about who we knew, what we had done and how we saw the world, I felt like I had known her all my life. I found her attractive, intelligent and interesting. I had no idea whether she was actually interested in what I said and who I was, or whether she was just being polite, but I knew I had to see her again.

When I asked her about work, she said something very vague about working in the family business. At this point, Clive stepped into the conversation to override what I was later to learn was Rina's natural inclination to downplay her own achievements. The family business was Viro Locks, one of the most recognisable brands in South Africa and the country's major manufacturer of padlocks. She was doing far more than working in the business – she was running it. Her father, Les King, had built Viro Locks from nothing. Rina had left TAG and gone to work with him in the late 1980s. In 1991, Les' health had deteriorated and he had died on her thirty-third birthday in February 1992. Rina was now running the company single-handedly. Clive knew Rina because he was part of the team working on the company's annual audit. If I thought that my plate was full, dealing with the many things I was engaged in, it was nothing compared to the size and responsibility of Rina's role. Viro employed hundreds of people and each of them depended on her for their livelihood and the welfare of their families.

As we were leaving Clive, I asked Rina how I could contact her. She gave me her business card: "Rina King, Managing Director, Viro Locks (Pty) Ltd" with a company phone and fax number. This was before email addresses and cell phones. The next morning, I contacted her to make an arrangement to meet again. I felt a bit shy phoning her via the company switchboard and imagined being put through to some personal assistant who would grill me and ask complicated questions, so I decided to send a fax. Clive had mentioned how Aviva prepared delicious peanut butter sandwiches for him each day. Both Rina and I said how nice it would be to have someone prepare lunch for us. I sent a fax saying something like, 'Hi Rina, I tried to fax you a peanut butter sandwich, but it got stuck in the fax machine. Sorry! Would you like to meet again some time?' I included my phone number. I know it was a very corny chat-up line, but it worked! A few minutes later, Rina called me and we agreed to meet up the following evening.

Over the next few months, we got to know each other well and soon realised that we were the life partners we had both been seeking. I had fallen in love for the first time in my life. We started sharing secrets. I told her a little about my secret underground life and the work I was doing on the ANC's secret communications system. I had never shared this with anyone. It was 1992 and, although the ANC was now legal, the political situation in South Africa was still on a knife-edge. Even though I trusted Rina completely, I was still cautious about what I shared.

I wasn't at all surprised when she confided in me that

she had also been engaged in underground activity. I had guessed as much when we had talked at Clive and Aviva's dinner table about who we knew and what we did. When I had first visited her home in Westdene, she had introduced me to the person she shared the house with, none other than Janet Love. The same person who was all over the news when Operation Vula was exposed. She had gone into hiding and was branded in the local media as a dangerous terrorist. At first, Rina was very vague about how she knew Janet and how they had landed up sharing a house.

It was only later, maybe even years later, that I put all the pieces together.

In the late 1980s, when Janet and other Vula operatives returned secretly to South Africa, internal underground operatives were assigned to support them. Janet, heavily disguised, had become Cathy, and Rina became her assigned helper who assisted her in various ways. They soon developed a real and lifelong friendship. For some time, Rina only knew Janet as Cathy. She bought a car which Cathy used and a house in Westdene which they shared. One of Janet's key roles in Vula was to manage secret communications. She had been trained in London by Tim Jenkin in the use of his system and she trained others. She was responsible for coordinating the operation of Tim's secure communications system within South Africa. Rina supported her in this task. Unbeknown to either Janet or Rina, someone called Barry Dwolatzky arrived in South Africa in July 1989, set himself up at Wits University and in a flat in Hillbrow, and became Tim's secret agent working on refining and improving the communications system they were using.

In May 1992, when Rina introduced me to her housemate Janet in Westdene, she was working openly as a key member of the ANC's negotiation team led by Cyril Ramaphosa at CODESA (the Convention for a Democratic South Africa), a forum set up in 1991 at which the ANC, the National Party and others met to negotiate the route to a post-Apartheid South Africa.

The house in Westdene was intriguing. The huge downstairs area was equipped with state-of-the-art carpentry equipment. When I first visited the house, Rina told me that she was learning carpentry, and sometime later showed me a door she had made with a secret compartment for hiding documents. She also had a large and expensive satellite phone packed in a silver metal suitcase. I had seen one of these before in Tim's flat in London.

Rina and I soon became part of one another's lives. While we both had very busy and separate working lives, our social lives merged into one. Although of slightly different generations, our friends and acquaintances were entirely connected. Everyone we knew seemed to be happy to see us coming together. Rina's mother Ilana and brother Michael welcomed me into their lives without hesitation. Ilana was overjoyed that Rina was entering into a relationship with a 'nice Jewish boy'. My family, then living in Israel and Australia, were equally thrilled.

Every Friday night, we would go for Shabbat dinner to Ilana, who laid on a delicious four-course meal. Ilana usually invited some of her friends, and dinner-table conversation inevitably focused on the news of the day. It was a time of great fear and uncertainty amongst affluent white South Africans. Apart from newspapers and TV news, the major source of information and opinion within Ilana's circle was 702 Talk Radio. It was an echo chamber in which affluent white English-speaking South Africans spoke to themselves. 'What did the future hold?' Mandela and the ANC had been vilified by Apartheid propaganda for decades, and now "we" were sitting down and negotiating with "them". 'How can you trust them?' The "communists" who ran the ANC would take away "our" property and businesses. Chaos and anarchy would break out when "they" took over the country. Each week, the news brought more and more horrific stories of crime and hijacking, violence in the townships, civil war in Natal. Ilana and her friends fearfully recounted these stories, while Rina and I tried to avoid getting into arguments with them. Sometimes things got heated. Rina was much less willing than I was to avoid confrontation with Ilana's friends.

The evening usually ended with Rina slipping off into the lounge where she curled up on a sofa and fell asleep, exhausted after another stressful week at Viro. I sat with Ilana and her friends until the last of them left. I would then wake Rina to drive her home either to my house in Orange Grove, or hers in Westdene. We were always sent off with a hamper of left-over food which would provide treats for the coming week.

Rina and I began discussing holiday plans for the end of

1992. We were both interested in visiting Egypt. Since most of both of our families lived in Israel, we agreed that we should include Israel in our travel plans. My parents would be able to meet Rina. We agreed that if we were to ever get married, it would make sense to do so in Israel, and progressed to the decision that the end of that year was as good a time as any to do so. I never formally proposed to Rina. In the first few months of our relationship, I knew that I loved Rina and that I would be very happy to spend the rest of my life with her. She felt the same about me. We agreed that I would formally ask Ilana for her approval and blessing.

On the way to Ilana for Friday night dinner that week, Rina and I discussed how we would break the news to Ilana that we were planning to get married in Israel in December. There were some guests for dinner that evening, and I sat waiting for them to leave, feeling quite nervous. Before dinner ended, Rina disappeared into the lounge. Later that evening, as Rina lay sleeping on the sofa, I asked for Ilana's blessing and spoke to her about our plans. Unsurprisingly, she was overjoyed. From then on, she took charge of making the arrangements for our wedding. Rina and I were very happy to leave the details to her as we got on with our busy lives and that arrangement worked out really well.

———

THE TWENTY-FIRST OF NOVEMBER 1993 WAS A BEAUTIFUL summer's day. Rina and I were having our last weekend

away on our own at Mountain Sanctuary Park in the Magaliesberg, an hour and a half northwest of Johannesburg. She
was in the eighth month of her pregnancy and the baby had
stubbornly adopted a breach position. The baby, a girl
according to the obstetrician, was due to be delivered by
caesarean section at the Marymount Maternity Hospital in
Kensington Johannesburg a week later. As I waded in a
rockpool near the secluded cabin we were staying in, Rina
hopped from rock to rock enjoying her last child-free
outing. We headed back to the cabin in the late afternoon
and sat on the bed enjoying an icy mixture of grape juice
and sparkling water. I suddenly realised that the bed
was wet.

'Oh shit!' said Rina, 'I'm in labour!'

Memories of the next few hours are a blur. While I
packed our stuff and threw it into the car, Rina walked to
reception to use the phone. She alerted the Marymount that
we were on our way. I'm a notoriously slow and careful
driver, but with Rina's instructions issued through clenched
teeth as the contractions became stronger, I completed the
journey in under an hour, recklessly overtaking on the left
and inching through red traffic lights. At the Marymount,
Rina was immediately taken into an operating theatre
where a stand-in obstetrician, as ours was on the golf
course, and anaesthetist, who I had seen racing into the
carpark on a motor scooter, were preparing for the
caesarean.

'I'm sure you already know it's a boy,' said the nurse
who was monitoring Rina's contractions.

A sheet had been suspended between the upper- and lower-half of Rina's body. As I sat chatting to her on a chair near her head, the doctor and nurse did what was required behind the sheet. A few minutes later, the doctor lifted something above the sheet to show us. I was shocked. He was holding up a frozen chicken. Suddenly, a tiny human leg appeared from the side of the pale white package he was holding. It wasn't a chicken, it was our perfectly healthy firstborn child. Our son Leslie.

Two-and-a-half years later, on the thirtieth of July 1996, our daughter Jodie entered the world in a far less dramatic fashion. She was born at the active birth unit at Garden City Clinic with our friend Janet Love assisting in the delivery.

After successfully running, and growing, Viro Locks, Rina sold the company to the Swedish multinational Assa Abloy in 2002. Since then, she has taken on many diverse and interesting projects. These include working with others on the development and marketing of a fuel-efficient wood-burning stove called the Vesto, training as a teacher, teaching science at Greenside High School where she taught both Leslie and Jodie, working as an activist on numerous committees, and becoming an accomplished potter. Everything she does, she takes on with passion and energy. She is the glue that holds us all together.

I could fill many pages recounting stories about my family and the wonderful years I've spent with Rina King as my wife, my friend, my companion and the amazing mother of our children. Instead of this, I will sum up these years with one word: happiness. We have supported each other, grown older together, and have been blessed with an uncountable number of happy memories and special moments.

Watching our children grow up and being part of developing them into the adults they are today has been the most fulfilling and rewarding part of my life. Leslie and Jodie are two wonderful human beings. They both have a strong social conscience and a solid sense of the difference between good and evil in the complex world we live in. I have no doubt that they will, each in their own way, play a part in working for a better world. I also love their sense of humour, their kindness and the friendship and love they show to Rina and me, and to each other.

———

MY MOTHER MASHA DIED IN 1999. HER BODY, A TINY BUNDLE wrapped in a white shroud, was gently lowered into a neatly dug hole in the earth. I glanced down into the grave, trying desperately not to allow my imagination to see that shrouded form as my mother's body. My stomach turned as the first shovel-full of dark earth thudded onto the shroud. I remember forcing myself to raise my head and stare into the distance as the assembled mourners took turns shovelling soil into the grave. When I next looked down, the hole in the ground had been replaced by a small mound.

Masha's remains and those of my father lie side-by-side in the tiny cemetery at Kfar Etzion on a tree-covered hillside between Jerusalem and Hebron. My father, Jock, had died in 1996 after a long struggle with depression and failing health. They left behind three sons and nine grandchildren.

After Masha's funeral, my brother Hilton and I spent the next seven days sitting shiva in his house in Efrat. Jewish custom has done an excellent job at codifying the mourning process. During the shiva period, the closest relatives sit together on low chairs as those who knew the deceased arrive to sit with them for a short time. As they sit, the visitors describe how they knew the deceased and share stories about their qualities, deeds and attributes. Twice a day, a minimum of ten men, a minyan, gather to recite the morning and evening prayers.

My parents had moved from Australia to Israel to live in a flatlet attached to Hilton and his wife, Shelley's, house in the mid-1980s. Efrat was at that time a small town on the West Bank between Bethlehem and Hebron. Many of the earliest residents had come together as a group of young families from South Africa. There were very few older residents, and my parents became the substitute grandparents for many of the young children. My mother enthusiastically embraced the role as Bobba Masha. She ran a creche in her flatlet, looking after very young children while their parents went to work. She was constantly knitting baby clothes, remembering birthdays, sending cards and keeping up with family events. It was only while I sat shiva during that week, listening to stories from an endless procession of complete strangers, that I fully appreciated the impact Masha had had on the lives of literally tens, or even hundreds of people. She was always available for a chat.

She offered words of advice and a shoulder to cry on and was never judgemental, offering instead her wisdom where appropriate. Even Hilton and Shelley who lived with her were astonished at how many lives she touched and how popular she had been in their community.

Although my mother had been ill with cancer for some time, her death came as a shock. A few weeks earlier, she had visited Rina and me in South Africa after her first round of treatment had, we thought, left her cancer in remission. She was able to see her brother Abe and other relatives and friends in South Africa. She also had quality time with our children Leslie and Jodie. Towards the end of her stay, she had terrible abdominal pain. Rina rushed her to Rosebank Hospital where she was examined by Dr Werner Bezwoda, the oncologist who had treated my leukaemia when I returned to South Africa from the UK. The cancer had returned, and he started treatment immediately. Hilton flew to South Africa and as soon as Masha was stable enough to travel, he accompanied her back to Israel. We all hoped that she would respond well to this latest round of treatment, but it was not to be. As soon as I heard she had died, I flew to Israel, arriving just in time for her funeral.

I believe in the importance of role models in shaping who we are and how we behave. In the earliest years of our life, parents are the most important role models. As we grow older, teachers, friends and outside heroes and villains become our most important influencers. As parents to Leslie and Jodie, I believe that Rina and I can claim some credit and possibly blame in shaping who they are today. In the same way, it was my parents who shaped me. In reflecting on my life, it seems important for me to reflect on my own parents and immediate family.

My parents Joseph Kalman ("Jock") Dwolatzky and Masha Len were the children of Lithuanian Jewish immigrants who fled the impending holocaust to find refuge on the southern tip of Africa. Neither Masha nor Jock had a tertiary education, in fact neither of them passed the matric exams. Before they married, Masha had worked as a secretary for the company L Suzman, a wholesaler who sold tobacco products. Jock was a salesman at the wholesaler Jaggers. After they married, Masha became a housewife, settling down in the house they bought in Orange Grove, one of Johannesburg's middleclass suburbs. They had three sons, Leon Elias born in 1947, me born in 1952 and Hilton born in 1955.

In the early 1960s, Masha and Jock bought their own small retail business where they worked extremely hard. When we were older, my siblings and I often helped in the shop.

The values they instilled in my brothers and I are ones we express and share to this day. All three of us have a very strong work ethic, indeed some see us all as workaholics. We also share a very high regard for education. Both Hilton and I are academics. Hilton is a Professor of Geriatric Medicine at the Technion in Haifa. He is a highly accomplished and respected researcher and clinician in his field of specialisation. Leon picked up a taste for academia later in life.

After spending many years living and working as a financial advisor in Melbourne, he began lecturing and researching at Monash University in the field of business management. In 2016, at the age of 69, he received his PhD from Monash for work on change management and innovation. He now lives in Jerusalem and, like me, is semi-retired but working as busily as ever.

The most important attribute instilled in all of us by our parents is the sense of caring for and being part of a larger community. This has manifested in each of us in very different ways. In my life, the bigger community is South Africa. In the case of both Hilton and Leon, it's Israel. Our world views may be different but all three of us care deeply about how we can contribute to what we see as the greater good. I believe that we learnt this from Masha. For her, this greater good was her extended family, friends and the communities in which she lived.

Our Wedding 1992. [Photo: Family Album]

With nieces Chani and Nikki and nephew Yehuda. [Photo: Family
Album]

Our Wedding 1992. [Photo: Family Album]

My Bobba on Durban Beach circa. 1958 [Photo: Family Album]

With Leslie, Jodie and Rina in 2022. [Photo: Sean Mongie]

chapter
seventeen

DISCOVERING I AM A TEACHER

I n February 2020, I stepped into a crowded lift in one of Sandton's newest steel and glass corporate palaces. As the lift doors closed, a voice from somewhere behind me said, 'Hello Prof Dwolatzky.'

I turned around, trying to see who had spoken. None of the faces looked familiar, but a young man with a smart cornrow hairstyle, dressed in a tie and jacket, smiled back at me. He saw the confused look on my face and said, 'You taught me at Wits. My name's Kenneth. Do you remember me?'

'Oh. Hi Kenneth. Of course I remember you,' I lied, as the lift shot upwards and some of the other passengers listened attentively to our conversation.

'I'm a team lead now,' said Kenneth proudly. The lift stopped, the doors opened, and he moved towards them. 'Thank you so much for all you did for me,' he said as the doors closed between us and the lift continued its upward journey. I wasn't exactly sure what it was that I had done for him but it's always nice to receive thanks.

When it was my turn to step out of the lift, the man who had been standing next to me said, 'You taught me too. I learnt a lot from you. Kenneth works for me. Thanks Prof.' I looked at him, an older man with messy greying hair and glasses. He was wearing a T-shirt with a Dilbert cartoon. I recognised his face but couldn't remember his name.

'Hi,' I said as the lift door closed between us.

This type of random encounter happens to me all the time, often in the strangest of places, the checkout queue at supermarkets, at airports and on the New York Subway or the London Tube. I've been teaching at Wits and running industry short courses since July 1989 and the number of people I've taught probably runs into tens of thousands. As time goes by and the numbers increase, I struggle to remember names, faces, and timelines. When did I teach Kenneth? Was it last year or ten years ago?

The two things I generally love about meeting former students is that they always make a point of greeting me and chatting if there's time, and they usually have nice things to say about the positive impact I've had on their lives and their careers. What better affirmation can a teacher want?

I strongly believe that being a teacher is one of the most noble and impactful professions. There is very little that is more rewarding than helping someone develop their abilities to improve not only themselves but the world around them. I'm in my happiest and most fulfilled state when I'm teaching and simultaneously learning, because it's always a two-way process for me.

Teaching, however, was the last thing I ever imagined myself doing when I was growing up. I had a bad stutter and dreaded speaking in public. I lived in fear of being asked to speak in class. The thought of standing up three or four times a week in front of a huge lecture theatre filled with hundreds of engineering students would have been my idea of hell.

This started to change when I became a post-graduate student at Wits in 1976. I was given a bursary from Wits and one of the conditions was that I had to work as a demon-strator, i.e. a tutor, in some of the undergrad laboratories. I became the chief demonstrator for the control engineering third-year labs and one of my tasks was to gather the nine or ten students taking the lab each week and give them a short pre-lab talk. After being a bundle of nerves the first few times, it suddenly changed. Not only did I enjoy doing it, but I received really positive feedback from the students. I suddenly realised that I have a special ability to explain things. The more I did it, the better I became and the more positive feedback I received. This is a classic example of a feedback loop, and a useful practical demonstration of control theory, which is exactly what the students were learning in my labs each week.

My other revelation was that there is a strong link between teaching others and learning oneself. Albert Einstein said, 'If you can't explain it simply, you don't understand it well enough.' This sums up my approach to teaching. I love finding simple ways to explain complex things, and according to those I teach, I'm very good at precisely that. I've also learnt so much by teaching others.

In the late 1970s, as a postgrad student at Wits, I began seeking out opportunities to teach. I decided that offering private tutoring to Wits students was a good way to earn the money I needed to support myself. My friend Colin Mendelowitz made a poster for me. I became "SuperMath" and I went around Wits Campus pinning my poster onto notice boards. I took on a few students who referred me to others. Soon I was running a nice little business on the side, teaching maths and physics to undergrad engineers, medics and even the odd physiotherapy and radiology student. I also volunteered to run free extra tutorial sessions in my Department as a way of getting myself in front of small groups of students, explaining stuff. I still avoided public speaking, although it's hard to remember how I saw this as being different from lecturing.

———

WHEN I RETURNED TO WITS IN JULY 1989 AS A SENIOR Lecturer in the Department of Electrical Engineering, I was thrown into the deep end with a full teaching load. The then-Head of Department, Prof Hu Hanrahan, handed me a box file containing a course outline, some old notes and past exam papers for the third-year course on Digital and Microprocessors Engineering, also known as Micros, and told me that I would start teaching it a week later. I knew very little about the hardware aspects of computing as I'm actually a "software guy", but I learnt as I taught, working hard to keep ahead of the students as the course unfolded. I taught this course until 1992 and I managed to do quite a good job of it.

On joining the Department, I had to align myself with one of the existing sub-disciplines and its associated research group. I naturally gravitated toward the software engineering group led by Prof Alastair Walker, who had lectured me fifteen years earlier. Alastair's research group was called SEAL (Software Engineering Applications Laboratory) and had a strong focus on software quality. At that time, there was only one software-related course in the undergraduate curriculum, called Engineering Applied Computing (EAC). It was taught by our Department to all second-year civil, mechanical and electrical engineering students. In addition, Alastair taught an elective on Software Engineering in the fourth year.

In 1991, I was asked to chair an internal Departmental Working Group that would develop proposals for a stream of computer-related courses within the electrical engineering curriculum. Based on the recommendations of this Working Group, the Department accepted major changes in the structure and content of a number of undergraduate courses. I was given the task of developing and lecturing two of these courses: a new-look EAC in the first semester of second year, and Engineering Software Design (ESD) in the second semester. In 1994, we changed the name of EAC to Software Development I. I "owned" and taught this course until 2000. From 1993, I also taught ESD, which we moved into the third year in 1994 and changed its name to Software Development II. I taught this course until 2001. In the late 1990s, I also took charge of the fourth-year elective Software Engineering and helped design another new elective unsurprisingly called Software Development III.

My approach to developing the computing stream in the Wits electrical engineering curriculum began in the UK where I became a firm believer in the concept of Object Orientation (OO). For readers interested in learning more about the concept of OO, read the SIDE BAR at the end.

In 1991, when I took over teaching EAC, the first programming language that engineering students at Wits learnt was Pascal. This language had been invented in the early 1970s by the Swiss computer scientist Niklaus Wirth. He developed Pascal as a tool for teaching his students at ETH in Zurich 'good programming practices using structured programming' based on functional decomposition. By the early 1990s, a significant proportion of people learning computer programming anywhere in the world were taught Pascal as their first language. Since this became their computing "mother tongue", all of these programmers, and others who learnt languages like C, FORTRAN or COBOL, thought about programming in terms of functional decomposition. It meant that an entire generation of programmers were wired from birth to think in terms of functions.

The language I had started using in the UK, and the one I wanted to introduce at Wits as the first language for engineering students, was C++. This is a variant of the language

C and was invented in 1979 by the Danish computer scientist Bjarne Stroustrup. C++ was one of the first complete implementations of object-oriented programming (OOP). It wasn't until 1990, when the "Annotated C++ Reference Manual" was released and Borland launched a cheap and simple commercial compiler called Turbo C++, that universities started to consider introducing it as a teaching language. I decided to introduce it at Wits as the first language taught to all engineering students.

Internationally a war of words was raging around the pros and cons of OOP. The large majority of academic and industrial computing experts believed passionately in the virtues of structured or functional programming. They argued vehemently against OO, supporting their case with umpteen examples of situations where OO led to bad code and poor performance. There is also a lucrative business sector in support of software development. This sector is focused on the sale of tools, methodologies, consulting services, textbooks and training courses. In the early 1990s, the sector had a huge vested interest in maintaining the status quo, i.e. functional decomposition. They funded the war against OO. I had been reading articles about the resistance certain academics at major international universities faced in attempting to move from Pascal to C++ and I prepared myself for a similar fight at Wits.

When I suggested making this change, very few of my colleagues appreciated how radical this was. Most were not even interested in computer programming and the second-year EAC course. Being given responsibility for running this course was generally seen as having drawn the short straw. The classes were big, drawing students from several engineering departments, and running the computer laboratory was a huge headache. My colleagues were overjoyed to have found someone enthusiastic about this course and were happy to let me get on with it. Whether I taught Pascal or C++ was irrelevant to most of them.

Alastair Walker, as the head of the software group, was interested in software quality and had read articles on OO and the claims that using it led to code that was more reusable and maintainable, which met with his approval. He had some doubts about us teaching C++ as a first language but was prepared to back me in making the change. There were other Departments at Wits teaching computer programming, but there was no University-wide policy on which languages to teach. Each Department did its own thing. I did pick up chatter on the Wits grapevine that the experts in our Department of Computer Science (CS) and their colleagues in CS departments at other South African Universities thought that I didn't know what I was doing, but I wasn't openly challenged. To make my intentions clear, I presented a paper on "Teaching Smalltalk as a first programming language" at the annual national SACLA (South African Computer Lecturers Association) conference. Smalltalk was the first and some would say the purest OO language. My paper said that teaching Smalltalk would be ideal, but C++ was a good compromise. The consensus at the conference was that OO was a bad idea, and we should wait until other international universities had experimented with teaching OO to students. My CS colleagues were happy to be followers rather than leaders, which really irritated me.

When I introduced the new version of the EAC course in 1992 with C++ as the first language students would learn, Wits became the first university in Africa and one of the few in the world to introduce computer programming to students via OO. When this change became known within the local commercial IT community, I met with a great deal of criticism. My Head of Department, Hu Hanrahan, called me in one morning to say that he had been phoned by the parent of one of our second-year students. This parent ran the IT Department in one of our major banks, where he was in charge of one of the biggest mainframe systems in South Africa. He told Hu that this 'new Dwolatzky chap' should not be allowed to ruin the future of Wits engineering students by teaching them 'this obscure language C++'. Hu didn't interfere but did ask me to phone the parent. I did so and was subjected to a lengthy tirade about 'sticking to the tried and tested basics, and not following every fad and fashion that came along'.

While the consensus in the local IT community was that using OO and C++ was a terrible idea, I did pick up a little support. I met John Ballinger, who was head of a software development group at the local company Techlogic. Independent of me, John had been learning about and had started using C++. Another connection I made was with Kevin Ryan, who had been in my electrical engineering class at Wits in the 1970s. We had also shared an office while we were postgrads. Kevin worked at Rand Merchant Bank (RMB) and had been driving a large project implementing financial systems in Smalltalk.

Throughout the 1990s, Alastair Walker ran a number of short courses for industry on software quality through his SEAL group. I decided to offer some courses on OO programming and OO design through SEAL and I invited John Ballinger and Kevin Ryan to assist me in teaching some of these courses. They brought knowledge, experience and credibility within the local software industry to the courses we offered. These courses became very popular and earned SEAL a great deal of money. Between 1992 and the early 2000s, we taught increasing numbers of working professionals in the local IT sector about OO. Gradually, the idea of OO as the way to design and develop complex software gained acceptance in South Africa and around the world.

In the current world of software development, OO is now the dominant paradigm. Some would say that by promoting widespread reuse and maintainability, OO has underpinned the software innovations that lie at the heart of digital transformation and the so-called Fourth Industrial Revolution (4IR). C++ is still taught as the first programming language in the Wits School of Electrical and Information Engineering. In general, an OO language, either C++ or a newer generation OO language like Java, C# or Python, is now taught universally when programming is introduced.

I do feel a great deal of pride when I stop to reflect on the fact that I was one of the pioneers who strongly influenced the introduction of OO programming and OO design in South Africa.

THE WITS ELECTRICAL ENGINEERING DEGREE IN THE EARLY 1990s had a curriculum jam-packed with science and engineering courses. Although the issue of bringing in some flavour of the humanities was an ongoing conversation in the Department, there didn't seem to be space in the timetable to do so. However, soon after I joined the Department in 1989, the Washington Accord was signed. This was an international agreement between English-speaking countries covering mutual recognition of engineering qualifications. It meant that a graduate with an engineering degree from any of the co-signatories could work as a professional engineer in any of the other countries. One of the prerequisites for recognition of a qualification under the Washington Accord was that a certain percentage of the curriculum must consist of non-technical content. My Department was now forced to introduce a humanities course, and I was given the task in 1990 of designing the curriculum and having it approved and implemented.

We called the course Engineer in Society and it was to be taught in the third year of study. I teamed up with the Wits Sociology Department to design the curriculum. My relationship with the Sociology Department went back to the 1970s when my politicisation had brought me into contact with the radical left, many of whom studied sociology under Eddie Webster, one of the leading progressive thinkers on Wits Campus at the time. Before I left for Britain in 1979, I had worked with Eddie and others in an informal study group that dealt with technology and work in the coal mining industry. Another connection I had with Eddie was that he is the step-father of one of my closest friends, Helene Zampetakis. In 1990, Eddie was Head of the Wits Sociology Department and he was very keen to formally collaborate with the Department of Electrical Engineering around the new course. He assigned his colleague Judy Maller to work with me on it.

The course we developed was relatively innovative, certainly far more political than Wits engineering academics and students were comfortable with at that time. We designed the course to cover issues such as how the world economy worked, how South Africa's economy related to this world economy and how South African capitalism worked. We then focused on the South African industrial workplace. We dealt with race and class, and trade union-ism. We also dealt with the typical organisation of labour in the twentieth century, mass production, Fordism, and new forms of production, post-Fordism. Each week we brought in a guest speaker, who spoke to the whole class and fielded questions, and we also prepared a reading pack from which students were expected to read in advance of each weekly session to be discussed in a small group tutorial. Each year, Judy and I put together an impressive list of guest speakers including trade union leaders, like Jay Naidoo, General Secretary of COSATU, business leaders, like Clem Sunter, a senior executive at Anglo American, economists, political scientists and sociologists. We tried to strike a balance, having a factory manager one week and a shop-floor worker the next.

The early 1990s was a very exciting time to be presenting such a course. Apartheid was on its last gasp as the future of South Africa was being negotiated at the CODESA talks. Globally, the Soviet Union had collapsed and international relations were being realigned. Everyone, including our third-year electrical engineering students, were filled with doubts about the future. Our guest lecturer sessions and tutorials became active, and often heated, debates about the future of South Africa and the future of our still mainly white and male students. If I were to generalise, I would say that our students were conservative, racist and fearful. Their world-view was strongly influenced by our local media and the opinions of their parents.

While I don't believe that the Engineer in Society course made a large impact on our students, it did provide an opportunity for them to hear a range of different views and hopefully a few of them acquired some of the skills needed to read critically and discuss events more analytically.

Judy and I ran the course together from 1990 to 1993 as well as collaborating on some research dealing with post-Fordism in the South African workplace. In 1993, the UK-based Institution of Electrical Engineers (IEE) visited our Department to accredit our degree and were particularly enthusiastic about the Engineer in Society course. In 1994, we handed it over to other lecturers. It's still part of the electrical engineering curriculum at Wits and is still taught by a sociologist.

SIDE BAR

Functional decomposition versus Object Oriented Design

In the 1970s and early 80s, the size and complexity of computer programs grew rapidly. There was a need to engineer software, rather than just knock something together that worked. It's the difference between building a garden shed and a multistorey building. A skilled builder can easily start with a pile of bricks, some pieces of timber and a doorframe, and then construct a pretty decent garden shed without much more than an idea in their head of what it should look like. But even the best builders cannot build a multistorey building in this informal way. They need to work with an architect and other professionals who will design the building and develop detailed plans before any building can start. The same is true when building software.

The discipline of software engineering covers issues like how to analyse the purpose of the required program, how to develop the architecture and design for the program, how to manage its construction, and how to test, deploy and maintain it. There are many theories and schools of thought about how to do each of these tasks, which makes software engineering a fascinating field to study and to teach. There are a few overall objectives that any software engineering methodology aims to achieve.

Two of the most important of these are called reusability and maintainability. Reusability deals with finding ways to reduce the effort of developing a program. It asks whether there are ways to take pieces of one program and reuse them in another. Maintainability is about the ease with which one can change a program after it has been deployed. One might ask: 'Why would we want to change a finished program?'

One of the characteristics of computer software is that only after a program has been put to use in the real world do users see its true potential. Consider, for example, the development of a program that aims to digitise some paper-based office tasks. At first, we would use the existing paper-based process to specify the requirements for the computer program. Once the new program has been put to work, people begin to understand what it could be doing. They might say, 'Wouldn't it be great if this program could also do X and Y?' Before long, there is a long list of refinements that need to be made to the original program. In software engineering, we call this perfective maintenance.

Reuse and maintainability are two of the so-called non-functional requirements when a program is designed, but software design also aims to reduce complexity. In other words, how do we divide and conquer the task of building a huge and complex program?

In the 1970s, several methodologies for designing software were developed. They all used the concept of functional decomposition as the mechanism for divide and conquer. What this means is that the program as a whole was seen to be implementing one or more big tasks or functions. For example, a banking system implements functions like "deposit money" or "withdraw money". Each of these big functions can be broken down (or decomposed) into a number of smaller and simpler functions. And then each of these smaller functions can, in turn, be decomposed into still smaller functions. Proceeding in this way, we eventually get to the smallest and simplest functions that can be turned into manageable pieces of computer programs. Functional decomposition became the accepted way to deal with complexity in the world of computing. University courses and textbooks in computer science and software engineering taught students how to do this.

In the late 1980s, some of the limitations of functional decomposition began to become obvious. Firstly, even the smallest and simplest functions were very specific to a particular application. It was very difficult to take a function from one program and use it unchanged in another. This meant that reusability was poor. Secondly, the focus was on functionality, not on data. When we use functional decomposition, we place data, in other words the information that the functions receive, manipulate and pass on to the next function, in a common pool where it is accessible to all functions. This is reasonably acceptable unless anything changes. Suppose, for example, that a program was originally designed and built on the assumption that every person has only a first name and a last name. What if after the whole program is designed, coded and released someone realises that most people have a middle name and that this is important information. This would mean that we will need to change every function that deals with a person's name and this can get messy. In this case, we would say that maintainability is poor.

The most dramatic example of the maintainability issue became huge news around the world in the 1990s. Up until then, programmers had mostly assumed that any date can be represented as six digits, i.e. ddmmyy, rather than eight, i.e. ddmmyyyy. For example, my birthday which is 29th April 1952 would be represented in a program as 290452, rather than 29041952. This was a very important assumption at that time because computer memory, which is where data is stored, was very expensive. Saving two digits of storage for each date had considerable benefits in large programs. Every function, sub-function and sub-sub-function in a functionally decomposed program was built on the assumption that dates are represented by 6 digits. In addition, the common pool of data used by all of the program's functions contained dates stored in that way. Everything worked well until it dawned on us that we really should have stored dates as eight digits. It became clear that using six-digit dates as we moved into the 21st Century would no longer be adequate. When the date changed from 31st December 1999 to 1st January 2000, the six-digit dates in software would go from 311299 to 010100. Calculations done on dates might start to return negative numbers.

How would programs know how to deal with that? They would either crash or start to give nonsensical answers.

This became known as Y2K (for the Year 2000) and everyone running computer software from the huge and complex systems that run banks, to the safety critical systems onboard aircraft and in nuclear power stations, to the software embedded in the controller of a lift in an office block, became concerned about what would happen when the date changed from 31st December 1999 to 1st January 2000.

This seemingly innocuous change created havoc in the computing world. Skilled programmers would need to go through every line of computer code in every function that makes up every program in the world and manually change the way it dealt with dates. Every tried-and-tested program that had worked perfectly for years would now need to be changed. And every change opened up the very real possibility that the programmer would make a mistake and introduce a bug into the program.

In the late 1990s, billions were spent ensuring that existing systems were "Y2K compliant" or replaced with new ones. In spite of all of this preparation, and because of a large amount of hype and scaremongering, many people believed that the dawning of the new millennium would lead to global chaos and disaster as millions of computer programs would start malfunctioning. My family welcomed the arrival of the new millennium camping in a remote, and beautiful, part of the Drakens-berg Mountains far away from technology-dependent civilisation just in case power stations blew up and planes fell out of the sky.

There was another path, however, and it began long before Y2K threatened the dawn of the 21st Century. In the 1980s, software engineers, myself included, began reading and experimenting with a different way of decomposing software called "object-orientation" or OO.

The major difference between functional decomposition and object-oriented decomposition or design (OOD) is that the focus moves from functions to data. Suppose, for example, that a program is needed for managing a hospital ward. In the functionally decomposed view of the world, we would have a number of high-level functions such as: Admit_patient( ), Prescribe_patient_meds( ), Record_patient_blood-pressure( ), Discharge_patient( ). Each of these functions draws in data about individual patients, and as I pointed out earlier, each piece of patient data is stored in a common, or global, pool of data.

In the object-oriented view of the world, we would create a black-box entity or encapsulation in our program representing a Patient. When we write the program, we decide firstly what information we want to hold for each Patient. We could, for example, decide that for each Patient we will store a name, ID number, contact details for next-of-kin, list of prescribed medications, blood pressure, etc. We call these attributes. Secondly, we decide how we will manipulate these attributes in our program. For example, we will Admit(), Prescribe_meds(), Record_blood_pressure() and Discharge() a Patient. Each of these is called a method, and methods store, access, manipulate and display attributes. We call the Patient entity a Class.

When we write an OO program, we can treat the Classes we have defined as data types. Just as all programming languages have "built-in" types such as Integer, Real, Character and String, our OO program will now have a type called Patient. And just as we can declare 3 integer variables called a, b, and c, we can declare 3 Patient variables called tom, dick and harry. In the program, it would look like this:

int a, b, c;

Patient tom, dick, harry;

We call these Patient variables "objects". It is this very powerful conceptual idea which distinguishes functional decomposition from OOD and also results in a high level of reuse and maintainability. Faced with a crisis like Y2K, an OO program could be upgraded in a few minutes without needing to rebuild and recode many thousands of lines of code

chapter
eighteen
CHANGING COURSES

Soon after arriving back at Wits, I became aware that many of our Wits electrical engineering students were not entering conventional engineering jobs after graduating. Instead, they were being recruited into the somewhat invisible Information and Communication Technology (ICT) Sector, which had an insatiable hunger for people with very specific skills, and Wits electrical engineers met their requirements best. In the mid-1990s, I had a discussion with Simon Shapiro, the then-Chief Information Officer (CIO) at Investec Bank. I asked him why he employed as many of our students as he could get. He replied: 'I can teach engineering graduates a little about banking, but I can't teach computer science and commerce graduates a lot about engineering. The systems we are developing are complex engineering systems. They are real-time distributed and mission critical. Only engineers have the skills to design and build such systems.'

Following this, and other similar conversations with senior industry people, I thought long and hard about what it was that made our Wits electrical engineering graduates so attractive to the ICT sector, and what we could do to make them even more attractive. I looked at the entire curriculum of our Department and thought about which specific courses prepared graduates for top ICT jobs in the financial services and other non-traditional engineering sectors. I realised that there were very few specific courses I could identify as being good training for the sector. What I found was that there were some common themes running through all of the courses that made up the four years of a Wits electrical engineering degree. These themes developed a set of skills that were drummed into our students throughout the four (or more) years they were in our Department. There was a strong focus on developing foundational knowledge, an ability to critically sift through information and engage in self-learning, and skills in problem-solving. This was coupled with a focus on professionalism, ethics and technical communication. Anyone looking at the Washington Accord accreditation process will identify these as the required outcomes of a good professional engineering education. The Wits electrical engineering programme didn't pay lip service to these outcomes but embodied them at its very core.

I did, however, believe that the content of our curriculum could be changed to include more ICT-related material. The core outcomes listed above are the attributes of all flavours of engineering education. However, the content of the curriculum for each specific type of engineer needs to reflect the body of knowledge needed by that engineering discipline. One would obviously teach very different content to a chemical engineer compared to a mining engineer, even though there might be some overlap. I believed and still believe that a new branch of engineering called software engineering needed to be established alongside the older disciplines of civil, mechanical, chemical, mining and electrical engineering.

Such programmes did exist internationally and I familiarised myself with best practice in software engineering education. The authoritative IEEE Computer Society had developed SWEBOK, the Software Engineering Body of Knowledge. The IEEE and ACM, another authoritative international body, had also jointly developed guidelines for undergraduate curricula in Software Engineering. In the late 1990s, working with one of my colleagues, Professor Ian McLeod, we developed a proposal for a new stream within the Wits electrical engineering curriculum. This stream would cater for the roughly half of our students who landed up working in the ICT sector after graduating. Without going into too much detail, the general shape of our proposal consisted of a common first and second year for both electrical and software engineers. At the end of second year, students could opt for either one of the streams. Those choosing software engineering would follow a third-year curriculum in which courses with a strong power engineering flavour, such as Electrical Machines, would be replaced with core software engineering courses.

In the fourth year, there would be elective courses and project topics only open to students in the software engineering stream.

My intention was that the initial proposals put forward by Ian McLeod and I would be the first step in a multi-step process. Each subsequent step would further diverge the electrical and software engineering streams, until Wits would ultimately have a fully-fledged and distinct Software Engineering Department offering a programme that was aligned with SWEBOK and the IEEE/ACM guidelines and other international models. This software engineering degree would be accredited as a professional engineering qualification in South Africa by ECSA, the Engineering Council of South Africa, and internationally via the Washington Accord. Having developed our proposals for a Software Engineering option, the next step was to have it approved within Wits, and it was here that we faced our first obstacle. While our Faculty was fully supportive, the Wits Department of Computer Science in the Faculty of Science raised a major objection.

Our Computer Science Department believed that any course or programme that had the words "computer" or "software" in the title belonged to them. In the third year of their degree, they already offered a single semester course called Software Engineering and they felt that if we offered Software Engineering as a stream within Electrical Engineering, we would confuse potential students. The irony was that, from 2001, I taught the Software Engineering course to their third-year students, since they had no members of staff with any interest in software engineering. The underlying reason for the Department of Computer Science objecting to our new option was that they feared they would lose students to us.

While from the outside one might believe that there is a single publicly funded tertiary education system in South Africa working in harmony to optimise the number of skilled graduates entering the economy, the dynamics inside this system are fiercely competitive. Deeply entrenched weaknesses in our secondary education system have resulted in there being relatively few matriculants finishing secondary education with good results in maths, science and English. These subjects are the prerequisites for entry into science and engineering degrees. All our universities compete for this small pool of suitable qualified matriculants. The competition is not only between universities but also between departments within each university.

I believe that the Wits Department of Computer Science might have feared that the best matriculants interested in working in the ICT sector would flock to our Software Engineering option, leaving Computer Science with those who we decided not to accept. Their strategy seemed to be to block us from offering the Software Engineering option and, if that failed, to confuse the market. Since we needed to gain approval from the University's Senate, our then-Dean, Professor Charles Landy, came up with a compromise. We would not call our new option Software Engineering but would opt for the term Information Engineering. While this compromise helped us to bypass the objections from

Computer Science, I've never been happy with this name. I feel that it's a misnomer and that it has done what Computer Science intended, which is to confuse potential students. Neither matriculants trying to decide which degree they should register for nor companies employing our graduates have ever quite understood what Information Engineering is. In my mind, it is simply an alias for Software Engineering, a term which is clearly understood internationally.

In 2000, our Department of Electrical Engineering became the new School of Electrical and Information Engineering when Wits reorganised and rationalised its departments and faculties. I worked hard to get the new option off the ground and to produce its first graduates. I also coordinated the accreditation of the programme by ECSA. While the Information Engineering option is still offered as a stream in our School, it has not diverged from the mainstream electrical engineering programme as I had intended. It has rather moved the other way in that the distinction between the two streams has narrowed. While I'm very disappointed about this, I accept some of the blame since from the mid-2000s my focus turned elsewhere, and I began paying more attention to the ICT Sector as a whole.

———

IN 2003, I TURNED MY ATTENTION TO OUR SCHOOL'S POST-graduate programme. After several years of developing and offering short courses on objected-oriented design (OOD) to people working in the local ICT Sector, I decided to expand my engagement with these working professionals by offering a Master of Engineering (MEng) in Software Engineering. I managed to slip this name past my Computer Science colleagues and call it Software Engineering rather than Information Engineering. It consisted of five core courses at a post-graduate level, plus three electives. Students were also required to complete two capstone assessments, a design exercise and a small research report. It could be completed in one year full-time or three years part-time. While I thought that some of our electrical engineering or information engineering graduates, or even computer science honours graduates, might wish to spend an extra year at university learning more about software engineering, my real target market was working professionals. I hoped that working software development professionals would see this as an opportunity to sharpen their professional knowledge.

I met with several senior people in the local ICT Sector to discuss offering this MEng to their staff members and during these discussions made a very important discovery. Very few people working in the local ICT Sector had a formal academic qualification in ICT. They did not have degrees in computer science, IT, information systems or engineering. The vast majority of working professionals had come into the ICT Sector straight from school or had somehow drifted into the Sector. I even met a chief enterprise architect, which is a very high-level role in the ICT hierarchy, who worked at a major bank and had a degree in classical music.

At first glance, it would seem that the lack of a formal qualification did not prevent people from finding employment in the ICT Sector. However, in speaking to some of these people, I learnt that the lack of a relevant ICT-related degree blocked prospects of promotion once they had reached mid-tier positions within their organisations. One of the people I met who was in his late thirties had been a team leader in the software development division of a major bank for twelve years but he was stuck at that level.

Another issue I soon became aware of was that while the MEng in Software Engineering offered an exciting set of cutting-edge courses, there was very little uptake. We were struggling to recruit sufficient numbers of students, full- or part-time, into the programme. The problem was two-fold. Firstly, the prerequisite for entry into the MEng was a four-year engineering degree or an honours degree in computer science or information systems. Secondly, the Faculty timetable had scheduled these courses during normal working hours, making it very difficult for part-time students to get time off work to attend classes. Solving this latter problem was fairly simple and involved changing the timetable so that courses were taught in the late afternoon and early evening. The issue around prerequisite qualifications was far more difficult to solve.

In 2004, I had several discussions with Dr Piet van Vuuren, who was then CIO at FNB's (First National Bank) new online division. Piet bemoaned the fact that, while the

MEng was a perfect fit for upskilling people in his development teams, none of them had the academic prerequisites to be accepted by Wits into the programme. We explored ways in which we could offer a tailor-made version of the programme for FNB. I found out that Wits has a little-used rule that deals with "mature students". A "mature student" is defined as someone who has a certain number of years of relevant experience depending on what other academic qualification they might have. Acceptance into the MEng is, however, not automatic. After the prospective student has applied to be accepted, a committee considers the application and decides whether to accept the student, and therein lay the problem.

The Faculty of Engineering's postgraduate studies committee had a reputation for being very reluctant to approve applications from "mature students". They were particularly risk-averse, saying that unless there was strong evidence that an applicant could cope with a post-graduate level course, they would prefer not to set them up for failure. In most cases, they rejected such applications. With support from Piet van Vuuren, I offered the five core courses in the MEng programme as short courses. Students could register for them individually for non-degree purposes. Although they were offered as short courses, they were identical in all respects to the course in the MEng programme. Students attended the same lectures, did the same assignments and were assessed in the same exam. If a student passed three of the five core courses with better than a 60% average and had the required number of years of relevant work experience to be accepted as a "mature student", I would personally submit a motivation to the graduate studies committee asking for the student to be accepted into the MEng programme. Any courses they had passed as short courses would be recorded as credits towards the MEng. It was thus possible for someone with matric plus ten years of experience to end up with a highly prestigious Wits University MEng in Software Engineering.

In 2005, we offered this option to a group of twenty FNB software development professionals. In 2007, we grew this number to about thirty-five per year and opened it up to everyone. Over the next ten years, we received hundreds of applications per year and accepted about forty each year. Many of these completed the MEng and went on to fill senior technical and managerial positions in the local IT Sector. A few even went on to register for MSc(Eng) and PhD degrees via research. I believe that this programme was a huge success and did a lot to raise the level of high-level skills locally. It also gave a significant number of people the opportunity to improve their qualifications and their future.

In 2017, because of a Government decision to do away with all masters by coursework qualifications at South African universities in favour of masters by research, Wits decided to stop offering the MEng qualification. We offered students a route into a lesser qualification, namely a Post Graduate Diploma (or PGDip) in Software Engineering. This proved to be far less popular than the MEng and the number of applications dropped significantly.

———

SINCE THE EARLY 1990S, I'VE OFTEN BEEN ASKED TO ADVISE and mentor prospective and existing Wits students who struggle to understand how to decide on which qualification best equips them for a career in the ICT Sector. In broad terms, Wits and most other South African universities offer three distinct qualifications. These are: (i) a BSc(Eng) in Electrical Engineering, with or without the Information Engineering option, (ii) a BSc with Computer Science as a major, and (iii) a BCom with Information Systems as a major. A matriculant wanting to go into ICT would need to choose one of these three options. The question I was often asked by matriculants and their parents was 'What's the difference between these options?' I developed a clear way of answering this question and helped many people make the right choice, but it is still confusing for many. I've also been asked to help students who have progressed part of the way into one of these options only to find that they should have chosen one of the other two.

In 2010, I developed a detailed and somewhat revolutionary proposal for a new breadth first three-year computing curriculum. Instead of there being three different options, all students wanting to work in ICT entered a common first year. This first year consisted of subjects that provided a strong foundation, such as maths and applied maths, together with an introduction to programming. The second year was also common, giving students exposure to software engineering, information systems and computer science. The third year allowed the students to specialise. They selected courses from one of the three specialisations.

On successfully completing the third year, the student receives a degree, but then has an option to specialise further. They can do an honours in either computer science or information systems, or they would be allowed to enter the third year of the BSc(Eng) in Information Engineering. Making this choice would mean that students can end up with two degrees, namely the initial degree plus an honours in computer science, information systems or an engineering degree. The advantage of this broad-based approach is that matriculants who are uncertain about which "flavour" of qualification they wish to follow can make a choice after two years of being exposed to all flavours.

In developing the proposal for this programme, I consulted broadly with senior people in the local ICT Sector. They were extremely supportive and positive about it. When it came to implementing it, however, Wits management decided that it should not fall under my School but that it should be managed by the School of Computer Science. The reason for this was that Computer Science was the smallest school at Wits and there was pressure on it to either grow or merge with another school. The then-Deputy Vice-Chancellor: Academic, Professor Yunus Ballim, offered Computer Science the opportunity to "own" this broad-based programme and to use it to grow in size and become viable. The programme was called Applied Computing and was launched within the School of Computer Science in

2011. After three years, students received a BSc in Applied Computing. For reasons I fail to understand, Computer Science showed no enthusiasm for this programme. Neither did Information Systems nor my own School. After producing a few cohorts of graduates, the programme was shelved. It stopped producing graduates in 2018. I kept track of some of the graduates and I can say with some pride that they are highly regarded in the local IT Sector.

Over my many years at Wits, both as the head of Software Engineering in the School of Electrical and Information Engineering and as Director of the JCSE, the challenge of producing the right skills for South Africa's ICT sector has been my major passion. My success can be measured by the large number of people I can point to and say 'She or he was one of my students'. These ex-students can be found in top positions in South Africa and around the world. My failure was that some of the most innovative changes I worked to implement failed to gain traction and grow. For example, I would have loved to see Wits becoming the first South African university offering a fully-fledged branch of engineering called Software Engineering. I believe that programmes I introduced such as the MEng in Software Engineering and the BSc in Applied Computing should have been grown rather than phased out. I partially blame myself for these failures. I planted seeds and then moved onto my next idea. I should have stayed more focused.

chapter
nineteen

THOSE LIGHTBULB MOMENTS

Dressed in her Sunday best, the elderly woman stood in the kitchen of her tiny house. In the corner was a wood-burning stove. Although it wasn't in use, a strong smell of smoke filled the room. She stood near the door welcoming the small party of VIPs into her home with a big smile on her wrinkled face. A small child clung anxiously to her skirt watching the cameraman setting up his equipment in the far corner of the kitchen. The Mayor was there, a youngish man dressed in a sharp suit and a red tie. He sported a small ANC badge pinned to his lapel. A young woman, who I recognised as a provincial spokesperson, bustled into the kitchen clearing space for the MEC for Social Development, who followed her into the room. The MEC was an elegant elderly woman wearing a purple headscarf and expensive shoes. The regional head of Eskom Distribution, a dour-looking middle-aged white man who had been standing with me and the consulting engineer,

Sakhi, stepped forward to greet the MEC and the Mayor. The dimly-lit room had become overcrowded and claustrophobic.

The Mayor said a few words in Sesotho staring directly into the camera's lens, and then the Eskom man stepped forward to flick the main switch on the Ready Board mounted on the wall near the front door. The room was instantaneously filled with bright light from the 60-watt light bulb on the Ready Board. We all applauded, and the elderly woman beamed. The small child blinked in amazement, fixing her bright little eyes on the even brighter lightbulb. The provincial spokesperson stepped forward with a brand-new kettle filled with water. The kettle was a gift from the provincial government to the smiling houseowner. The spokesperson handed it to the MEC who plugged it into the three-pin socket on the Ready Board. The photographer captured some posed pictures as the water in the kettle boiled.

This small house and every other building in this small Limpopo township was now connected to Eskom's national grid. Eight hundred more South African homes had just been given access to electricity for the first time ever. It was 1998 and every week similar scenes were playing out throughout South Africa as thousands of homes were being connected to the national grid.

We moved from the house to open ground across the road where hundreds of people had gathered under a marquee to celebrate the community's "switch on" day. The smell of cooking meat filled the air as the VIPs took turns making speeches punctuated with much laughing and ululating.

I was there because the design software I had written, which I had named CART, for Computer-Aided Reticulation of Townships, had been used to design the electrical system that had just been turned on. This was the first time that CART had been used to design a township reticulation system that had then been built and switched on. From where I stood, I could see a sturdy wooden pole on the side of the road outside the house we had just come from. Four thin cables looped from the top of the pole to that house and three others. A thicker cable spanned from that pole to the next one 50m down the road and on to others receding into the distance. At the end of the road, I could see a small transformer mounted on a pole. I knew that this transformer was connected to cables that were carried on poles along the main road for several kilometres to an Eskom substation which provided a connection to the national grid. Every home connection, pole, cable and transformer that brought electricity to this township had been specified using CART. The position of each pole, the size of each cable and the specifications for each transformer had been determined using CART. CART had also optimised the system, making sure that it was built at the lowest possible cost per connection while meeting Eskom's very demanding technical standards.

I felt incredibly proud. Developing CART and its underlying algorithms had occupied me and some of my research students at Wits for the past six or so years. The electrification of this small township in Limpopo, and hundreds of others that were yet to be designed using CART in the future, represented my ideal of the purpose of research.

I'M SOMETIMES ASKED BY PEOPLE BORN AFTER THE LATE 1980s to explain what Apartheid was like. An easy way of understanding the lived reality is to focus on access to resources such as water and electricity, which can be seen in simple statistics.

The rate of electrification is defined as the percentage of homes that have access to electricity. The highly developed countries of Europe and North America have electrification rates of 100%, or very close to that. In the least developed countries or regions of the world, the electrification rate might be as low as 10%. In the 1980s, the electrification rate for the one in five South Africans with white skin was close to 100%, while only about 10% of black South Africans had access to electricity.

In other words, all white South Africans had electricity at home, even those living in tiny towns or in remote farmhouses. Eskom, the national electricity utility, and municipalities spared no expense to connect white areas to the national grid. In spite of this, the price they paid for electricity was the lowest in the world. The reliability and quality of supply was at a standard expected in Europe and North America. White SA was very much part of the Global North.

The situation for black South Africans was completely different. Even old established urban black townships in major cities were not electrified. Soweto, the huge sprawling township to the south of Johannesburg, wasn't electrified. A common image was of black families using candles for light and wood, coal, and paraffin for heating and cooking as Eskom's giant power pylons carried the national grid over, but not into, their homes. For white South Africans, energy was cheap and available at the flick of a switch. For Black South Africans, access to energy was a daily struggle. Sources of energy were polluting, expensive and difficult to access. The irony of this was that in the 1970s Eskom had built several huge new power stations that turned out not to be needed. This resulted in an over-supply of electrical generation capacity. Several huge power stations were mothballed while millions of black women and children spent hours each day collecting wood and dung for cooking and heating.

This is what Apartheid was about. The same stark inequality and weird logic existed around access to water, housing, health care, education, food and the other essentials of life.

In the early 1990s, I became deeply interested in mass electrification and in the years that followed the challenge of bringing electricity into the homes of millions of black South Africans became one of my major obsessions. It also allowed me to make a small contribution to one of the greatest development success stories of post-Apartheid South Africa.

In the late 1980s, Eskom's CEO Dr Ian McRae had initiated a programme he called Electricity for All. Well aware of the Apartheid-era stigma represented by South Africa's shameful electrification gap, and eager to position Eskom at the forefront of the unfolding arrival of the new South Africa, McRae and Eskom's executive leadership decided to launch an ambitious programme to narrow this gap. It became hugely successful. Between 1990 and 2000, the overall electrification rate in South Africa grew from 35% to 71%. Over two and a half million homes were connected to the national grid. At its peak, the electrification programme was connecting more than a thousand houses per day and all of this was funded by Eskom itself. Rather than looking to government, or international agencies, Eskom drew on its own resources and reserves to pay for this ambitious programme.

Soon after returning to Wits in 1989, I started collaborating with a colleague in the Department of Electrical Engineering, the now late Alan Meyer. Alan was an expert in power systems and suggested that we join forces to develop software tools to support the national electrification drive. We also both became involved in forums discussing policies and strategies for mass electrification. Bear in mind that, at this time, I was living a double life as a Wits academic and as an underground ANC operative. It was therefore ironic that the recently unbanned ANC, unaware of my underground role, invited both Alan and I in 1992 to become ANC representatives in a multi-stakeholder initiative called NELF, the National Electrification Forum. Participating in

NELF helped me to understand the many practical problems associated with Eskom's ambitious electrification rollout. Over the next ten years, Alan and I led a large research and development project focused on creating software in support of this programme.

———

THE OVERALL AIM OF OUR RESEARCH WAS TO PROVIDE AN integrated digital environment for engineers tasked with designing the low voltage distribution networks. At first, Alan and I made our own assumptions as to how the designer of a low voltage network should work. We came up with ideas for software tools that we believed would make the engineer's task more efficient. We spoke to senior Eskom managers and representatives of companies who supplied cables and transformers. Our main focus was on developing novel algorithms and implementing them as stand-alone programs. I worked on loosely integrating these programs into a commercial CAD (Computer-Aided Design) system called Microstation. This was the CAD system used by Eskom Distribution and the consulting engineers working with them.

Alan and I had a number of research students working with us. The first MSc student I supervised after returning to Wits in 1989 was James Nicholson, whose research topic was the development of an algorithm to select the optimal combination of different sizes of low voltage cables in an electrical distribution network. Since thinner and cheaper cables have higher resistance, and therefore higher voltage drops, James' challenge was to ensure that the voltage level at the consumer's house was sufficiently close to the nominal 220 volts, while the cost of the cables was as low as possible. Using the algorithm developed by James, I wrote a cable selection program that could be run from inside Microstation. Nicola West did her PhD under my supervision on optimising the routing of a network of cables along predefined paths such as the roads in a township. Raj Rajakanthan did his MSc on optimising transformer zones and Steve Levitt did his PhD research on automatically recognising buildings on an aerial photograph of a township. Each building was a "connection point" for electricity. Marios Moutzouris, working on his PhD, developed a system that could help a designer visualise the performance of a distribution network. I supervised Estelle Trengove's MSc(Eng) research which built onto the work James Nicholson had done. Estelle developed a method for optimally selecting medium voltage cables.

A large number of other students, both fourth-year students and postgrads, developed methods and tools which aimed to support the design of low voltage distribution systems. Either Alan Meyer or I supervised these students. Where appropriate, these contributions were loosely integrated into Microstation as additional tools. I did this integration work myself. We called this collection of integrated tools CART 1.0. The work of the students and some additional research that Alan and I did was also published in international and local journals, or presented at conferences around the world. Over a ten-year period, more than thirty MSc's and four PhDs were awarded for research carried out as part of the CART project. We certainly made a significant contribution to the knowledge and practice in the area of computer-based low voltage electrical network design.

While CART 1.0 offered a very useful toolbox of digital design tools, it wasn't enthusiastically adopted by the engineers tasked with designing the hundreds of electrification projects. This was in spite of the fact that we offered the software for free to anyone who wanted it. I found this really puzzling.

In 1997, I was due a year of sabbatical leave and chose to use the year as a make-or-break time for CART. I intended to devote all my time and energy to either getting CART to be broadly adopted, or to understand why it was always going to be little more than an academic exercise. I set a target for the year: 'By the end of this year,' I told myself, 'the first electrification network designed using CART must be built and energised.' I wanted to see actual households benefiting from the work I and my students had done in developing a bunch of very innovative algorithms and tools.

To start with, I needed to return to the basic assumptions that Alan and I had started from. How exactly did engineers design low voltage electrical networks? I realised that we had never spoken to the actual design engineers. I had relied on Alan's advice on how he, as a very experienced electrical engineer, thought these systems should be designed. We had also only spoken to other experts, senior managers at Eskom and representatives of equipment and cable suppliers, none of whom had ever designed a complete low voltage network from scratch. My first step was therefore to undertake what we in the software engineering field call requirements gathering. And instead of interviewing engineers who worked at the electrification coalface, I went a step further and decided to spend the first three months of my sabbatical working in a consulting engineers office on the detailed design of electrification networks.

I contacted a consulting engineering company called Karabo Engineering, one of the first black-owned consulting engineering companies in the new post-1994 South Africa. It had been founded by two electrical engineers, Sakhi Dumakude, a UCT graduate, and Philip Chaba, a Wits graduate. They had offices in Centurion between Johannesburg and Pretoria. Karabo was one of the mid-sized consulting companies contracted by Eskom Distribution to do design and implementation work for the mass electrification programme. Eskom achieved its impressive electrification targets by adopting a shared regional approach. Annual electrification targets were set for each region of the country, and in each region townships and villages were selected to be connected to the grid in that year. Each of these townships and villages was defined as a project and each project was assigned to a local consulting engineering company. Karabo Engineering was assigned a few projects each year, whereas larger consulting firms took on tens of projects annually.

In terms of Eskom's methodology, the consultant and his technical team were responsible for developing a detailed design of the entire low-voltage network that brought power from a medium-voltage transformer on the Eskom grid into every home, school, shop and other important buildings. They then had to oversee the construction of the network and ensure that it met rigorous technical and construction standards set by Eskom. The consultant also had to manage the cost of the project. A target cost per connection had to be achieved for each project, an amount which was annually reduced, encouraging consultants to work hard to optimise their designs.

I asked Sakhi and Phil to take me on as a member of their electrification team and treat me like any other team member. I worked as a volunteer since Sakhi said he couldn't justify paying me because, in spite of the fact that I had a PhD in electrical engineering, I had no experience or expertise in electrification design. It was both a humbling and rewarding experience.

The two things that I realised very soon were, firstly, that the design work required very little skill or deep knowledge in electrical engineering. For this reason, most of the work was done by draughts- men and women, rather than engineers. Sakhi or Phil signed off on the designs, but the bulk of the work was done by people whose main area of competence was in the use of the Microstation CAD software.

Secondly, the work was tedious, repetitive and slow. There was no time at all for developing optimal designs. Instead, all the designer focused on was getting a design that worked and satisfied all of the many design constraints.

Once all constraints were satisfied, a detailed design could be prepared. The network was drawn neatly on Microstation with every pole and other piece of equipment accurately represented. A bill of materials containing a complete list of everything that would need to be delivered to the site of the project was created. The cost of material was also entered so that the overall cost of the project as a whole and the all-important "cost per connection" could be calculated. This was the critical number in obtaining Eskom's approval. If this number was too high, the design as a whole or parts of the design would be reworked to reduce it.

Since each iteration could take many days, it was never possible to say, 'I have a design that meets all the constraints, and that has an acceptable cost per connection, and I can't do any better.'

I learnt about all of this sitting in the Karabo offices in Centurion, sometimes until well after midnight, struggling to get acceptable designs out. I learnt about how difficult and inefficient the manual processes were and discovered how computer-based tools could assist.

Another important learning opportunity for me at Karabo was to accompany Sakhi on site visits. We travelled together to townships, which allowed me to be a fly on the wall at the initiation of projects where, together with

Eskom's regional officials, Sakhi walked around the unelec-
trified area, chatted to residents, local leaders and business-
men, agreed on where the site office and materials store
would be, and generally brought the lines, symbols and
dots on the Microstation drawing to life. This meant that
when I sat later in the Karabo office trying to decide where
to place a transformer or pole on the drawing, I had a
picture in my mind of where it would be built in the real
world. We also visited projects as construction was underway. I sat through site meetings where Sakhi berated
contractors and the site foreman for falling behind schedule
or not doing the job properly. Sakhi was a stickler for
quality and had a sharp eye for incorrect and sloppy work.
Eskom set very high-quality standards which were rigor-
ously enforced, and poor quality work cost the consultants
money and damaged their reputation. I also attended
several very rewarding "switch on" days.

After my three-month stint as a junior draughts-
man/electrification designer at Karabo, I was ready to start
working again on CART. I decided to completely reimple-
ment it from scratch as "CART 2.0".

I rented a small office in Norwood, close to where I
lived, since working at home had too many distractions,
and sitting in my office at Wits made it hard for me to
disengage from students and Wits work. The following nine
months was one of the most productive and rewarding
periods of my working life. I spent literally hundreds of
hours sitting alone in front of my computer writing software. Psychologists talk about the flow state, a state of

complete immersion in an activity which takes one out of conventional ideas of time. This was where I spent those nine months and I absolutely loved it.

By the end of 1997, CART 2.0 was finished. It had become a huge piece of very well designed and implemented software. I had built all of it myself. My goal was to provide the electrification designer with a tool that would allow them to follow the same workflow that I had experienced working at the coalface in the Karabo design office. The aim was to support electrification network designers by automating as many of the tedious manual tasks as possible, while not replacing the role of the experienced human designer. Whereas previously the human designer might spend many days on a single design, the intention was that CART would allow them to develop the same iteration in a few hours. I very consciously decided not to bring many of our cleverest optimisation methods into CART 2.0 as I felt that these undermined and intimidated the human designer. I rather saw CART 2.0 as a support tool.

At various stages of developing the CART 2.0 software, I showed it to Sakhi and some of his designers. They were very enthusiastic and I worked with them on a few actual projects using CART. I also demonstrated CART to senior engineers at Eskom and they were equally enthusiastic.

The main advantage of CART is that all of the tedious tasks are done by the computer. It results in significant time saving and allows designers to optimise the design while reducing the overall cost of the project. CART has made a hugely positive contribution to mass electrification in South Africa and has saved Eskom millions of Rands.

The question I sat with at the end of my sabbatical in 1997 was how to get it out into the world. This is the problem faced by academic researchers around the world. This was the issue Alan Meyer and I needed to address as we sat together late in 1997, talking about how to proceed with CART.

Without doubt, there was a need for CART. Eskom's electrification drive was gaining momentum and, as my stint at Karabo had shown me, the current way of designing reticulation networks was too labour intensive, slow and haphazard to meet the growing demand for the design of new networks. There were also no similar computer-based tools available at that time. My experience working at Karabo also helped me to understand that consulting engineers working on township reticulation designs worked under huge pressure and carried enormous responsibility. If the tool being used crashed for any reason, the user needed to be able to shout into a phone and get support immediately. This meant that for CART to be useful, it would need to be backed up with 24/7 support together with user training. There would also need to be ongoing development and refinement of the system to keep pace with emerging requirements and user needs.

Alan and I decided to set up a start-up company dedicated to the commercialisation of CART. We registered a company called Terrasoft. It was my second foray into the world of software entrepreneurship. One of my MSc students, Raj Rajakanthan, joined Terrasoft as a shareholder and full-time employee, and worked on supporting the product and the growing user community. Although it never made big profits, Terrasoft became a sustainable commercial entity that allowed us to put CART to work with tens of consultants across South Africa and neighbouring countries. Many hundreds of electrification projects bringing electricity to the homes of hundreds of thousands or even millions of people have been designed using CART over the past twenty years and it remains in use to this day.

Over the years, competing systems emerged, some of which shamelessly copied some of CART's best features. We also came up against some of Eskom's very dubious commercial practices that favoured a competitor's system over CART. The bottom line, however, is that Alan and I successfully navigated the technology transfer hurdle faced by academic researchers. We were able to turn invention into an innovation that had both economic and social benefits.

chapter
twenty

WITS UNIVERSITY – MY OTHER FAMILY

I t was a Saturday morning in 1998. I parked my car in De Beer Street in Braamfontein and walked around the corner into Jorissen Street to my Standard Bank branch. I was there to collect a new cheque book. In 1998, we still bought stuff and paid our bills by writing out cheques. About ten minutes later, cheque book in hand, I returned to my car.

As I dug into my pocket trying to fish out my car key, I noticed someone hovering nearby. Every parking spot in Johannesburg is "owned" by a car-guard who watches your car and expects a small payment in return. As I turned to the hovering man, thinking he was a car-guard, I saw a knife clasped in his hand. He didn't speak to me. He didn't ask for money, or my car, or anything else. He simply raised his arm with the knife above his head and then brought it down, striking me hard in the centre of my chest. I looked down, expecting to see blood gushing out of me, but the knife hadn't penetrated my chest. Maybe the blade wasn't sharp enough, or it had struck a bone, or the man wasn't strong enough? Who knows? I grabbed the man's wrist. He was still clutching the knife. I looked into his eyes and saw no emotion. No fear, no anger, no explanation. I let go of his wrist.

I started shouting loudly, 'What the fuck are you doing! He has a knife! He tried to stab me!'

He turned away from me and walked slowly toward Jorissen Street. There were lots of people around. There was a security guard standing outside a shop nearby.

'Help!' I shouted. 'He tried to kill me! Catch him!'

The man sauntered around the corner. Nobody moved towards me or the man. Nobody looked at me. With shaking knees, I found my keys, opened my car door, started the engine and drove off, my chest aching as a huge bruise started to form.

All I could think was that someone had tried to take my life without even giving me a chance to save myself. If the knife had gone into my chest, I would be lying in a pool of blood next to my car. Would he then have taken my wallet or my car, or would he still have just sauntered off round the corner? Would passers-by have stopped to help me, or would they have looked the other way as they went about their Saturday shopping?

I swore then that I would never go back into Braam-fontein.

———

As a student in the 1970s, I had spent a lot of time in Braamfontein. There were several popular student hangout spots in "Braamies", as we called it. One was the bar at the Devonshire Hotel in Jorissen Street known as The Dev, which I hardly ever went to. Some of my engineering class-mates spent many lunchtimes there before coming back drunk to campus to do their laboratory sessions. The other popular hangout was Pop's Café on the corner of Jan Smuts Avenue and Ameshoff Street, close to where the Eland Statue now stands. It was a place for cold drinks, coffee, ice cream, toasted sandwiches and hot chips. There was a small seating area, a jukebox and a row of pinball machines. Pop's Café was always busy, crowded and noisy. In the 1970s, I often hung out with my non-engineering friends at Pop's.

In those days, Wits had no fence around its campus. Students and anyone else could walk onto the Wits campus from Braamfontein. The University and the City were connected. While at school in the 1960s, I would take a bus to Braamfontein and walk over to the Wits Library to find information for school projects.

When I returned to Wits in 1989 from England, things were beginning to change. Braamfontein and the neigh-bouring city centre had for decades been the throbbing heart of Johannesburg. Doctors, lawyers and other profes-sionals had their offices there. Retailers had their smartest shops there. During the 1980s, many of these offices and stores had relocated to the newly developed malls and office towers in the now fashionable Sandton and Rosebank areas to the north, leaving behind empty buildings. Crime and grime triggered a vicious circle, making Braamfontein and the city centre less and less desirable as a place to do business.

In the early 1990s, after several major criminal incidents on the Wits campus, a fence was erected between Wits and Braamfontein. An access control system was installed and for the first time in its history the physical link between University and City was cut.

I, however, continued to see Braamfontein as an extension of the Wits Campus. I shopped there, had my hair cut there and visited my bank there. That incident in 1998 changed this for me.

———

I'VE BEEN CLOSELY ASSOCIATED WITH WITS UNIVERSITY FOR over fifty years, and the relationship is still ongoing with an exciting new chapter having opened when I was appointed at the age of sixty-nine to a role in the Office of the Deputy Vice Chancellor for Research and Innovation. Apart from my years in the UK in the 1980s, I've spent my entire adult life at Wits. As the University celebrated its centenary in 2022, I was one of the few people who could claim to have actively participated in half of that history.

On joining the Wits staff in 1989, I found myself drawn toward serving on committees. Most of the detailed workings of the university are assigned to a broad range of committees which provide those who serve on them a unique vantage point to see and influence the institution as a whole. Over the years, I've served Wits in many ways, and in doing so became passionate about it and its role in society. At some moment of time in the 1990s, I fell in love with Wits and started to see it as my family. Decades later, I feel the same.

Another community with which I've had a long and passionate association is the South African Information and Communication Technology (ICT) sector. My interest in this sector grew out of my mission to infiltrate it and expose its secrets in the early 1990s. Very soon, however, I developed a deep respect for it and a passionate desire to help grow it and make it succeed. How did I hope to do this? By marrying my two passions and developing the relationship between Wits University and the ICT sector.

The digital computer was invented during and after the Second World War. The first commercial computers became available in the 1950s. At this early dawn of the Age of Computing, South Africa became a trail blazer. The world's second oldest professional organisation for ICT professionals was established in South Africa in 1957. The Computer Society of South Africa, now called the Institute of IT Professionals of South Africa (IITPSA), is only a few months younger than the British Computer Society. South African programmers notched up many world firsts in the early history of computing. Applications were developed for sectors such as mining, banking and insurance. The public sector also enthusiastically adopted computer technology.

Wits University played a pivotal role in the growth of

353

South Africa's ICT sector and became the first academic institution in Africa, and among the first in the world, to acquire a computer for teaching and research purposes. In the 1960s, the Head of the Department of Electrical Engineering, Prof GR Bozzoli, persuaded the university to lease a state-of-the-art mainframe computer from IBM. At that time, IBM never sold computers, they only leased them. Derek Henderson, a lecturer in Electrical Engineering, taught the first courses in programming at Wits. Eventually a degree programme in Computer Science was offered by Wits. The university appointed Henderson as the first Professor of Computer Science in South Africa in 1967. Later in his career, he served as Vice Chancellor of Rhodes University.

In the 1970s, as international pressure on South Africa grew, the spotlight focused on the ICT sector. It became known, for example, that the Apartheid government used IBM computers to support the extensive and complex administrative systems that underpinned the notorious pass laws. Trade unions in the USA exerted huge pressure on IBM, eventually forcing them to withdraw from the South African market. The camera company Polaroid was also supplying equipment to the South African government for use in producing the notorious passes, or "dompas", carried by all black South Africans. It too was forced by shareholders and unions in the USA to disinvest from South Africa, with other international technology companies following suit.

Ironically, in response to international sanctions in the

1970s, the South African ICT sector entered a golden age. ICT professionals are notorious for their preference to reinvent the wheel. Sanctions gave local software developers an opportunity to operate in a bubble of their own without facing international competition. In the name of sanctions-busting, proprietary applications and systems owned by international companies were reverse engineered, and then improved. At the same time, the South African government allocated huge budgets to security and defence. A large slice of these budgets ended up in the local ICT sector.

In the mid-1990s, when I became particularly interested in the South African ICT sector, Apartheid had just ended and international technology companies were rushing to enter, or re-enter, this important and lucrative market. The local industry suddenly faced serious international competition. At the same time, South African companies had the opportunity to expand into other markets.

In 1999, the Canadian government sponsored an important study for South Africa's Department of Trade and Industry (DTI) on the local ICT sector. This study, called the "South African IT Industrial Strategy" or SAITIS, was carried out by Price Waterhouse Cooper (PWC) and involved extensive consultations with local experts. I was one of the experts consulted. The major conclusions of the study were that the South African government, through the DTI, should support the ICT sector by: (i) encouraging the adoption of international standards and best practices, (ii) growing the size of the sector, (iii) transforming the workforce in the ICT sector by encouraging more young people, women and people of colour to join the sector, (iv) encouraging innovation and entrepreneurship, (v) marketing and promoting the sector internationally, and (vi) finding ways to expand access to, and reduce the cost of, the Internet.

I thought deeply about these recommendations and concluded that Wits University could play an active role in implementing all but the sixth proposal. I set to work on creating a new entity at Wits, called the Joburg Centre for Software Engineering (JCSE) within the School of Electrical and Information Engineering. The aims of the JCSE matched the first five SAITIS recommendations. At a glitzy gathering on the top floor of Johannesburg's Civic Centre on the evening of 15th May 2005, the Wits Vice-Chancellor and Principal Professor Loyiso Nongxa, and the Mayor of Johannesburg, Councillor Amos Masondo, signed an agreement that launched the JCSE. A number of commercial sponsors also agreed to support this venture.

We appointed Rex van Olst, a veteran of the local ICT sector, as the first Director of the JCSE, while I focused on fundraising. In 2007, my Faculty agreed to second me full-time to the JCSE and I took over from Rex as Director. My arrangement with Wits was that the entire JCSE budget, including my own salary, would be funded through income generated by the JCSE and donations received. It's an arrangement that continues to the present.

Setting up and managing the JCSE opened up many opportunities for me to work at improving the fortunes of the South African ICT sector. It also allowed me to reinforce

Wits University's reputation in the ICT sector, both within South Africa and internationally.

I established a formal partnership between Wits and the Software Engineering Institute (SEI) at Carnegie Mellon University in Pittsburgh, USA, which is the leading global institution in software engineering, software quality and cyber security. With financial support from the DTI, I used the relationship with the SEI to bring the very important CMMI process improvement model to South Africa. I also piloted the adoption of the SEI's Personal Software Process (PSP) and Team Software Process (TSP) in our local ICT sector.

In 2005, and again on several other occasions, I arranged for Kent Beck, one of the world's most famous and influential software engineering gurus, to visit South Africa and run masterclasses for local ICT professionals. Kent is one of the signatories of the very important Agile Manifesto and originator of innovative software development methods such as eXtreme Programming (XP) and Test-Driven Development (TDD). Kent and other leading international experts, such as Ivor Jacobsen, have become good personal friends and have enthusiastically supported the aims of the JCSE.

By 2012, I had made very good progress in achieving most of the aims we had set for the JCSE. However, the important SAITIS recommendation relating to encouraging innovation and entrepreneurship had not progressed very far.

Around that time, I travelled extensively attending

conferences, joining outgoing trade missions as an expert spokesperson promoting the South African ICT sector, and meeting with partner universities and companies in other countries. On most of these trips, I began to observe an interesting development. Most major cities seemed to have a thriving digital innovation district and my hosts would talk about an area in their city where digital innovators and entrepreneurs gathered to hatch and incubate interesting digital start-ups.

As early as 2007, soon after the JCSE was established, I had started thinking about an African Silicon Valley. The question was where? I found inspiration in the writings of Michael Porter and other authors who wrote about clustering as an important concept in economic and regional development. I also asked people working in some of the best digital innovation districts I visited to identify reasons for their success.

My research led me to conclude that the most successful digital clusters were to be found close to major research universities, in existing business districts that were well provided with necessary infrastructure, such as good digital connectivity. They were in areas that offered convenient and conducive lifestyle factors that would attract digital innovators to the area. Typically, these innovators were young and geeky. Such people would require suitable places to live, work and play in that area.

Considering these success factors and thinking about the most successful digital innovation hubs I had seen else-

where in the world, it seemed to me in 2012 that Braamfontein ticked all the boxes.

————

IT HAD TAKEN ME FOURTEEN YEARS, BUT IN SPITE OF MY VOW TO
never venture into Braamfontein again, I re-engaged with
the area. Although it was still quite a scary place, and was
dirty and rundown, I now saw it as a place with great
potential. I began to believe that, with my help, this area
could, and would, turn into Africa's version of Silicon
Valley. I had seen other derelict and dangerous inner-city
areas elsewhere in the world transform. I thought of
Boston's Kendall Square and London's Shoreditch area.
These were both wonderful examples of such transformation.

I formulated a bold and ambitious plan, but I needed to
find a suitable place to plant the seed. I imagined a digital
innovation hub in the centre of Braamfontein acting as a
bridge between Wits University and this part of the City of
Johannesburg. I was certain that, once established, this hub
would act as a catalyst, leading eventually to a high-tech
cluster on the southern fringe of Wits. I met some of the
major landlords in Braamfontein. One of them, South Point,
offered me a small space at a relatively high rent. Someone
else offered me a space above a restaurant in De Korte
Street at a reasonable rent, which subsequently became The
Orbit Jazz Club. Then I thought of asking Wits University

management whether the University owned any property in Braamfontein.

Patrick Fitzgerald was then the Wits Deputy Vice-Chancellor: Finance. One of his responsibilities was property and infrastructure. He had been a student at Wits in the 1970s at the same time as me and was a very colourful and popular member of the White Left at that time. When I asked him about Wits-owned buildings in Braamfontein, he pulled out a long list of properties the university owned.

After taking a few walks through Braamfontein, Patrick and I inspected a row of buildings in Juta Street in the area south of the Wits campus. These buildings covered half a city block and included two office blocks, a small warehouse, and a former nightclub. I immediately fell in love with these derelict and neglected buildings as the future site for the digital innovation hub I planned to create. Wits had bought the buildings with a view to tearing them down and building a new student residence on the site. This was a long-term plan and until that happened, the University had no use for them. They were a rat-infested eyesore, constantly being broken into and vandalised. Patrick was only too pleased to grant me use of the buildings until they were needed for something else.

The one condition that the university management set was that no university funds would go into renovating the buildings, equipping them and running my proposed digital innovation hub. If I was hoping to establish this hub, I would need to raise the funds myself. I accepted this condition and set to work fundraising.

I produced a PowerPoint slide-deck and set about seeking the funds I needed. I met countless potential sponsors. I moved the offices of the JCSE from the twelfth floor of University Corner, above what is now the Wits Art Museum, to one of the semi-derelict buildings in Juta Street, and I started to use parts of the old buildings to run some of the activities that would eventually be offered in the envisaged innovation hub. My JCSE team and I ran hackathons and challenges and initiated a digital arts festival called Fak'ugesi. Slowly, sponsors signed up, money came in, and my dream took shape. Two or three times a day, I would either go out to meet with potential sponsors or I would bring them to Juta Street and, with torch in hand as the old nightclub had no electricity and no windows, I would show people around.

'And here we will have a large co-working space. And there we will have a coffee shop,' I would say, pointing to debris-covered floors and broken toilet stalls, as the sound of rats scurrying in the dark made my visitors look anxiously around them. Most visitors thought I was a complete loon, but some could see the potential and became enthusiastic supporters and sponsors. Soon there was enough money to begin drawing up plans and appointing a builder.

We needed a name for this digital innovation hub, and I asked one of my team, Xoliswa Mahlangu, for a suggestion. She went away to think about it and came back a day or two later with the name Tshimologong. It's a seTswana word which means a place of new beginnings. I loved the name. The place I was building represented new beginnings in a number of different ways. It was a place where we would incubate innovative new digital businesses, revitalise Braamfontein and Johannesburg's inner city, and encourage Wits University to once again venture beyond the physical and psychological barriers it had constructed around its campus. It was indeed a new beginning and so the place I was building now had a name – The Tshimologong Digital Innovation Precinct.

The renovations were carried out in phases and by September 2016 we were ready to formally launch the Tshimologong Precinct. Sponsors and friends gathered in Founders Square for the official opening presided over by the Vice-Chancellor and Principal Adam Habib. The seed was planted and the vision was clear. All that remained was the hard work of implementation.

––––––––

IT WAS 11PM ON FRIDAY 18TH OCTOBER 2015. I SAT AT HOME staring in amazement at video images being streamed live from Wits University's Senate House Concourse. An app called Periscope linked the screen on my iPad to the camera on someone's cell phone as a drama unfolded in the large open area on the ground floor of the university's administrative building. Well over fifteen hundred singing and chanting students filled the Concourse. Some were sitting on the floor, others were dancing or standing and watching on the fringes. In the centre of the crowd, the former head of the Wits Student Representative Council (SRC), Mcebo Dlamini, stood shouting into a megaphone. He wore jeans, a yellow ANC T-shirt and military-style camouflage cap. In front of him, some of the university's senior management and members of Council sat silently on chairs on one side of a row of tables. They looked as though they were on trial. They appeared irritated, impatient and a little frightened. Students were shouting at them, saying that their chairs should be taken away and they should all be forced to sit on the floor.

Mcebo said, 'Comrades, it is the first time in the history of universities that all of its important stakeholders have met. We, the students are here; the vice-chancellor and his team are here. The chairperson of Council is here. These,' he said pointing at the students surrounding him, 'are the children of taxi-workers, the unemployed, the deceased. Their only hope is education. These are the children of miners, farmworkers, and domestic workers. The country and the world is watching.'

He paused, staring into the faces of the university's management, 'Be leaders. No one is being held hostage. We are here to say no fee increment.'

Cas Coovadia, one of the members of the Wits Council, stood and tried to address the gathering. To my generation of activists, Cas is an instantly recognisable and highly respected veteran of the struggle against Apartheid. The students, however, had no idea who he was. They shouted him down. As I watched on my iPad, comments popped up as they were posted by viewers. 'Who's this old man?' 'He must sit down and keep quiet!'

Adam Habib and Randall Carolissen, the chairperson of Council, attempted to speak. They too were met with heckling and booing from the crowd and insulting comments on Periscope.

This standoff continued well into the early hours of Saturday morning. I remained connected, unable to tear my eyes away from the live streaming of the spectacle. Eventually, a resolution was reached after the management team had been allowed to leave the Concourse to hold a discussion. They returned and Mcebo announced to the exhausted crowd of students that the decision by Council to raise student fees – the trigger that led to this dramatic protest – would be suspended. Other student demands had also been accepted. He waved a signed piece of paper as proof.

This was one of the iconic moments in a protest movement called #FeesMustFall. Students at universities throughout South Africa were protesting about the fact that access to a university education was becoming increasingly more expensive and unattainable each year.

———

FAST FORWARD TO ANOTHER INCIDENT THAT HAPPENED ALMOST exactly a year later. A symbol of the reversal of Braamfontein's fortunes from a run-down inner-city area to hi-tech cluster was a jazz club called The Orbit. It opened in

2014 and soon became one of Johannesburg's best venues for live music.

On Friday 14th October 2016, I was at The Orbit with my wife Rina and Val, a visitor from Canada. One of South Africa's most acclaimed jazz singers, Sibongile Khumalo, was performing and The Orbit was jam-packed. As we arrived at the club, I saw a brand-new outside broadcasting vehicle parked in the street in front of The Orbit. It was emblazoned with the logo of the SABC – South Africa's national broadcaster. I paused to look inside. A technician told me that they would be recording the concert for later broadcast on one of the SABC TV channels.

As we settled down in our seats, I felt my cell phone vibrate in my pocket. I sneaked a peak and saw it was a message from a colleague at Wits to a WhatsApp group I was on. Protests were again taking place at Wits and other universities, and a large group of students and others were marching from the Wits campus into Braamfontein. Earlier that day, Wits management had announced a night-time curfew on campus, confining students to their residence buildings. Students objected to this and had been marching on campus to show their rejection of this restriction.

As I sat in The Orbit, I felt guilty about being in an entertainment venue while these serious events were unfolding a few hundred metres away. In the distance, I heard the dull thuds of stun grenades and the siren of a passing police vehicle.

Sibongile Khumalo began her performance. Her voice was as wonderful as ever and the prospect of a very special evening was certainly on the cards. Looking toward the entrance, I saw some of the club's security people whispering to the manager. More stun grenades, still far away but definitely closer. More police vehicles driving past the club with sirens blaring and flashing blue lights visible through the curtains covering the windows. And then the unmistakable sound of breaking glass and an angry crowd very close by.

The manager of The Orbit climbed onto the stage as the music stopped. 'There is unrest in the streets outside. Anyone who wants to leave may do so now, but we have been advised by the police to ask everyone to remain inside the club. Please move away from the windows on the right,' he said. 'Police reinforcements will soon be here and we will all be evacuated. Please keep calm.'

More breaking glass and more stun grenades followed, this time right outside. Through gaps in the curtains, we suddenly saw huge orange flames as something burnt outside the building. We smelt smoke and could feel the heat. We heard shouting and screaming. Sibongile Khumalo and her musicians stood up and started playing again. She sang a quiet soulful song in a tear-filled voice. It was a prayer. She prayed for the students, "our children", fighting outside for access to quality education in our new democratic South Africa. She sang with her eyes closed and a look of calm on her face. And then she led us all in a heart-wrenching rendition of the beautiful hymn Nkosi Sikelel' iAfrika, 'God Bless Africa. May her spirit rise high up. Hear our prayers'. As I joined the others in singing this song, I realised that we were not singing a stanza of the hotchpotch national anthem of the new South Africa. We were again singing the rallying cry of the liberation movement that I had once sung with an aching heart at anti-Apartheid meetings and protest marches in London and Manchester.

I felt deeply conflicted listening to Sibongile's voice against the backdrop of the sounds of fury coming from the streets outside. Whose side was I on? I strongly supported the #FeesMustFall movement, but I hated the fact that destruction and violence had become part of it. I was comforted to think that the police were protecting me and this wonderful venue in Braamfontein, while at the same time I was angry that they had been called in to confront our students.

Several hours later, I was driven in an armoured police vehicle to fetch my car that I had parked a block away. Miraculously it was intact, but the SABC's outside broadcast vehicle was a smouldering wreck. The Orbit's huge glass windows had been smashed and the streets resembled a war zone. Small fires burnt and barricades partially blocked the streets. At that moment, I was filled with despair for the future of Braamfontein, the future of Wits and the future of South Africa.

————

THE #FEESMUSTFALL PROTESTS BROUGHT TO A HEAD A KEY issue that had been brewing since the early days of post-Apartheid South Africa. What were the duties and responsibilities of the government in relation to education? The Freedom Charter, which was the statement of core principles of the ANC and its Congress Alliance partners during the liberation struggle, made very clear commitments about access to education in a future South Africa. Among other things it stated, *'Education shall be free, compulsory, universal and equal for all children; Higher education and technical training shall be opened to all by means of state allowances and scholarships awarded on the basis of merit.'* The South African Constitution entrenched this principle in Section 29 stating that everyone has the right to a basic education, including adult basic education. In terms of further education, our Constitution says that the State, 'through reasonable measures, must make further education progressively available and accessible'. This imposes an obligation on the State to promote and provide education by putting in place and maintaining an education system that is responsive to the needs of the country.

The sad reality that was highlighted in 2015 when #FeesMustFall started was that our education system was broken. Education, like many other aspects of life in South Africa, remains hugely unequal. Each year, the gap grows wider as government subsidies to universities fail to keep pace with inflation and universities are forced to raise their fees to balance their budgets.

The major protagonists in the battle for affordable and equitable university education are students and their parents on the one side, particularly those with limited financial resources, and the government on the other side.

While university councils and management have very little room to manoeuvre, they are also key role players.

I was firmly on the side of the #FeesMustFall movement, which was fighting for the same outcomes I fought for in my years of student activism. We fought for an end to our racially segregated and hugely unequal education system and for the rights of workers and a better society.

In 2016, two important factors entered the #FeesMustFall movement. One was a level of violent confrontation. Wits management and other universities brought the police and private security companies onto our campuses. This led to violent attacks on peaceful student protestors as poorly trained police officers and security guards randomly fired rubber bullets, teargas and stun grenades. On the other side of the coin, university buildings were burnt, property was damaged and fellow students and staff members were intimidated. As in any conflict that becomes violent, it's very hard to objectively say who started the cycle of violence. The net result, however, was a level of violence on and around our campuses that was reminiscent of the worst days of Apartheid.

The second factor was that #FeesMustFall became a proxy for the politics of the day. Factions of the ANC and the EFF (Economic Freedom Fighters) saw student fees and access to university education as an opportunity to raise the national political temperature and appeal to their national support bases. The DA (Democratic Alliance) also sought to capitalise on the situation by coming out on the side of the silent majority. These political parties infiltrated and co-opted the student movement. I strongly suspect that the ANC worked hard to move the spotlight away from its own short-comings and responsibility as the ruling party toward the universities, while the Jacob Zuma faction in the ANC began punting an anti-intellectual narrative.

A clear and long-term decision from government on how to make quality, affordable education available to all South Africans has yet to be made. The future of our country depends on this.

———

IT WAS A WARM JOHANNESBURG EVENING IN EARLY DECEMBER 2016. A small stage had been erected in Founders Square, the central entrance area of Wits University's Tshimologong Digital Innovation Precinct in Juta Street, Braamfontein. Senior Wits colleagues were gathered for the annual Senate and Council Dinner. The Registrar, Carol Crosley, stood at a lectern announcing the names of those who had been selected to receive Vice-Chancellor's Awards for research and teaching. She then came to the award for academic citizenship, which recognises "service to the university".

'... and the award goes to Barry Dwolatzky', she read.

There was loud applause. I stepped forward to receive a framed certificate and a handshake from Adam Habib. He made a short speech, recognising my role as the founder and the visionary behind the Tshimologong Precinct, the venue we were now in. I made a short speech in response.

It was one of the highlights of my long association with Wits University.

A few weeks later, Rina and I were in Cape Town at a New Year's Eve party. At midnight, we all shouted 'Happy New Year', hugged old and new friends, and sipped champagne. A few minutes into the new year, my cell phone vibrated. My first email of 2017 had arrived. I read it.

It was an automated message from Wits University that went something like *"Note that your appointment at the university will be terminated on 29 April 2017. On that date, all access to university campuses and IT systems including email will be removed. Ensure that you make the necessary arrangements."* In 2017, I would turn sixty-five and was expected to retire from Wits and instantly disappear from sight. The email, its timing, its tone, and the information it shared struck me as being insensitive, even brutal, uncaring and unfriendly. This was one of the low points of my long association with Wits University.

Luckily, it wasn't to end like that. In the course of 2017, I was able to make arrangements to remain at Wits beyond my compulsory retirement date and continue as part of the Wits "family".

———

WITH RESPECT TO EACH OF THE SAITIS RECOMMENDATIONS, the JCSE has, since 2005, been very successful. My contribution to the South African ICT sector was recognised by my peers in 2013 when I was named by the IITPSA as joint recipient of South Africa's IT Personality of the Year. I shared the award with Mteto Nyathi, a good personal friend and enthusiastic supporter of the JCSE. He was head of Microsoft South Africa at the time. He went on to become CEO of MTN and then CEO of Altron. In 2016, I was recognised again when the IITPSA gave me their award for Distinguished Service to the IT Profession in South Africa.

In all I have done through the JCSE and in setting up the Tshimologong Precinct, the key objective has been to reinforce and enhance Wits University's leading position and reputation in relation to South Africa's IT sector. With the growth in the digital economy and the approaching "Fourth Industrial Revolution", Wits still has a key role to play developing digital knowledge, skills and innovations.

Opening of Tshimologong Precinct in 2016 with Joburg Mayor Parks Tau and Christo Doherty. [Photo: Edwin Wes]

Opening of Tshimologong Precinct in 2016 with Janet Love. [Photo: Edwin Wes]

chapter
twenty-one

RETIREMENT

My conditions of employment at Wits University were always very clear. The contractual arrangement between Wits and all employees is that appointments end on the date that the employee reaches their retirement age, namely sixty-five. The university does provide some flexibility in that it can be arranged, by mutual consent, to postpone retirement to the end of the year in which one turns sixty-five. For me, this would have been the 31st December 2017.

While retirement on one of these dates was always part of the deal, I had never thought much about it as I was always busy and as 2017 got closer, I seemed to become busier. I was running and growing the JCSE, setting up the Tshimologong Precinct, assisting the Wits Research Office in building strategic partnerships with top international universities and companies, including MIT and IBM Research, and raising funds for ICT-related activities. I served on several key university committees and had a finger in many pies. Wits was my family, and I was a very important member of the family. In addition, Wits didn't even pay my salary as I raised sufficient income through the JCSE to cover my salary and more.

I imagined that as 2017 approached, I would have a friendly chat with Wits management and find some way to take the issue of retirement off the table. I certainly had no desire to retire. I had never even thought about what it would mean for me.

However, as the calendar flipped over to 2017, Wits' Human Resource retirement processes kicked in and correspondence relating to my impending retirement followed in the weeks after that. I didn't attach much importance to this as I was still confident that it would be easy to arrange for me to continue doing the important work I had started. I was particularly eager to remain in charge of Tshimologong, which had been my obsession since 2012. Early in 2017, someone sent me a word cloud generated from everything appearing on the Internet and social media over the past year associated with my name. Three words loomed large: Tshimologong, Wits and Braamfontein. I'm ashamed to say that the names of my wife and children appeared in the tiniest of fonts.

I had some off-the-record conversations with senior Wits colleagues and these left me feeling that the university appreciated all I was doing and wanted me to continue in my current roles, but towards the middle of 2017, I received very different signals. Although it was never formally discussed with me, it soon became clear that there was no possibility of me continuing with what I had been doing after the end of 2017. Senior management had reached a decision about my future, and I would have to hand over the Tshimologong project to someone else.

There was some flexibility within Wits about me staying on at the university beyond my retirement. I would be appointed as an Emeritus Professor, and I would be given a post-retirement contract to continue as Director of the JCSE. I should explain that although the Tshimologong Precinct began as a project under the JCSE, a decision was made in 2017 to create a new entity to run and grow Tshimologong. This entity was a new company called Wits Incubator (Pty) Ltd, wholly owned by Wits' commercial entity called Wits Commercial Enterprise. Since the JCSE and Tshimologong were so intertwined, most of the interesting and revenue-generating programmes I had built under the banner of the JCSE would now fall under this new company with a new CEO who would definitely not be me.

I was very unhappy about these developments, but it became abundantly clear that it was not something that was open to discussion. I had to decide whether to walk away from it all and accept retirement, or whether to remain involved in another role. I never seriously contemplated walking away and instead hoped that a new role for me could be defined in a way that Tshimologong and Wits would continue benefitting from my continued engagement.

Once I recovered from the initial shock of realising that I

would not be able to continue driving the Tshimologong Precinct initiative and my greater plans for the transformation of Braamfontein into South Africa's Digital Cluster, I resolved to not give up on my ambitions. I had to find other ways to move my strategy forward.

Firstly, being given the title of Emeritus Professor ensured that my connection to Wits would continue. I asked an older colleague who had the title of Emeritus to explain what it meant. He thought for a moment and then said, 'I guess it allows you to keep your Wits email address'. While it is certainly more than that, his statement does sum it up well. The title doesn't come with a salary or any financial benefits. It allows you to continue accessing the Wits library and other university resources and infrastructure. You can also elect to do some teaching, supervision or mentoring of younger staff. For such activities, you might be paid. Most importantly, however, it allows you to still remain associated with Wits, albeit in a rather tenuous way.

Being given a post-retirement contract was another huge advantage. I arranged that I would continue for another three years as Director of the JCSE. All that remained of the JCSE in terms of staff was myself and two incredibly competent and loyal support staff, my Programme Manager, Ashleigh Gormally, and my PA, Jassika Sheikh. There were a few other people who worked on an *ad hoc* basis with the JCSE. I could call on them as the need arose. Since the bulk of the JCSE's activities had been handed over to Tshimologong, I would need to reconceptualise and rebuild the JCSE.

In negotiating my post-retirement contract, I was also able to retain a formal role within the Tshimologong Precinct as Chief Visionary Officer (CVO) and would work under the newly appointed CEO as part of the executive management team. My post-retirement contract set aside a nominal 40% of my time for this role, with the remainder being devoted to the JCSE. I would also remain as a member of the Tshimologong Board.

In the latter half of 2017, Lesley-Donna Williams was appointed to the role of CEO of the Tshimologong Precinct. I had known Lesley for several years. We first met as panellists at a conference organised by Microsoft in 2013. She was the founder of the first co-working space in Johannesburg called Impact Hub, and she shared my vision and enthusiasm for Braamfontein and even lived in Braamfontein. I was very happy that she was appointed to run Tshimologong and spent the rest of 2017 doing my best to hand over to her.

Since I was owed many leave days, I chose to go on holiday at the beginning of December 2017 before retiring from Wits at the end of the year. My new contract with the university would start on 1st February 2018, leaving me with two months of holiday, my longest break for decades. Rina and I went with our children on a trip to Europe, including a cruise off the coast of Norway. The two-week cruise on the famous Hurtigruten route took us from Bergen along the Norwegian coast to Hammerfest, close to the Russian border. We saw the Northern Lights and some of the most spectacular winter scenery in the world. I also revisited Trondheim, the university town I worked in as an engineering student on my first-ever trip out of Southern Africa in the 1970s.

In February, I returned to Wits as an Emeritus Professor and on a post-retirement contract as Director of the JCSE and CVO of the Tshimologong Precinct. A new phase of my life was about to begin.

———

HOW DID IT FEEL TO BE RETIRED? I'M SURE THAT THE experience is different for everyone. I expected life to continue almost unchanged. There would be a change of role and a new contractual relationship with Wits, but this should have had no significant effect on my day-to-day activity and how I felt about myself and my place in the world. I was in for a huge surprise.

The most profound and unexpected aspect of having retired was in the way people related to me. In 2017, I was connected and involved. People at Wits sought me out, asked my advice, fitted in with me. Any conversation at Wits that related to ICT, Braamfontein or Innovation would have to include me. Meetings were scheduled around my availability. People outside of Wits with an interest in any of these issues would come to me if they wanted the university's involvement.

In 2018, this all changed. I heard after they had happened that meetings about Braamfontein or Wits' involvement in some ICT-related issue took place without me. If I asked why I hadn't been invited, the response was 'But you're retired.' This happened on numerous occasions. I suddenly felt like an outsider whose opinion, expertise and experience had no value.

It was extremely frustrating as I still felt on top of my game and had so much to contribute. I struggle to understand what it was that "flipped the switch" at the end of 2017. Does this happen to anyone who retires from an organisation? Or were there other reasons? I don't know.

———

BEING FORCED TO CONFRONT THE CONCEPT OF RETIREMENT LED me to reflect on many of those existential issues we miss as we rush through life dealing with day-to-day concerns. In particular, I thought long and hard about South Africa and the world my children will inherit.

When Nelson Mandela became South Africa's first democratically elected President in 1994, the struggle against the social and economic system that underpinned Apartheid entered a new stage. Institutionalised racism and inequality did not magically end with the swearing in of a black president.

Many of those who had fought Apartheid turned their energy to building the post-Apartheid state. Some entered politics or joined the civil service. Others decided to use their skills to play a role in building a developmental state. I would place myself in this latter category.

While some rolled up their sleeves and set to work to

build a new South Africa, others did not. Many ANC cadres and reputable struggle veterans entered the post-Apartheid era with a sense of entitlement and proceeded to build their own wealth and their own power at the expense of the masses. Others, who had already been rotten and corrupt under Apartheid, remained rotten and corrupt.

Looking at the shape of South Africa in 2022, I feel disappointed and let down. Twenty-eight years into our new democracy, inequality, unemployment and lack of service delivery remain major problems. Our primary and secondary education systems are broken, and huge structural problems persist in tertiary education. The ANC has failed us. Our government and the ruling party have not only failed to deal with corruption and greed but have actually been the source of this scourge. All other political parties have also failed us. I've never had much faith in politics, and I now have even less.

There is, however, a brighter side. Since the 1990s, I've been privileged to work at a wonderful university. Over this time, I've come to know many young South Africans who were born after the end of Apartheid. Within the current generation of young South Africans, there are many who are creative, talented and socially conscious. At Wits, and in the work I've done at Tshimologong and in the ICT sector, I have met many remarkable young people. I believe deeply in this generation and its ability to solve large and complex problems.

The issues facing young Africans are large and complex. They include climate change, urbanisation, migration, globalisation and energy. Digital transformation provides solutions and brings with it its own challenges. The current political class in South Africa and elsewhere have proven themselves incapable of dealing with most of the challenges to be faced in the future, but I believe that the young generation will transcend politics as we now know it. New ways of organising will emerge.

Some might see this as idealistic and naïve, but that is who I am. Through the life I've lived, I've discovered that idealism and naivety coupled with bold dreams and determination can get one very far. Although I might not live to see it, I believe that the future is bright.

about the author

Barry Dwolatzky is an Emeritus Professor and Director of Innovation Strategy at the University of Witwatersrand, Johannesburg. He is also the founder and director of the University's Joburg Centre for Software Engineering (JCSE) and founder of the Tshimologong Digital Innovation Precinct in Braamfontein Johannesburg.

Barry holds a BSc(Eng) in Electrical Engineering and a PhD from Wits University. Apart from a nine-year period in the UK in the 1980s, Barry has spent more than fifty years at Wits where he has educated generations of software engineers. He was named as the co-winner of the South African ICT Personality of the Year Award in 2013 and has played a pivotal role in developing and growing the South African digital economy.

He is married to Rina and has two children, Leslie and Jodie.

Connect with Barry here:

Website: https://www.SoftwareEngineer.org.za

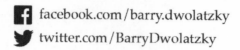

facebook.com/barry.dwolatzky

twitter.com/BarryDwolatzky